BLOODY
ST ALBANS

Edited by

JL Merrow, Steven Mitchell
and Wendy Turner

COPYRIGHT NOTICE

CONTENTS

SINISTER ST ALBANS

St Albans—affluent, historic, quaint. On the face of it, an idyllic Hertfordshire city. But below the surface, its alleys run with blood, flowing past the clock tower, snaking around the Abbey, down to the River Ver and lake of Verulamium Park. Fighting, robbery and deceit overflow in the history of sinister St Albans.

Some stories in this collection are based on actual events, and some pure fiction, but even fiction comes from truth—truth about ourselves. The law-abiding Verulam Writers members have turned to their criminal undercurrents to write these stories, demonstrating their ability to turn their talent to any genre with imagination and style. I can no longer look some members in the eye, thinking their hearts have turned dark. Are they reaching for a pen to scribble something down, or a knife? A notebook, or an axe? Does their smile mask an untold villainy? Still, I'm very honoured to share a writing group with them.

I thank our local guest authors, best-selling crime writers Howard Linskey, Rachel Blok, and Candy Denman for their contributions and for supporting and providing inspiration to Verulam Writers.

And thank you to everyone involved in creating Bloody St Albans. I'm extremely proud of this anthology, and I hope you enjoy it as much as I do.

Phil (Steven) Mitchell
Chair of Verulam Writers
October 2022

ABOUT ST ALBANS
FOR REFUGEES

St Albans for Refugees was founded in 2015 and was formed to give local St Albans residents the opportunity to provide support to people from around the world who have found themselves in the unimaginable situation of seeking refugee status as they flee from war, oppression, natural disasters, climate change or persecution.

A significant proportion of the charity's activities is focused on providing vital support through the collection and distribution of aid both locally and internationally, providing life changing relief from financial hardship.

For those who are granted refugee status in the UK and settle in St Albans and the surrounding areas, the charity gives important assistance in both education and training, allowing refugees and their dependents to gain important skills which help them to adapt to their new community. Support and advice in areas including employment and mental health are also provided – with the aim of creating safe spaces in which those seeking asylum can adjust and settle into life in the UK.

The charity's activities have included using their expertise to support Syrian refugees settling into St Albans; sending clothing shipments to Lebanon; and providing ESOL (English for Speakers of Other

Languages) lessons to local asylum seekers. Most recently St Albans for Refugees are aiding the huge relief effort to those fleeing from the current Ukrainian conflict, delivering aid directly to the region and working hard to help Ukrainian refugees already in St Albans to settle.

St Albans for Refugees has been named as the Mayor of St Albans' chosen charity for the 2022-2023 year. Verulam Writers are proud to support their efforts and will be donating 50% of the profits from the sale of this anthology to this incredible charity.

You can find out more about the work that St Albans for Refugees undertake, and also make your own donation, by visiting:

www.stalbansforrefugees.org

INTRODUCTION
Howard Linskey

I have been involved with the Verulam Writers group for a number of years now, ever since they first asked me to pop along one night to talk about my books and how I became an author. I found an enthusiastic, friendly group of people, with varying levels of writing experience. Some already had novels published, others aspired to reach that point but most enjoyed writing for their own enjoyment then sharing their words with like-minded people. What they all had in common, with me and the other members of their group, was that they were all writers, so it's no wonder we got on. Writers instinctively understand other writers. Even close friends and family members who are non-writers cannot possibly understand how it feels on a good day, when the words are flowing, or a bad one, when we are staring at a blank page, searching in vain for inspiration. That's when a group like Verulam Writers comes in very handy.

I've been coming back to the group regularly ever since that first chat, sometimes to update them on books I am writing but also to judge the annual 'Howard Linskey Crime Writing Short Story Competition', which they were kind enough to name after me. Every year, I get around a dozen entries of a very high standard. I love reading them but hate judging them. Writing is such a subjective exercise and I know how fragile an author's self confidence can be. Somehow, I have to pick a top three and a winner. The winners are always pleased, the ones who don't quite make the short list are gracious and happy for their friends who did. It's that kind of group. Coming first in that contest is almost as prestigious as winning the now famous 'Gnome De Plume' award, given to the writer who comes up with the best Pen Name, which is judged by their peers in a lively open vote. Last year's winner was 'Lady Quelle-Heure'. I can only admire and envy that level of creativity.

What I like most about the Verulam Writer's Group is their solidarity and support of one another. When I was an aspiring author, I lacked the self-confidence to come along to a group of fellow writers and actually read out something I had written. I don't know what I imaged would happen; ridicule, stinging criticism, the end to any fragile dreams I might have had of becoming an author? Having seen them at first hand, I know I wouldn't have experienced any of that at Verulam Writers. I wish I had turned up there much sooner. I probably would have been published years earlier if I had. Long may they continue as a group and I hope they carry on inviting me to judge their dark, twisted, often quite brilliant crime tales for many more years to come. I hope you enjoy this collection of their latest short stories as much as I will.

Howard Linskey
October 2022

LOCAL CRIMES FOR LOCAL PEOPLE

TRAPPED

Rachael Blok

The air is rank—stale, fetid. Something runs over her foot and in the dark, Zoe screams. A rat? She's always hated rats.

She pushes her hands as far as they'll go, up above her head. The wet, slimy stone is repellent. The stone is the same either side of her. Rounded, almost. It feels like a tunnel of some kind. She takes a step forwards, but there's a tug on her ankle.

She bends, feeling around. A chain.

Squinting, summoning all the light she can, she can vaguely make out the end of the chain in an old hook on the wall. She knows it's old—her fingers find the rough giveaway of rust on the ring.

Trapped.

*

Fear bites, and she can't remember what's happened. She was on a date. Cocktails in a bar. Then dinner. Did they walk down Holywell Hill? He was holding her hand. It was going so well. Time is loose in the dark. She woke recently—an hour, two hours? How long was she unconscious? The date could have been hours ago. Or maybe days.

Then what? Holywell Hill, walking—there was something; what was it? She felt dizzy, that's right.

They were by the bookshop. She leant against the glass, cool against the palm of her hand.

Oh my God. Had there been something in the wine?

When she woke in this tunnel, she opened her eyes to the thick pitch of black; for a second, she worried there was something wrong with her eyes.

Instead, there's something very, very wrong.

*

DCI Maarten Jansen looks round the restaurant. Zoe Lattimer has been missing now for 11 hours. Not enough time for anyone to really worry—most likely she's stayed over at a boyfriend's and hasn't got in touch with her mum. But her mum teaches yoga at the class Liv, his wife, does each week, and she called first thing, in floods of tears.

'We have a code! On a first date, she messages every hour. If she's staying over, then she always messages first. There's just the two of us—she knows I worry.'

The station wasn't busy that morning and he couldn't ask anyone else to look into it yet. He'd been tied up with a case that had only been resolved the previous day, so an hour away from paperwork was welcome. He wandered down, and Adrika, his DI, came along.

'The restaurant remember her being here. They're looking for the CCTV footage, but I made a call to her date—Zoe passed the details on to her mum. He says he put her in a taxi on Holywell Hill about 11 p.m.; she wasn't feeling very well.'

The sun is bright as they walk back to the station. A cold April sun—the promise of more heat in a few weeks.

'Does he have the taxi details?'

She shakes her head. 'It was one they flagged. He walked home.'

'Let's head back to the station. I'll phone her mum. Chances are, she's been in touch by now if she's gone home with him.'

Adrika takes a call as they arrive at the traffic lights. 'Another one!' she says, hanging up.

Maarten feels his stomach plummet. 'Another missing woman?'

'No. A break in. The bookshop—Books on the Hill.'

'Someone's stolen books?' Maarten thinks of the first editions in there, thousands of pounds in the cabinets.

Adrika's face wrinkles. 'Nothing's gone. The door lock has been smashed in, the security system disabled, a few books on the floor and the counter the till sits on is upended, but nothing taken. It's the second time it's happened in a month.'

'The morning needs more coffee,' Maarten says, stretching his tall frame. 'They have a coffee shop in there. Let's drop in. That paperwork isn't calling me. We've worked round the clock recently. Let the station know we'll pay a visit.'

*

'It's the mess, really.' The woman who owns the shop is clearly upset. 'I haven't touched anything, as I thought you'd need to check for fingerprints. But we can't open today. That's another day lost. Insurance will cover the damage, but it all takes time. We need to open.'

Maarten nods in reply, as Adrika asks questions.

Strange, Maarten thinks. It's not even gratuitous destruction. It's almost as if a mini whirlwind sped through. What does anyone get out of this?

*

Zoe's head aches. She must have cut it at some point. Her forehead feels swollen and spongy. Sticky too. She must look a right state.

She's tried shouting, but no one has come. The shouting has left her throat aching and she's almost dry of tears. Her ankle is raw, and she's so desperate for water she can feel her fingers swollen as though she's been on a flight. Her back aches from lack of movement.

'Mum,' she whispers, in the dark. She knows what kind of state her mum will be in. She would always call; her mum knows that. Since Dad died it's just been the two of them, and yes, renting is almost unaffordable, but she opted to stay living with mum a little longer. At some point she'll move out. Just not yet.

Her school—they will wonder why she isn't there. Year 6 will be missing a teacher today—that won't have escaped anyone's attention.

Between her mum and the school, they must have raised the alarm?

She prays they have.

Maarten sips at the hot coffee he carried back to the station. Something niggles. He can't put his finger on it.

'Adrika, there was another woman a few weeks ago—someone thought she'd gone missing, then her flatmate said she was going travelling. It came to nothing. Can you pull the details?'

Once Adrika returns, he scans the file.

'What is it, sir?'

'This case—it ended before it began. A young woman—she had tickets to go travelling and went out for drinks the night before. But a friend on the night out said she didn't think she'd gone home. The flatmate said she'd left the next morning, and then there was a post on her Instagram, a photo of Thailand—her first stop. It came up while the friend was in the station, so she apologised, as the woman didn't seem to be missing anymore. But that was a few weeks ago—the same date as the first break in at the bookshop.'

Adrika looks at him, and her shiny bob swings forward as she reaches for the file. She runs her finger down the details. 'The mobile number on this.' There's a note to her voice; a professional excitement kicks in, tinged with dread. It's a tone Maarten is familiar with, and it doesn't bode well. 'The number of the flatmate here is the same as that of Zoe's date last night. Different names, but then he could give any name. I don't like this.'

*

Zoe reaches as far as she can, hoping she finds anything: a dropped phone, rock to hit the chain with. Anything.

What she does feel stops her cold. It's a hand. A cold hand. She's not alone in here, but from the feel of it, she's the only one still alive.

The scream dies in her throat—fear holds it tight and she trembles.

*

'He's ready for questioning,' Adrika says. 'The name he gave as the flatmate of Lana Cole, the first woman reported as missing, was Joss Burton. The name he gave Zoe Lattimer last night was Jessie Brown. Joss Burton is his real name—Jessie Brown is fabricated. It's not hugely unusual on dating apps, but it doesn't help his case.'

Maarten nods. 'And CCTV for Holywell Hill?'

'From the angles of the cameras we have them heading towards the bookshop. Then a bit later, he walks home alone down the hill. Like he said. He maintains the time in between was spent flagging a cab. We can't see her in any of the cars leaving the hill in either direction. But there's no sign of her on the street. She's vanished into thin air. We can't disprove his story. It looks like maybe she was in a cab; we just haven't got the angle right from the camera, and we can't see her.'

Maarten is tired. His patience is thin. These last few weeks have been long and he's ready for a break.

'Let's go. If she is in trouble, then there's not much time left.'

*

Zoe's eyes are heavy. No one is coming. The things she thinks of: her mum's birthday present is hidden in the cupboard at home; she hasn't marked the practice SATs papers for Year 6; she'll never visit California.

Panic takes hold, and she gives one last surge. One last pull on the chain.

Is it enough?

*

Joss Burton is giving nothing away. Maarten's left him to stew in the interview room. He was cocky and rude. *'What are you saying I've done? I walked home alone—you can see that. What, you think I hid her in my pockets?'*

'Can you check fingerprints on the bookshop? Was it him in there?' Maarten looks outside. The April sun is falling and it's getting dark. It will be Easter soon. He's supposed to be at an event in the cathedral tonight, but he doubts he'll make it.

Something stirs at the back of his mind.

'No fingerprints—they're going over the scene again at your request. Because nothing was taken, they'd just classed it as vandals. You want SOCO in there?'

Maarten nods. 'Yes. And don't let Burton go. Keep him in for a bit longer.' What niggles? The cathedral.

Kak—of course. People don't disappear into thin air. But they can disappear underground.

*

Zoe is trying to scratch into the wall—there's a button on her cardigan, and she's pulled it off. She's tried to scratch a message to her mum, but it's so dark she can't see anything. It's too black.

And she's so tired.

Not here, she thinks. Not like this.

The tiniest fleck of light flashes down the tunnel. Just a speck.

'Mum!' she screams. 'Mum!'

*

'Oh Maarten,' Zoe's mum hurls herself at him in the hospital. 'Thank you. Thank you.'

Adrika smiles as she watches his discomfort with physical contact.

He can cope just this once.

'How did you find her?'

'I went on a tour of the cathedral last year; they mentioned there are secret tunnels all around here. I'd heard the same thing in the bookshop. The main mess was in the front of the shop, so no one had thought to go to the cellar underneath. The tunnels are bricked up, but when we pushed, they gave way. Someone has smashed part of the wall through and replaced it with new bricks but no cement—there's small opening you can crawl through. The bookshop was broken into last year. He must have been planning this for a while.'

Zoe's mum is ashen. 'Zoe said there was a body down there? She felt a hand. I can't think what—'

'Don't think about it. Zoe is safe, and that's what matters,' Adrika says, quietly. 'The other woman was not so lucky.'

Maarten nods. 'We checked, and Lana Cole never boarded the plane. Joss Burton had taken her phone, and was updating her social media, sending the odd message to her parents. You can check-in on social media anywhere in the world, it seems. You don't actually have to be there for it to work. A few photos of Thailand, and a few check-ins in foreign bars. It would have crashed at some point, but who knows how many women he could have hurt or killed by then?'

'Why?' Zoe's mum shakes her head. 'Why would anyone do this?'

'I don't know. Power? Some kind of fantasy? There's no point wasting time thinking about him.' He thinks of Lana's family. He'd spoken to her parents only half an hour ago. They were coming to the station later.

It wasn't all happy news.

'You want to come and say hello? Zoe wants to say thank you.'

It wasn't all happy news. But he can be pleased about Zoe—if she'd stayed down there for much longer it would have been a different story.

'Yes, I'd love to say hello.' He smiles.

FIREWATCH DUTY

Steve Seaton

Outside the ancient, gnarled door of the abbey, a teenager was missing his 'girlfriend' and stamping his feet against the cold. Usually a genial-enough young choirboy, Basil found himself giving voice to a grumble or two. His breath steamed out under the frosty Yew Tree.

'Oh *yes*! 'Don't be late tonight young Saville,' Basil muttered to himself. "Hitler can strike on Christmas Eve as well as any other night.' What on earth's happened to old Big Ed? Late—and him normally a stickler.'

Mr Edison the Choirmaster, the Big Ed in question, was also the leader of the Cathedral Firewatch Team, and was a strict but respected disciplinarian both in rehearsals and in Firewatch shifts. *Worse than Dad,* thought Basil.

His father was with his RAF squadron, somewhere in the wreckage-strewn sandy hillocks of the north-eastern Sahara, where he'd been attacking the war-weary Italians in his rocket-armed Beaufighter aircraft.

'Edison says, 'you needn't make that face, young fellow-me-lad—a Doodlebug fell on Elstree yesterday, so we have to keep a keen eye out. So make sure it's 8 o'clock, sharp!" Basil kicked at the ground and scoured a mark in the frost with his heel. His grounds for grievance were mounting. 'Huh. 'And don't forget your torch, young man—no lights allowed on inside or the wardens will have our guts for garters.' Just my luck my choirmaster's the Firewatch boss too.'

But Basil smiled as he remembered his own riposte later in that rehearsal:

'Basil, you sang that D Flat sharp!'

'Yes, Sir. You keep telling us we have to look sharp...'

Under his brusque manner, Henry Edison had a soft spot for his choristers, and when the choirboys burst into laughter, he'd had the good grace to smile tolerantly. But now it was Christmas Eve, and Basil yearned to be at the carol singing in the Market Place. Alice would be there.

Alice... Instead of mooching here, he could be smooching there, with nice Alice. If only girls were allowed in the choir—stupid rule!—what close harmonies he and she might make together...

If only.

He still wasn't sure where he stood with Alice. But the thought of her sweet face and sparky company warmed him through a little as, rubbing his hands, he glanced up at the starry sky.

Oh! There was a sudden rustle in the gloom behind the yew tree. Startled, Basil stood stock still. What was that? A shape...just...over there...?

Silence. Stillness. Basil hardly breathed, tense, heart thudding.

Alice's Mum's recent 'warning' flashed into his mind: 'You choirboys should be careful about messing around in the Abbey Yard—it's been cursed since Benedictine times! If that yew tree is circled at midnight, evil things happen. They say that the Devil himself has even appeared!'

She'd had a twinkle in her eye as she'd said it, as she often did, Mrs Gordimer—she was nice too. But standing rigidly alone outside the great empty cathedral, as chilled and immobile as the tomb statues inside, Basil felt a twinge of terror at the thought of facing the might of Satan, as well as of the Luftwaffe, all by himself.

Then as the heart-stirring sound of age-old carols drifted down faintly from somewhere near the Town Hall, Basil pulled himself together, again grinning to himself. 'Yeah, yeah, yeah—fairy story rubbish!'

And there'd be roast chestnuts later, and cocoa too, now there were more rationed goods in the shops at last. Maybe he'd even be invited back for some of Mrs Gordimer's mince pies....

A twig snapping. A low growl. Basil clutched at his heart. There *was* something there, over by the yew. What in heaven's name? Whatever could...?

A fox! It was a stealthy fox, circling the tree. It halted, snuffled. Its red eyes shot a sharp gleam at Basil in the soft moonlight.

It glared for a moment, arrogantly holding Basil's stock-still gaze. A long, long bated-breath stand-off.

Then at last, turning, it padded silkily away, off down the slope towards the river.

This time, Basil really was unnerved. Where were his Firewatch shiftmates? How was he expected to handle flying bombs alone, in a haunted yard, terrorised by savage night-time creatures? *Time to chuck it in—let the cathedral burn for all I care,* he thought. *I don't want to... I feel like...*

I'm off!

And he actually did scurry a good few steps, round and along the graveyard path, homeward. But then Alice's words from yesterday came back to him: 'Bazza, I think you're brave doing that Firewatch duty. Them Doodlebugs scare the living daylight out of me.'

'Well, Firewatch scares *me* to death,' he blurted out loud in the ancient cemetery gloom. But then he faltered. How could he explain it to Alice if a V1 *did* come, and he'd chickened out of his duty because of some silly legend or whatever? What if St. Albans' beloved cathedral burned to the ground, over a thousand years of history wiped out, and it all had been his fault?

Would Dad back out any time he *was scared? Even if badly scared? Had Alice's Mum gone to pieces as an ARP in that awful Hatfield disaster two months ago?*

He hesitated; then steeling himself, he squared his shoulders, turning back towards the Abbot's Door. 'OK, so the others haven't come. Someone's got to do it. I guess that'll be me then.'

Basil retraced his steps.

He fumbled for his key. The ancient, studded abbey door creaked open and, feeling a bit shaky at the knees, he forced his reluctant self into the huge cathedral, a cavern of echoing gloom.

Fumbling for his torch, Basil made sure the abbey door had clunked shut behind him before he cautiously flashed the beam on. Even a pinprick of light glimpsed through a stained-glass window could serve as a beacon to the Nazi airmen, like when the Luftwaffe pilots had killed his schoolmate's cousin in the Camp bomb blast four years previously. Mr Edison was always reminding the Abbey Firewatch Team that their historic cathedral was used by enemy airmen as a landmark for the Nazi mass-murder attacks on civilian populations in London and its environs.

Basil shuddered. The thud of the door was still echoing around the huge space in counterpoint to Basil's thumping heart as he made his reluctant way across the South Transept. He flicked off the torch again. Glancing up across the High Tower, he could just make out in the metallic moonlight the roses of York and Lancaster commemorating the battles of St Albans, fought during the Wars of the Roses.

Lancaster. Those poor Berliners must be as scared of our bombers as we are of theirs…

Unexpectedly, he stumbled over something on the floor—a drape? Someone's abandoned greatcoat? There were two cloaks, or something, which he'd tripped over. He risked his flashlight for a few seconds. *Monks' habits?* What would *they* be doing there? (How *could* they be there?)

Now, he had the queasy feeling that he wasn't alone – that someone was watching him. Something flitted in the corner of his eye! – he wheeled, gasping. Two hooded figures were hurrying towards the shrine area! Gaping, Basil struggled to breathe, his head pounding.

No, no. *NO.*

All that nonsense about the Yew Tree outside had left him imagining things, of course. He shook his head sharply to drive all this rubbish out of his head.

With teeth clenched, he took a very deep breath, and willed himself to get on with the fire-fighting equipment checks. He stumbled on towards the Shrine Chapel.

Right. St Amphibalus's shrine next, he lectured himself grimly. *Help me please, Amphibalus. Right now, I could do with some of the guts you showed, facing a brutal foreign enemy.*

Although he still felt very uneasy, soon he'd completed the fire equipment check, and had looked in on the Lady Chapel, his favourite. The three-quarters moon had helped him find his way around, although the light shining in through the high stained-glass windows could also cast disturbing shapes and shadows.

OK, maybe I'm doing a bit better now. Now for the Tower.

The Tower was the huge Norman edifice from where they were supposed to keep watch for bombers. Panting a little as he neared the top of the endless stairs, he heard a strange creaking sound above and to his right. *Pigeons?*

There it was again. A rough, rasping sound. A creak. Louder, more prolonged this time.

Creeaakk...

Basil was stunned as, startling him half out of his wits, the stentorian clamour of one of the cathedral bells began to clang deafeningly just above his head! It was so, so *deafeningly* loud that it hurt.

But—this isn't possible*! The bells've all been stowed away. To protect them from war damage, Henry said! Oh, but maybe they've replaced one so it could serve as an air raid warning after the V1 strikes started, or something?*

Galvanising himself, Basil rushed up the remaining steps to the belfry. The mighty din from the bell tower continued unabated, like enough to waken the dead.

The belfry loft. Dimly lit by the three-quarters moon.

But nothing. No-one. Empty bell shafts, completely unmoving.

Face screwed up, fingers in his ears, Basil stood there, rocking on his tiptoes, petrified, willing himself just to survive, to withstand his overpowering terror amidst this impossible, unholy cacophony. He found himself screaming, '*WHAT THE HELL'S GOING ON?*' but his bellows were inaudible amidst the diabolical maelstrom of shattering noise.

Will it never stop?

But bit by bit, Basil began to realise—*thank God, thank God*—that the thunderous peals were gradually abating. He found himself staring around the belfry in stupefaction, wondering whether *he* was the problem. *Am I going barmy tonight?* By now the deafening clangs were mere reverberations in the dusty reaches of the bell tower, echoes of that infernal ringing lingering in his ears, and in his brain.

At last, it was over.

Still shaken to the core, panting and bewildered, Basil staggered unsteadily across the belfry to try to get a grip on himself in the freezing air on the tower roof. He peered through the open slats to gaze over the frosty roof tops of his historic home town, all aglow and glinting in the moonlight. There was the medieval Eleanor Tower, the august Town Hall, the pleasant boulevard of St Peter's Street and at its head, lovely St Peter's Church.

And he could just make out a large-ish crowd of carol singers in the marketplace, dimmed lanterns glowing faintly. *Alice.* Perhaps Alice would be amongst them. The strains of 'Silent Night, Holy Night' drifted up to him as his body slowly unclenched, his terror gradually evaporating with the frosted exhalations of his calming breaths.

At last, Basil could wipe his brow with the back of his hand. No sign of any bombers, anyway. But what else could possibly happen on this weird, weird, wartime Christmas Eve?

Wintry though it was, the air at the heady top of St Albans Abbey Tower had done Basil some good.

Perhaps you can get used to being shaken rigid by unexpected terrors, he pondered. He'd only left school a few months ago, and although war had been declared before he'd even started at the Boys' School, he'd had more to disconcert him this Christmas Eve than in the whole of the previous five war-torn years. Except, perhaps, for his first day as an Articled Clerk last September. And, of course, Dad's posting to North Africa. And...Alice—did she like him? Or not, really? A particularly disconcerting thought.

Shivering a little, he wondered whether Henry and the team had finally arrived yet and decided it was time to descend. But as he approached the quire area, he was startled by a glimpse of a light on in the organ loft. *Who's arrived? And why on earth are they being so careless?*

He hurried from the transept, calling out a sharp, echoing reminder about the blackout.

But instead, organ music started to sound! Organ music! Music he recognised and loved, a thunderous masterpiece which Henry had once played to the dumbstruck choir. *Is this Henry now? What can he be playing at?* Angry now, Basil rushed up the organ steps to berate whomever it might be…

…but there was no-one.

An empty organ stool. A Bach passacaglia, the mighty C minor, now swelling to its spine-chilling tidal wave of spiritual energy, filling the abbey with its majestic sonorities. But no-one was playing it! All he could see were the notes on the keyboard manuals…. and the foot pedals…. depressing themselves! Activated by some invisible agency. And - the pages of the music score were *solemnly turning themselves over entirely by themselves.…*

Dazed and rooted to the organ loft floorboards, Basil gaped with disbelief as he struggled to comprehend the surreal scene he was witnessing. But the bizarreness intensified when the magnificent organ music gradually faded, only to be replaced with a swelling chorus of male voices, apparently from the far end of the nave. The music was ancient, beautiful, and somehow Basil recognised it—a haunting renaissance Mass, strangely familiar.

A glorious ancient Agnus Dei continued to spread across the Cathedral, sweetening every chapel and dark corner of the abbey as a group of richly-voiced, hooded—*monks! –they're monks!* — came into view. Too astonished to marvel at anything now, nor even to feel frightened anymore, Basil found himself joining in with their worship in his oaken young baritone, singing instinctively along to the beautiful words:

'O, Lamb of God, that takest away the sins of the world, grant us thy peace.'

Scalp prickling, tears streaming, Basil was transfixed by the sublimity of it all.

The figures of the monks, led by the abbot, each holding a lighted candle, were now approaching the high altar. They did not stop nor deviate. One by one they passed through the holy screen, fading from view as they did so, the glorious music diminishing with the disappearance of each couple until, as the last pair vanished from view, Basil too stopped singing, lingering on the final chord of the Amen, the very end of the Missa Albanus, Robert Fayrfax's mass for St Alban.

This time ready for almost anything, when the Abbot's Door began to creak open, Basil faced it grittily with his shoulders pulled back.

It was Henry's voice! At last. What a tale, what an incredible story he had to tell.

'Unlocked—Basil must be in here somewhere.' There were fumbling noises.

Basil's voice returned from the shadows. 'Yes, I am definitely here!' He switched his torch on, shielding it with his hand, to indicate where he was standing. A torchlight flashed in his eyes.

'Ah! Well done, lad, for sticking to your guns without us. Everything all right?'

Then, Alice's voice this time. 'Bazza! You OK? You look sort of funny.'

'Don't know—but where have you lot all been? You've missed something absolutely extraordinary.'

'False alarm, love. We were sent to a call-out, down Folly Lane—wild goose chase.' replied Alice's Mum. 'Thank God it wasn't another one like the Hatfield attack.'

Henry was keeping his flashlight on. 'Have you done the equipment checks, Basil? Actually, *are* you all right lad? You do look a bit...odd.'

'Mr Edison, we need to talk. It's urgent.'

'Oh. All right – let's get into the Vestry, then we can have a light on proper and make some tea. If the Dean's left us any evaporated milk this time.'

The four of them groped their way uncertainly across into the vestry. With a sigh of relief, Alice shut the door and turned on the light. She also turned her dazzling smile on to Basil. His heart skipped a different kind of beat this time.

'Take your time, lad. You look as if you've had a bit of a shock of some kind.'

Sitting on a stool, head in his hands, Basil realised how hard it would be to put it all into words. But when the kettle had boiled, he took a sip of sweet tea, and began, haltingly.

'Well... My Firewatch stint started with this fox outside, round by the yew tree. I felt it stirred something up...Something weird, circling round the tree like that...You remember that old legend, Mrs Gordimer...?'

So, at first falteringly, keenly aware of how unutterably implausible it must sound, but then gathering momentum, Basil told them the story of his incredible experiences in the abbey during the evening. He ended, eyes shining, with a passionate description of his participation in the Alban Mass with the abbot and his hooded monks.

Henry had been listening with an expression of benign scepticism, Alice with excited wonder, but Janet had been looking concerned and thoughtful.

'So, Basil,' she responded after a heavy pause. 'Are we to understand that you think the fox unleashed some paranormal—even diabolical—forces?'

Basil shrugged.

Henry leaned forward. 'Oh, come on lad—an organ which plays itself? Singing monks? Bells which peal in an empty belfry? More like you've had bats in the belfry! You've told a great Christmas Eve ghost story, son but come on—really!'

Basil was crestfallen.

Janet intervened to save his feelings. 'Basil, you've done really well to do Firewatch without us, but don't you think your imagination might have run away with you, all alone in this massive space in the dark? Just stop and think a minute. If the bells had rung, we'd have heard them in St Peters Street.'

'I know, it doesn't make sense. But look, it really happened. I'm not making it up, Mrs Gordimer.'

Still looking thoughtful, Janet maintained her tone of reassuring common sense. 'OK Basil, love, tell you what, I'll just nip down and check the bell store, all right?'

'Yes Baz,' Alice put in encouragingly. 'And why don't you show us where you saw those monks' cloaks?'

They all got up. Alice switched off the vestry light, and while Janet proceeded cautiously off to the storeroom in the dim light of the north transept, the other three, led by Basil with his shielded torch beam, groped their way across the south transept.

'Somewhere over here, near the Abbot's Door.'

Henry clicked on his own torch, shielding it with his hand, and shone it around carefully. 'Nothing here, lad. You can see for yourself.'

'But they must be here somewhere. I just don't understand it—I actually tripped over them. I tell you it really did all happen. Look, I'll show you the music score on the organ if you like. It was that Bach you played us, Mr Edison.'

Basil hurried round through the quire, stumbling up the first few steps to the organ loft in the moonlit gloom, the other two following in his wake.

Guided by the light from Henry's torch, Janet was re-joining them. 'The whole set of thirteen are still safely stowed away, Basil,' she called out gently.

'But there *must* be one missing. Look, anyway, I'll show you the score of the organ music I heard!'

He switched on the light over the console.

'Oh. But it WAS there—I saw the pages turning themselves over...'

Basil was baffled and deflated. Now, Henry was looking concerned at his young protégé's distress.

'Basil, you mentioned the Missa Albanus. But that's all choral. There's no organ.'

'No, no, no! The organ had stopped by the time the monks appeared!'

Janet intervened soothingly again. 'Basil, we know you're a sensible lad. Maybe you're just a bit shaken up though?'

'I KNOW WHAT I SAW! And *listen,* I don't even know the Alban Mass. But somehow, I was singing it as if I did...I *knew* the bass part of the Agnus Dei though I've never sung it or seen it.'

The whole incredible evening had been too much, and now he was feeling a little hysterical. But Alice slipped her arm around his shoulders. 'My goodness, Baz, you certainly *look* as if you've seen a ghost.'

There. That word again.

'And I certainly believe you saw the fox, Baz. I've seen one in the graveyard before.'

Janet was smoothing down her hair wonderingly. 'Just thinking. Voices from the past, ghosts lighting up the dark, the Benedictines, Robert Fayrfax, maybe even St Alban himself. Henry, you don't think...?'

'What? What are you suggesting, Mrs Gordimer?'

'Could there be some *link* between Basil's experiences tonight? Something important we're being urged to understand?'

Henry sat on the organ stool, a sudden flash of recognition dawning on his brow. 'Voices from the past, Janet? Interesting. What Basil's been describing—ghostly musical emanations?' He scratched his beard. 'I remember now. It's happened before, I believe in Dean Glossop's time.'

'Yes! We were told about that at school,' put in Alice excitedly. 'They arranged one of those town centre history walks, and that ghost story about the cathedral scared me. I had nightmares after. It was about that famous Dean—he heard music coming from the abbey when the building was dark and empty at night.'

'Yes, that's right,' exclaimed Henry. 'And if memory serves, the music was...'

'The Fayrfax mass?' Basil's spirits were starting to revive with this unexpected possibility of vindication.

'Yes, lad. The Missa Albanus.' Bemused, Henry and his Firewatch team tried to assimilate the mind-bending implications of the links now being put together.

Soon, Janet spoke up again: 'So … supposing it wasn't malign forces which Basil's fox conjured up, but *voices from the past*? Our Saints, Alban and Amphibalus. And other great figures in our history, people who felt a passionate love for the cathedral. *Guardian figures watching over everything precious which this wonderful place has stood for during seventeen hundred years?*'

Another prolonged silence. Eventually, Henry shifted on the organ stool. He coughed demurely into the back of his hand.

'Well, who knows. Maybe I've misjudged you a bit, lad. And very well done for holding the fort all alone tonight. Good show. It'll take time for this other business to sink in though. Most odd. But meanwhile I reckon it's time for us all to lock up, go home, and start to enjoy Christmas.'

Prosaic as Henry's pronouncement was, all of them were more than happy to comply. They clambered down the organ loft steps and shuffled their way to the great oak door.

Outside, the bitter cold cut through them with a newly stirring easterly breeze.

Janet shivered as Henry locked the door of the ancient building. 'The last war was supposed to be the war to end all wars. But then came *this* dreadful war. There's talk of bringing the Nazis to trial for all their 'War Crimes' when it's finally over. *But isn't war itself the biggest, bloodiest crime?* So much senseless suffering, pain, loss, death, destruction.'

Henry nodded. Yawning, he stretched his arms out, then reached them behind himself to massage tiredness out of his back. 'You know what? I don't reckon Hitler's going to trouble us tonight. I'm looking forward to a glass of mulled wine and some supper. A very Happy Christmas to the three of you—but don't forget Firewatch tomorrow. You never know when those Nazi devils are going to darken our skies.' He waved goodbye, then strode off down towards Holywell Hill, humming the stern melody of Bach's C minor passacaglia in the wintry air, its echoes fading down Sumpter Yard.

'Come back with us, Basil,' Janet invited him. 'Your Mum said she'd pop in after carol singing.'

As they turned to walk past the graveyard, Basil's heart soared when Alice's hand crept into his.

But further up the slope, they stopped, clenching their hands together tightly, as away in eastern skies slashed erratically by searchlights, they heard the first faint throb of a V1 pulsejet engine drawing steadily closer.

***

This story is based on actual events and contemporary accounts at the end of 1944. Basil was a real person who became a successful local solicitor in adult life and was a respected member of the post-war St Albans Community. The other characters are fictional.

OVERKILL, MUCH?

J.L. Merrow

I heard about it from Vik at the off licence, who'd had it from Britney from the fabric shop when she'd popped in for some ciggies and a bottle of rosé prosecco, seeing as it was her eldest's sixteenth birthday.

I frowned at that one, distracted for a mo' from the no doubt mundane bit of gossip Vik had been about to impart. 'Don't you get in trouble for selling alcohol for consumption by a minor?'

'Hey, she never said who'd be drinking it. And parents are allowed to give their kids alcohol at home. Didn't your mum and dad let you have a crafty sip for Sunday lunch?'

'Well, yeah, but I didn't know it was *legal*. So go on then, what's this juicy gossip you've heard?'

Vik leaned on the counter. 'You know the Antique Emporium up the road?'

'I've never set foot through the door, but yeah. Think I know the guy who runs it by sight. Old-school flamboyant, with a touch of the Quentin Crisps?'

'That's the one. He's been done over. Fighting for his life.'

'He's been attacked?'

'Yep. Robbery. Bastards hit him over the head with an eighteenth-century blunderbuss. And then stabbed him with a medieval Scottish dirk. That one was a reproduction, though.'

I blinked. 'Okay, first, overkill much? And second, how come you know all about it?'

Vik shrugged. ''S what Britney said. She's into weapons. It was her what found him. She only went in to find out if he'd had any luck tracing a pistol ring for her.'

Well, after all that, there was only one thing to do. Develop a sudden interest into all things fabric-related.

The fabric shop was another Fleetville establishment I'd never set foot in. Clearly, I needed to make more effort to support the local economy. It wasn't quite what I'd expected—there was a serious lack of bright cotton florals and elderly ladies discussing the arcane art of quilting. Instead, there was a shed-load of Halloween themed stuff, although we were nowhere near October, and a poster advertising something called a 'Stitch and Witch' on Thursday evenings.

'Can I help?' called out the cheery lady behind the counter. She had blue hair, lightly tanned skin, and was wearing a black top embroidered with silver skulls.

'I'm, uh, looking for a present for my sister?' I improvised desperately.

'What's her craft?'

'Uh, cross-stitch?' I vaguely remembered Sis frowning over a bookmark once.

'Ooh, excellent. We've got some great new kits in. Traditional, goth, subversive...? This one's very popular.' She bustled over to a rotating display and pulled out a kit for a sampler. It looked sort of cottagey, until I read the text on the picture: *Some days, the supply of available curse words is insufficient to meet my demands.*

I screwed up my face. 'Maybe not?'

'Or this one?' She held out a similar sampler kit, this one asking visitors to *Please don't summon demons in the bathroom.* It had a cute little goat's head design, with an inverted cross.

I thought of my sister and her husband, the soon-to-be-bishop.

Ah, what the hell. She'd hate it, but *he'd* probably love it. 'Yeah, cheers, I'll take that one.'

As she rang up the sale, I said casually, 'Bad business about the antiques place.'

The lady's face went solemn. 'Terrible. Terrible! It was me what found him, you know?'

'You'd be Britney, then?' At her nod, I held out a hand. 'Tom Paretski. I live just round the corner.' Usually, at that point, I'd mention I'm a plumber, as a little extra advertising never hurts, but I didn't want to get her side-tracked into a discussion of any dripping taps or problematic drains.

She beamed. 'Lovely to meet you!' Then the smile vanished. 'Horrible, it was. He was all over blood, and when they hit him with that flintlock, they cracked the wooden stock. Terrible way to treat an antique.'

'Must have been a shock, finding him like that.'

'I hope he makes it. He's a lovely old bloke. Do you know him well?'

''Fraid not. Not really into antiques.'

'Oh, but... You know. You and him both being gay.'

I blinked. 'Is it written on my forehead?'

She cackled. 'I may not have been here long, but I've heard all about the famous Tom Paretski and his husband! Now, my Whitney reckons *he's* the good-looking one, but now I've met you all I can say is, you're a well-matched pair!'

'Er, thanks?' Also: Britney and Whitney?

'So, I know why you're here. Your other half is hot on the trail, isn't he?'

'Uh…' My other half, Phil, is a private investigator with an office only a hop, skip and a four hundred metre dash from where we were currently standing. But I didn't reckon he'd be too keen on me telling people he was employed on a case which, as far as I was aware, he hadn't even heard of. Even if this one was local. Practically personal.

Britney gave me a knowing smile. 'Mum's the word, eh? But I bet you'd like to hear it all from the horse's mouth. Well, I'll tell you what I told the police—'

The door jangled, and a skinny teen in a black hoodie stepped into the shop.

Britney gave them a smile. 'Here you go, love. Came in today.'

She handed a brown paper bag to the kid, whose age I was still trying to guess. Fourteen? Fifteen? School age, at any rate—this being the holidays there were a lot of kids about, although not so many this early in the morning. They paid and left, not having spoken a single word. 'Enjoy!' Britney called as the door jangled once more.

Then she turned back to me, her face serious. 'It was first thing this morning, before I opened up. Quentin's always half an hour before me.'

He was actually called Quentin?

'Well! It wasn't a sight for a woman before she's had her coffee, I can tell you that. Poor Quentin, lying bleeding on the carpet. And it's such a nice one, too. Kurdish, you know, with the indigo still so vivid.'

'Did you see anyone else?'

'Oh, they asked me about that, but I said, how could I have eyes for anyone but that poor old man? Laid out unconscious with one of those reproduction dirks in his guts! I told them, you could have marched seventy-seven elephants playing trombones past me right then and I wouldn't have noticed a thing.'

Fair enough. 'So did it look like they'd done the place over? Whoever attacked him, I mean?'

She pursed her lips. 'See, that's the funny thing. Now the police, they were all about it being a robbery, because the till had been emptied. But like I told them—tried to, anyhow—there was no point robbing the till at that time of day. How much could he have had in it? Just a float, that's all, and that's not worth risking prison time for. And there was nothing else taken that I could see.'

She had a point. And I didn't like the implication the poor old guy had been targeted for violence. Why? Because he was gay?

The door jangled again, and another teen walked in. This one was chunkier and wore a grey hoodie.

Britney smiled at them. 'Came in today. Here you go, love.'

Another brown paper package changed hands for money.

What the hell *was* this? I mean, surely it couldn't be the obvious?

If you were dealing drugs to teens, you wouldn't do it *this* openly, would you?

I was taking a rare, not to mention unexpected, day off, seeing as a job had cancelled on me at short notice; something about the wife deciding a new bathroom suite wouldn't improve her life as much as a new husband. The sun was shining, the bank account was firmly in the black, and I'd thought, why not?

My other half, Phil, would be slaving away over a hot desk, writing reports, poor sod. Maybe me turning up with news of a local crime would be just the thing to brighten up his day?

Or maybe... Maybe I could solve this mystery on my own? I'd been with Phil long enough to pick up a couple of tips, I reckoned. And it wasn't right, someone running round my home town stabbing people. Especially if it turned out to be a hate crime.

I unlocked my front door, paused only to dump the six-pack I'd got from the offie and Cherry's soon-to-be unwanted gift, and headed back out and up towards the antiques place.

Of course, I didn't go *in* the antiques place. For a start, 'famous Tom Paretski' or not, I didn't reckon the uniformed copper on the door would let me. She had that no-nonsense air about her. No, where I actually went was the dry cleaner's next door.

Presumably all the actual dry cleaning was going on out back, as the two women behind the counter had their heads together, putting the world to rights. 'Morning, ladies,' I called out cheerfully.

The older one gave me an arch look. 'Phil's got you picking up his suits now, has he? You need to watch out. It's a slippery slope.'

'Oi, I could be in here for something of mine.'

'From what your husband says, you don't own anything that needs dry cleaning.'

'Harsh, but true.' I grimaced as the younger one cackled. It figured they'd be well acquainted with my better half. In matters of sartorial elegance, he's pretty much a ten, whereas I'd need a wild card to even get on the scale.

'I'm pretty,' the older lady said.

'That you are,' I told her, truthfully. 'Oh—your name? Priti with an i?'

She gave me a knowing look. 'Two of them. And there are no discounts for flattery. Although you could give your Phil a few lessons anyway.'

Her colleague laughed. 'Please don't. She'll be useless all day if he starts paying her compliments.'

Priti batted her with a price list. 'Leila!'

Leila ducked and adjusted her headscarf. 'I tell it how I see it.'

I cleared my throat and said as casually as I could, 'Bad business next door, innit?'

Their smiles vanished, and two pairs of deep brown eyes widened. 'Awful,' Priti said. 'He's such a nice old man.'

'So did you see anything of what happened?' I asked.

Their heads shook in unison. 'I wish we had,' Priti said. 'We were very busy, first thing. People like to come in on the way to work.'

'What about beforehand? Did anything out of the ordinary happen? Notice anyone new around here?'

Leila made a face. 'Well, there was that woman yesterday. You know the one I mean, Prits?'

'The tall one with the sunglasses?' Leila nodded, and Priti turned back to me. 'She came in yesterday afternoon, asking about alterations. Although I think she was just killing time.'

'What was she like then, this tall lady?'

'Very skinny.' Priti's expression made it clear she'd be feeding the poor woman up given half a chance. 'And upset, I think. Nervy. But that was yesterday, not today.'

True—but that didn't mean it wasn't all grist to the attempted-murder mill. 'Blonde? Dark? Old? Young? How did she dress?'

Priti laughed. 'A white lady with dark hair. Older than you.'

'Older than my *mum*,' Leila put in. 'And she was wearing jeans and a long-sleeved shirt, and she hadn't ironed it very well. Creases in all the wrong places.'

'Anything else?'

They shook their heads.

'Well, cheers, ladies. I'll take Phil's stuff while I'm here. What's the damage?'

Priti named an unfeasibly large sum, which I paid with a wince. I clearly needed to leave the professional investigating to Phil. Me? I'd bankrupt myself within a week.

After that, being weighed down by garment bags wafting eau de dry cleaning right up my nose, I had little option but to toddle off home. I hung up the clothes and opened a window, which the cats promptly jumped out of. Then I grabbed my phone.

Like any PI worth their salt, me and Phil have friends on the Force. Well, one friend, anyway. DCI Dave Southgate, who I'd got to know a few years ago in connection with a missing kiddie case. See, I have this…gift, I suppose you'd call it (although I tend not to) for finding hidden things. As you can imagine, having overcome his initial healthy scepticism, Dave's made use of my so-called talents a few times since then.

Trouble was, there was nothing hidden in this case. Except, of course, the truth. And abstract concepts? Not really my area of expertise.

Dave answered on the third ring. 'Paretski. I might have known it. I heard there'd been trouble down your neck of the woods.'

That had been quick. I'd thought the news, even of a robbery with violence, might not have yet percolated up to the lofty spheres he now occupied. 'Do you have an alert out for anything that happens in Fleetville?'

'Ask me no questions and I'll tell you no lies. So what is it? Found the loot, have you?'

'No, and from what I hear, there won't have been much to find. You're treating it as a robbery, right? Are you sure about that?'

'Hang on, hang on…' There was a muffled sound of keys tapping and Dave cursing. 'They emptied the till.'

'Which had bugger all in it. And the bloke was hit *and* stabbed—why both? Unless it was personal. Was Quentin able to tell your lot anything?'

'Seeing as he'll have been rushed into surgery and probably hasn't come round yet, I doubt it. So what else do you know?'

'Not a lot. The ladies at the dry cleaners next door had a suspicious woman in yesterday, but I expect they mentioned that when the uniforms did door-to-door?'

There was another pause, then a heavy sigh. 'I bleedin' hate it when people don't do their job. Right. Leave it with me. Just got to set a few heads rolling.'

I said my goodbyes and hung up with the warm satisfaction of having done my civic duty. Mingled with the niggling frustration that I was now almost certainly off the case.

Then again... It wouldn't hurt to see if any of the other shopkeepers of Fleetville had noticed any suspicious strangers, would it? I shoved my phone into my pocket and headed out again.

I won't bore you with the details of my many conversations with the retail workers of my local area. Suffice it to say, I eventually struck gold at Suri's Saris. Rose, Suri's second in command, had noticed a woman acting oddly.

'But it was this morning, not yesterday,' she said. 'She didn't seem to know which way she wanted to go—walked past here three times. Looked upset. You don't reckon she had anything to do with what happened to poor old Quentin, do you?'

'Tall lady, was she?'

'Her? No. Shorter than average, I'd say.'

This was *possibly* a blow to my theory it was the same woman. Then again, Phil's told me often enough that the only time the police get really suspicious is when the witness statements actually agree. 'Blonde?'

'No. Dark hair, cut short—bit like mine.'

'What sort of age?' I asked cautiously.

Rose shrugged. 'Not mummy age, but not grandma age, either. She was dressed sort of posh casual, know what I mean? One of those stripey tops that look like you're about to get on a yacht, and a scarf.'

'Anything else about her?'

Rose shook her head. 'I had to help a customer after the third time she went past. I'm not just here to have a natter, you know.'

Was that a whiff of censure directed at yours truly, for taking up her time and not buying anything? 'Right. Sorry. Uh, how much are these scarves? Thinking of getting a present for my sister.'

Rose's eyes lit up. 'Your sister the lawyer? I've got just the thing.'

I left Suri's Saris carrying a paper bag so light it appeared to have nothing in it, although my bank card was telling me it should have weighed quite a few pounds. I hoped Cherry liked cerise silk. Maybe it would make up for the cross-stitch kit.

Still scanning my surroundings for a tall, short, dark, blonde woman I headed for Morrisons, where I could at least be sure of buying something I actually wanted.

Supplied with no new information but with a carrier bag full of cabbage, mince and tomatoes for golombki (Phil had been trying to persuade me to explore my culinary heritage) I ambled out of the store.

It was then, of course, that the sounds of an altercation caught my ear, and I turned to see a tall, blonde woman. And get this: the lady she was having a barney with in the car park was short and dark haired. In a stripey top. This couldn't be a coincidence. I toddled on over, trying to project the vibes of someone who'd forgotten where he'd left his car. *Forget me own head next, what am I like?*

As I got nearer, the darker lady snapped, 'That wasn't the plan!'

Blondie hissed, 'He des—' and glared daggers at yours truly. 'Can I *help* you?'

I got a worrying feeling she meant, *help me to an early grave*, and I took a step back, hands raised. 'Sorry, ladies. Didn't mean to intrude. Everything all right, though?'

'It will be, if you just *piss off.*' Dark lady growled.

Blondie looked briefly horrified at the language. Then her eyes narrowed. 'You're him, aren't you?'

'Um. Possibly?'

'The plumber. Who solves crimes.'

'Well, in between repairing your pipes—'

'Solve *this*, then!' She lunged at me, with a dagger, sorry, *dirk*, that had appeared from bloody nowhere.

I leapt backwards, holding my shopping bag up in front of me and fervently wishing Britney had got her facts right. *Nothing else was taken*, my mortally-imperilled arse.

Dark Lady screamed.

Blondie's face was twisted with hatred. 'You're all alike, you men! Treat women like dirt.'

'I'm gay!' I blurted out, dodging again. 'I don't treat women like anything!'

She snarled and lunged at me again.

My brain went offline. 'I've got a sister! I even bought her presents today!'

Blondie made another stab at me, and this time she got me right in the cabbage. The knife stuck, and I could feel her breath hot on my face as she yanked at it.

'Stop!' Dark Lady shouted. 'You'll kill him!'

Blondie got the knife free and pulled back her arm.

Oh, God. All I could think of was that I'd never cooked Phil anything Polish, and now I never would.

And then the police turned up.

Flippin' *finally*.

After all that, I only managed store-cupboard pasta for tea. The cabbage would have been a write-off even if Dave's underlings *hadn't* taken it as evidence; who knew where that knife had been?

Phil was still appreciative, bless him. While we ate, I tried to think how best to broach the subject of 'Tom's Day Off'. I still hadn't come up with anything by the time we'd finished eating, and I nipped off to the loo. When I got back to the living room, Phil was just putting my phone back on the coffee table.

'Checking for Grindr hook ups?' I asked mildly.

Phil sent me a hard stare. 'Dave rang, so I answered it.'

I swallowed. 'So, did he happen to mention anything about someone in Fleetville possibly having been in a teensy bit of mortal peril this afternoon?'

'As it happens, yes.' I swear that face was made of granite.

I gave a nervous laugh. 'Still, no harm done.'

The granite cracked. 'Christ, Tom, you have to tell me these things. There I was, writing up reports about husbands who can't keep it in their trousers, and you were facing sodding *death*?'

Shit. 'Not death as such. Malicious wounding, maybe. Grievous bodily harm at most. Probably.'

Phil huffed and opened his arms. 'Come here.'

I went.

After a while, Phil said, 'I suppose it's expecting too much to ask you not to let it happen again?'

'Oi, you say that like I went out asking to be attacked with a knife.'

'Reproduction antique dirk.'

'Potato, potahto. So what did Dave tell you, then?'

Phil gave a long-suffering sigh. 'Those women who attacked you? They were Quentin's *wives*. And yes, plural. Seems the one in Harpenden found out about the one in Welwyn, and they teamed up to teach him a lesson. Only the Harpenden one took it further than they'd planned.'

I was still working my way through that, starting with point one: 'So he's not gay?'

'Don't sound so disappointed. You're a married man.'

'Well, apparently that isn't the barrier to new relationships you might think. But what, the bloke's a bigamist? Hey, if he had three wives, would that make him a trigamist?' I grimaced. 'Bit of a bastard thing to do, but almost killing him for it seems extreme.'

Phil shrugged. 'Maybe Mrs Harpenden had taken out life insurance. And we don't know that was the only grievance they had with him. Dave just gave me the bare bones.'

I shuddered briefly at his choice of metaphor. 'Did he say if Quentin will pull through?'

'Surgery was successful. Finding out about the charge for bigamy might put his recovery back a bit, though.'

There was still one more mystery to solve, though. Exactly what was Britney, who loved weapons, peddling to the youth of Fleetville in her brown bags?

So next day, I nipped into the fabric shop between calls.

Behind the counter was a tall teenager, with long hair and a vintage frock. They had Britney's eyes, though. 'Whitney?' I guessed.

It netted me a smile. 'You're Tom, aren't you? That plumber with the thing?'

I admitted to being guilty on all counts. 'Did your mum say I'd been in?'

Their eyes rolled. 'No. I saw your picture online. So, like, do you stitch?'

I hated to disappoint, but— 'Sorry. I was in here for a present for my sister. Uh, listen, I don't want to pry, but...' I let it hang, as saying 'actually, I totally do' probably wouldn't get the desired result.

Whitney's eyes narrowed. 'Yes, I'm trans. Pronouns: she/her.'

'Oh. Good for you? I'm he/him. I mean no, that wasn't what I was going to ask. I'm, um, a bit concerned about these brown paper bags your mum keeps selling to teenagers... Not that I'm asking you to grass your mum up or anything.' I cringed inside because that was *exactly* what I was doing.

Whitney gave a whole-body *huff,* and reached down under the counter, bringing out one of the brown paper bags. She shook the contents out.

It looked like the offspring of a sports bra and a bullet-proof vest. 'Is that a...binder?' I found myself making vague chest gestures and shoved my hands into my pockets, quick.

Whitney eye-rolled again. '*Obviously*. Mum's the main supplier round here. She doesn't even make a profit on them,' she added with daughterly pride. 'She didn't like to think of people using duct tape or getting cheap binders online that don't fit. She lets people try them on at home and bring them back if they're not right.'

I grinned in relief. 'Very public-spirited of her.'

'Yeah. Specially since this shop's our only source of income.' Whitney sent a needle-pointed look my way. 'So, is there anything you actually want to buy?'

And that's how I ended up with a *Homo Sweet Homo* cross-stitch kit.

Hey, everyone needs a hobby, right?

***

Tom and Phil also feature in The Plumber's Mate Mystery Series of novels.

FINAL BATTLE

Wendy Turner

It was only because the gate had been left ajar that I witnessed the events of that black day and came face to face with death. Real death. Not as in the many skirmishes of the past when those that fell meant little to me. This death was different. It was personal.

Now I know what death is. I know what love is too.

I had been a loyal servant for five years, ever since I was somewhat rudely plucked from my comfortable lodgings at Roman Verulamium, a little north of Londinium. I remember the daisy-strewn meadows within strong Roman walls, strong enough to last for centuries, the early-morning cooing of the doves in the dovecots, chickens scratching about in the spring sun and, best of all, the fiery cookshops and workshops. I overheard my master's servants saying that I had been chosen for my strength, stamina and adventurous spirit. Be that as it may, my memory is of the horrendous sea voyage with the non-stop heave and roll of the ship, and the stench of stale food and vomit. I felt mightily aggrieved at being torn away from such a green and pleasant place. I was even more resentful when forced to traverse the burning streets of Rome. But my master was kind. We bonded almost at once to the point where little instruction was needed. I knew his needs and it pleased me to anticipate them. He rewarded me with little treats which he fed me with his own hand. On occasion in deepest winter, he bedded down with me for warmth, much to the amusement of the citizens and the disgust of his peers. We are two oddities, he and I. We work tirelessly and then run free as the wind until we collapse from exhaustion. He says he will never find another like me and that is the greatest compliment.

As it was, I nudged open the gate. The day was somehow eerie. A chill wind whistled like a shriek from Hades. Swans and geese took off squawking and wild boar turned from rooting in the mud, grunting their disapproval. Dark clouds rolled low smothering the sulphur sky.

Disquieted and unsettled, I capitalised on my new-found freedom by taking the city road, passing bathhouses, laundries, bakeries, wine shops and other familiar sights. Poking my nose in here and there. Breathing in tangy aromas: soap, steam, bread. Intrigued, on I went identifying the clang of steel, hot soup, beer, the latrine.

Steps. They are no problem. Up into the atrium, my footfalls clanging on the tiles like muted bells. Something is amiss. The silence says so. Lack of people, buzz and chatter. My ears prick up and a familiar stab of fear like pre-warfare dread makes me even more uneasy. I suddenly come across the scene. I need time to take it in and when I do, I rear in sheer panic, rolling my eyes. My Master is motionless, sprawled on the ground. His bloody garments are rent into tatters and sticky with gore. After a while I take courage. I lower my head to his and push gently. Arise. Arise like you have done year after year when I wake you in yet another godless and savage place. But he doesn't move. I lick the trickling red river. It tastes of iron and the sulphur sky. I worry his robe with my teeth, shaking it to and fro, but I know it's futile. A storm breaks overhead. My anxiety levels rise like a flood.

The flip-flop of sandals on the flags. A man appears. I know him for Mark Antony, constant at my master's side. For a moment we stand frozen in silence. Abruptly he sprints, landing on one knee at my master's side, heedless of red streaks leaping onto his white robe. A cry of anguish. I know he loves Master as well as I.

A crowd of senators gathers apprehensively. I'm amazed that some clutch blood-stained weapons. Mark Antony is a commander of men and well used to giving orders. He eyes them coldly. 'Why?' he barks.

A man steps forward. I know him for Brutus, my master's close companion. I remember him from Roman Verulamium. 'Caesar was my friend,' he declares. 'Only be patient till we have appeased the multitude, and then we will deliver you the cause why I, that did love Caesar when I struck him, have thus proceeded.'

Mark Antony is white with rage, his jutting jaw testament to his wavering self-control. He glances back at Master and his voice breaks. 'How like a deer strucken by many princes dost thou here lie,' he whispers.

But Brutus is brutal: 'Our reasons are so full of good regard that were you, Antony, the son of Caesar, you should be satisfied.'

Gossip buzzes like a plague of mosquitos. A crowd gathers. Brutus and Mark Antony tussle over who will first address them. Brutus's friend Cassius enters. Cassius and I go back a long way. I admired him when we lived at Roman Verulamium. He was ever vigilant and a shrewd observer of men. He foresees trouble and pulls Brutus roughly aside. 'Do not consent that Antony speak in his funeral,' he hisses. 'Know you how much the people may be moved by that which he will utter?'

He's right. Mark Antony could melt the frozen Tiber with his fair speech.

Cassius is suddenly aware of Caesar's warhorse. How I have grown since those far-off days in Verulamium. He smiles and runs his hands down my neck and along my nose, cleaning up splashes of my master's blood with his sleeve. 'I will take Toe-Ace,' he says, and leads me out. My official name is to do with the white markings on my hoof, but my Master had another: 'Great Heart,' secretly whispered in my ear before battle. But that heart now feels strangely cracked. I can almost feel it splintering.

The crowd becomes boisterous and demanding. Cassius holds onto my tether. I'm glad. I feel reassured near him and want to stay and hear what everyone has to say.

The noise abates as Brutus begins his oratory: 'Romans and countryman, hear me for my cause and have respect to mine honour. If any demand why Brutus rose against Caesar, it is not that I loved Caesar less, but that I loved Rome more. Had you rather Caesar were living and die all slaves? As Caesar loved me, I weep for him, as he was fortunate, I rejoice at it, as he was valiant, I honour him, but as he was ambitious, I slew him. There is tears for his love, joy for his fortune, honour for his valour and death for his ambition.'

Before Brutus can further plead his cause, there's a disturbance. Mark Antony enters unbidden, head bowed, followed by bearers carrying Caesar's body in an open coffin on a bier.

I see you, Mark Antony. Your entry timed to perfection. Will you interrupt Brutus's speech so rudely?

Mark Antony falls to his knees once more. He ignores Brutus and begins, 'I speak not to disprove what Brutus spoke, but here I am to speak what I do know. You all did love Caesar once, not without cause. What cause withholds you then to mourn for him? My heart is in the coffin there with Caesar and I must pause till it come back to me.' Mark Antony is still and pale as a marble statue. Eyeing the crowd, he whispers to them, 'If you have tears, prepare to shed them now.' He clutches my master's ripped and bloody cloak, and his voice wavers. 'You all do know this mantle. I remember the first time ever Caesar put it on. 'Twas on a summer's evening, in his tent, the day he overcame the Nervii.' The crowd is enthralled. Everyone as focussed as hawks circling above, seeking prey.

Cassius spits into the sand. 'I warned you, Brutus,' he snaps. 'Mark Antony has a silvered tongue. Listen to him! Look at them! See how they hold his every word with sighs and tears. Our cause is lost. Mark Antony will snatch away our victory with his pleas. They will seek us out as surely as thunder follows lightning.' He turns and strides away, leaving me bereft and Brutus staring in his wake.

Everything has gone quiet. No-one heeds Great Caesar's warhorse. I seem to have the freedom of the city again and mingle with the murmuring crowd until the sun sets. I make my way once more into the vast hall which has become the final resting place for Caesar's body, away from the stink of the market and overflowing gutters outside. It is a sanctuary of peace. Great bowls of lavender give out their heady aroma mixing with that of incense and spices. Dishes of rosewater stand next to soft hand towels. Barrels of burning pitch transform the white walls into a delicate shade of rose, the reflected flames leaping in polished shields hung along the walls. Despite the warmth, I tremble in my new aloneness.

Now I know what death costs. And what love costs too.

Death is the final barrier. Time is another, parting us slowly but oh so surely. Like a ship setting out from the shore and fading in the distance. Never again will I see the like of my great master. Never again feel his solid weight on my back or his gentle fingers caressing my ears. The echoes of that black day will live on in my great horse heart. May we meet again one day, my dearest Master, and run free once more in the spring meadows of Roman Verulamium.

***

With thanks to Shakespeare's Julius Caesar

ONLY ONE FOOL THIS APRIL

Candy Denman

As she stepped off the train, Callie tucked her blonde hair behind her ear and hoisted her small weekend bag over her shoulder. Once out of the station, she ignored the line of waiting taxis; she turned and walked up the hill towards the city centre. Not having been to St Albans before, she was relying on Google Maps to tell her which way to go.

It was a warm, sunny spring day and the market was busy as she made her way to the narrow road lined with tiny, terraced cottages that probably cost ten times what she had paid for her flat in Hastings. If Callie had been surprised by her old school friend's invite to spend a couple of days with her, she had been even more surprised that she had accepted. She told herself it had nothing to do with the turmoil she was going through, trying to decide on her own future, but there was no doubt she was looking forward to a few days away from Hastings and her life there.

Having located the tiny, terraced cottage where Sarah lived, she rang the bell. The only response was a frenzy of barking. Sarah had asked Callie if she was okay with dogs, she remembered, but she hoped the dog was not as big or fierce as it sounded. She had imagined something sweet and small, not The Hound of the Baskervilles.

When she had waited for a response long enough for the barking to have stopped and the only sound to be some snuffling behind the door, she rang the doorbell again, with, predictably, the same response. Sarah could hardly have failed to hear the first ring of the bell, let alone the cacophony of barks.

Callie pulled out her mobile and tried calling her, but Sarah's phone went straight to voicemail. She left a message and then checked the instructions her friend had given her 'in case I'm delayed.' It was a weekday after all, and solicitors might have to work long hours. Callie understood that because she was a GP.

The gate in the narrow alley between the houses was unlocked, and she went through to the small garden behind Sarah's house. The key to the back door was where she had been told she would find it, under the mat. Unoriginal and probably the first place a burglar would look, Callie tutted to herself. She unlocked the door and opened it, standing well back as a rust-coloured cockapoo hurtled out into the garden, jumping and barking, but stopping for a much-needed pee before starting up with the barking and yelping again, tail wagging wildly. Rather than ferocious, he seemed ridiculously pleased to see her.

Once he had calmed down a little, Callie went into the kitchen, stepping carefully over the mat inside the door which had a wet stain and a couple of piles of poop on it. The poor dog had obviously been shut inside for quite a while. She carefully manoeuvred the mat out of the door. Sarah could deal with it later, she decided. Buddy, as she seemed to remember the dog was called, was busy drinking from a flowerpot, and a brief look round the kitchen showed her two empty bowls. She filled one of the bowls with water and put it down for him as he came hurrying in. He drank some more, gratefully wagging his tail and looking at her with adoration between staring meaningfully at his food bowl. She was beginning to feel uneasy. It seemed to her that Sarah had been away longer than just for the day.

With still no answer from Sarah's phone, Callie put her overnight bag down in the living room and looked around the house. Everything seemed to be tidy; no signs of anything untoward in the living room, and a quick check of the upstairs, with its two bedrooms and family bathroom, revealed nothing out of place.

Callie was just trying to remember the name of Sarah's law firm, so that she could ring and check if everything was all right, when there was a knock at the door, sending Buddy into another frenzy.

The young woman looked surprised when Callie opened the door, holding onto Buddy to stop him rushing out into the street.

'Oh, hello,' the woman said. 'Is Sarah there?'

Once Callie had explained who she was and that Sarah was not at home, the woman told her that she was called Louise and that she worked for Sarah's law firm. Callie invited her in.

'Sarah left a message yesterday saying she wouldn't be in because she was ill,' Louise explained. 'It was a bit inconvenient because we had the auditors arriving.'

'I can imagine,' Callie encouraged her as she made them both tea. After all, Sarah's message had said to make herself at home.

'And then when she didn't come in again today and the auditors said there was, well something wasn't right…' Louise stuttered to a halt.

Callie thought about it. It seemed bizarre. Would Sarah really run off with the firm's cash? Somehow it didn't seem tó fit. She had never seemed overly interested in money. She didn't come from a rich family, but they had never been poor either; but then, Callie hadn't seen much of her friend in recent years and anyone could change.

'Is it a lot of money that's missing?' Callie asked.

'I don't know; they wouldn't tell me even if it was,' Louise admitted. 'I'm only admin, not a solicitor or anything. It's just that I like Sarah; she has always been nice to me and I can't believe she'd do this.' She looked at the dog. 'And she wouldn't leave Buddy. She always joked that he was her soulmate. Well, she did, until she met her new boyfriend.'

Callie's ears pricked up at the news that there was a new man on the scene. In her experience, love could make people do strange things, very strange things indeed. She tried to get more details from Louise, but it seemed that she didn't know anything much, just that his name was Dan.

Once Louise had gone, Callie set about doing a proper search of the house with Buddy following at her heels. He wasn't letting her out of his sight and even followed her into the bathroom. It didn't take Callie long to find an envelope addressed to herself in the spare bedroom, where she would expect to have been sleeping. Ripping it open, she quickly read the note.

Dear Callie,

I am so sorry to drag you into my problems, but if you are reading this note, something has happened to me. I am going to meet my fiancé, the love of my life I thought, but it seems that I was sadly mistaken. He said he needed money urgently for his sick mother who was in danger abroad. She kept needing more and more, and there was always a very plausible reason why his money was just out of reach. Having already given him all my savings, and maxxed out my cards and overdraft, he persuaded me to dip into the client accounts. He promised to pay it all back with interest in just a few days. But he didn't. And now the auditors are coming, and they will find out what I have done. I have also discovered that he has been lying to me about other things. His mother is dead, for a start, and has been for years. I am going to confront him. He absolutely has to give me the money back tonight! But I am frightened. He can be quite volatile and has even been violent, not to me, but I have seen him fly into a rage and hit others.

I am hoping that he will give me the money but if anything should happen to me, I know you will help.

Sarah

P.S. My mother will be happy to have Buddy, if you can take him down to her in Hastings, and please apologise from me because I borrowed money from her too.

Callie read the note several times. Then picked up the phone and called the police.

'No, I have no idea where she met her fiancé,' Callie told the police officer who came to take her statement. 'Like I said, I haven't seen Sarah in several years. Louise from the office might know more.'

She had already been told that an officer had been sent there to question Sarah's colleagues. It seemed that the Hertfordshire police were taking this seriously, not least because a large sum of money had already been confirmed as missing from the client accounts at the solicitor's where Sarah worked. A very large sum.

'So it was out of character for her to ask you to come and stay?'

'Yes, I suppose it was a bit out of the blue.'

'Wouldn't it have been easier to see her when she visited Hastings, where her mother lives?'

'Yes, but I've never been to St Albans before and I had a couple of days free. I thought it would be interesting.'

The constable nodded, accepting that explanation for now, but Callie was quite sure his more senior colleagues would question her more about it. Of course, it had been intriguing at the time, Sarah's sudden plea for Callie to come and stay, that she had something to show her, something urgent. Now Callie was in no doubt she had been summoned simply to take care of Buddy and deliver him to

Sarah's mother if anything happened to his owner when she confronted her fiancé Dan.

'And you have no idea where they were meeting?' the constable persisted.

'I know absolutely nothing other than what is in that note,' she reiterated, nodding towards the piece of paper that was now in a clear plastic folder.

Not long after the police officer had left, asking her not to go back to Hastings just yet in case other officers needed to speak to her, Buddy was sent into a fresh paroxysm of barks by the doorbell. Callie sighed. It seemed like she wasn't going to get a moments peace.

'I really can't help you,' she told the tall, middle-aged and smartly-suited man who had been despatched from Sarah's law firm to find out what she knew. Louise must have told them she was there. 'I haven't seen Sarah in quite a few years, and we've only spoken a few times on the phone in that time. She hadn't even told me she was engaged. I came, because I was at a loose end and it seemed a good time to reconnect.' Callie didn't want to go into details about her own relationship, which was going through a rough patch, or the work problems, not just with a new senior partner at her GP practice, but also with changes to her other part-time job as a police doctor, or forensic physician, to give the job its proper title. She had needed time away from Hastings to do some clear thinking, not to get caught up in someone else's drama.

'I just can't believe she would ever do something like this,' he said, and he had a point. Sarah was not the sort of person Callie would ever have believed would steal from her employers, or, more exactly, steal from her employers' clients. She had been Head Girl when they were at school, for goodness' sake! Straight as a die, honest as the day was long, calm, measured, responsible, sensible; these were the descriptions that came to mind when she thought of Sarah, not thief or embezzler. The only time she had ever seen Sarah angry was when someone had played a practical joke on her and she ended up, literally, with egg on her face. She had gone ballistic then but had got over it quite quickly. What on earth could have made Sarah do this? Callie could only suppose that Dan had been particularly persuasive. And she hoped that Sarah was wrong about the possibility that he would react with violence.

'How much is missing?' she asked.

He shuffled uncomfortably in his chair and ran a hand through his greying hair. 'A lot,' was as much detail as he was prepared to tell her.

'And you didn't notice?'

'It only happened in the last few weeks, a bit here, a bit there. The last withdrawal in the early hours yesterday morning was the only big one, the only one guaranteed not to go unnoticed, even in the short term,' he answered. 'Of course, the auditors would have picked up even the small amounts when they came. She would have known that.'

'Do you think she's run off with him, then?' Kate asked her when Callie rang her best friend and confidante later to tell her about the unexpected turn of events. Like Sarah, Kate was a solicitor, so she fully understood the enormity of Sarah's crime. It wasn't likely that she would be tempted to do the same as she didn't have much in her client account because she mostly did criminal work. Prostitutes, drug addicts and petty thieves never seemed to have any money of their own so they were mainly on legal aid.

'It's possible she's gone off with him I suppose,' Callie conceded, 'but I'm more concerned that he might have hurt her, when she confronted him.'

'What are the police doing about it?'

'Looking for her; they've identified the fiancé and been round to his flat, but there's no sign of him there.'

'That was quick.'

'Apparently he's done things like this before, so as soon as they knew the story, they were pretty sure who he was.'

'Done what before?'

'Dating scams. He meets women through a dating app, is charming and wonderful at first and then gets them to give him money, usually for a sick mother stuck in some foreign country. I can't believe Sarah fell for a scam like that. She's so sensible.'

'He must be very good at it.'

He must have been, Callie thought as she took Buddy for a walk around the lake. She hated to think how desperate her friend had been, how frightened when she realised her career was over as well as her engagement. Her whole life in ruins. How desperate she must have been when she confronted Dan. And what had he done? Hit her? Threatened her? Made her take that one last, major withdrawal from the client's accounts? And then what? Did he kill her? Or did they run off together?

'Do you think he killed her after he forced her to take that last, big, um, withdrawal?' Sarah's mother asked the detective sergeant who was leading the search of the tiny, terraced house where Sarah had lived. Apart from a slight break in her voice, Callie was surprised that she was so well-controlled. As soon as Callie had called, she had insisted that she would drive up. She desperately wanted to find her daughter alive and well but had already told Callie that she couldn't believe she would.

'It's possible,' he replied, uncomfortable to be discussing it. 'But it would be out of character. He normally just ditches one woman for the next one, and we know he was already working on that, from the dating app. In fact, he had a couple of other women on the go.'

Sarah would have hated that, if she had known, Callie thought. She would have hated being made to look a fool. That had always been her greatest fear.

They were standing in the garden, drinking tea, as Buddy snuffled around, peeing wherever he found a nice scent.

'And you've no idea where this Dan is now?' Callie asked.

'No. To be honest, with the last amount being so big, he was unlikely to hang around.' The policeman turned away to watch what was happening with the house search.

That seemed reasonable from Callie's point of view. He had made an absolute killing with that last amount. She shuddered as she thought that that probably wasn't a good turn of phrase under the circumstances, but he'd be able to use it to disappear for quite some time before reappearing in another guise, or even as himself once the furore had died down. And then he would be able to start all over again with his dating scam. Her thoughts were disturbed by Buddy barking.

'Buddy! Come here, Buddy,' Sarah's mother called to the dog. He was snuffling around the side of the garden shed and then started digging with his paws. Dead leaves and other detritus flew back as he dug, tail up and barking intermittently.

Callie had a sudden, awful thought.

'She didn't meet him here? Did she?' she asked the detective sergeant urgently, and hurried towards the shed, anxious at what Buddy might be digging up.

'Oh, God!' Sarah's mum said and covered her mouth with her hand, not daring to say more.

As soon as she reached him, Callie grabbed the dog's collar and pulled him out of the way. She stopped and looked at where he had been digging. The policeman who had rushed after her froze as well. Buddy had uncovered a shoe, and the foot was still in it. The partially covered body was lying face down and the back of the head was also visible.

'Is it her? Is it Sarah?' Sarah's mum called out as Callie led Buddy back to her.

'No, I don't think so,' she said. 'It's a man.'

As police and CSI's came to search the garden and process the body, part of Callie hoped that Sarah had managed to take enough money with that last withdrawal to start a new life somewhere, because she could never come back, not with Dan buried in her garden with the back of his head smashed in.

Sarah had never liked to be made to look a fool, and Dan had certainly done that. More fool him.

AT THE SOUND OF MY VOICE

Dave Weaver

'What do you mean, Jacko's dead?' Krasinski demanded.

'What I just said. Killed, murdered, deceased.' Mickey's grating voice on Krasinski's mobile rose with each word as if to hammer home the unwelcome message. 'He got into a fight with some guy in a pub, I don't know why, probably some woman or his damn football team. Anyway, he ended up with a knife stuck in his gut. Main artery, dead on arrival at State hospital. No more Jacko, that means no more boodle, brass, spondoolicks...' Mickey could have just said the word 'money' but he always repeated stuff three different ways whenever he got emotional. It usually irritated Krasinski, but tonight he suddenly had more important things on his mind. Like, how were they ever going to get the snatched bankroll out of the St. Peters Street bank they'd already stolen it from?

It had seemed such a bold, even artistic, concept when their brilliant ringleader Jacko Ricci had laid his latest plan before them. First, open a safety deposit box account in First National's vault, using Jacko's real name (no need for any alias, no-one had ever heard of him, nor indeed the rest of the gang; they were clean). Next, steal the money, wearing the monkey masks purchased on-line with the fake account they kept for such necessities. Finally, put the money back in the bank via Jacko's deposit box, deep in the vault that no-one would ever look in. They couldn't; it was private and secure. And who would think to search a bank for its own money? Wait the obligatory six months for the heat to die down, then repeat. The perfect recipe for the perfect crime. Only problem was Jacko's increasing paranoia regarding the other two members, Krasinski and Mickey. He'd recognised it as such and apologised to them but still, when it came down to it, decided to keep the key to the deposit box himself. Just until they were ready to split the money. Three ways of course; Jacko was still very democratic in his paranoia.

But now that little bit of trust they'd given him would mean they'd end up with zilch for their efforts. Damn! It was sad that Jacko had died as well, Krasinski added as an afterthought. Some way after in fact.

'What the hell are we going to do now?' Mickey posed the question as his voice gradually returned to normal. 'We're totally knackered, bollocked, balls up...'

The thought-flash should have lit up the bar around Krasinski like a thundercrack. Luckily for the patrons it stayed inside his head. 'Remember the Great Mystereo?' he asked Mickey.

'What about your stereo? This is hardly the time...'

'Mystereo, the hypnotist guy we used on that dame who was going to rat on Jacko, God rest his soul.' Krasinski added, automatically crossing himself. 'And the other time with that bent cop who was going to double cross us.'

'What about him?' Mickey asked.

'I've got an idea.' Krasinski replied, smiling. Jacko wasn't the only natural genius in the gang. As Krasinski was about to prove.

'I'd like to open a safety deposit box, please. I hope I've come to the right place?'

Nathan Smith jumped to his feet and proffered a chair to the man who'd addressed him. The bank staff got commission for every new client they introduced to the bank. A paltry amount but every little bit counts. You learn that in banking. 'Yes, you certainly have, Mr...?'

'Ness, Elliot Ness. I run a small securities firm in the city. We need somewhere a little more secure than the office safe to keep the petty cash and other financial commodities, if you know what I mean.'

Nathan didn't really know what he meant, he'd only been an assistant teller for the last three months and wasn't as up on the financial terms as he should have been, despite the chance the bank had given him. 'Right, well, please allow me to take you through the procedure, if I may be so bold?'

'You may.' Krasinski told him, thinking *this guy is too good to be true*. 'I believe you have a vault somewhere on the premises.'

'Yes, it's quite a simple process really. You open an account, for a nominal introductory fee, then we give you a security box of your own to keep your valuables in. If you come with me, I'll show you.'

Nathan led Mr Ness down some wide stairs to a large room with a metal cage down one side. He triple-unlocked the cage's door and showed him the shelves with the box fronts poking out. There were hundreds of them. He pulled one out, longer than Krasinski had expected it to be, and turned the key in the little lock. Then he lifted the lid. Obviously, there was nothing inside, yet.

'You have the only key apart from the spare we keep for emergencies.' Nathan told him.

'I see, very interesting. Thank you. I will definitely be taking out an account with your bank.'

'And when would you like that to start?' Nathan asked, calculating the commission.

'No time like the present.' Krasinski replied.

Now for the hard part.

Nathan only just managed to see the man in the long coat and hat standing in the road before he slammed on the brakes. It was raining hard and he slithered to a stop just inches away from the bedraggled stranger. 'What on earth are you doing?' he asked, not unreasonably.

'Oh, thank God someone's finally stopped. Thank you, sir. Thank you indeed.'

'What's happened?'

'My car, broken down a few miles up that way.' Nathan saw him point vaguely through the rain. 'Out of gas it seems.' He waved a red jerrycan to emphasise the fact. 'Could you possibly give me a lift to the next service station?'

'No problem.' Nathan replied, opening the car's door.

'I'll get in the back if you don't mind. This thing's a bit bulky.'

'Sure.'

They'd been driving for a few minutes when Nathan noticed the man staring at him in the driver's mirror. He seemed to be saying something; his lips were moving, repeating the same message over and over again. Nathan could make it out quite clearly. The message began with the words 'at the sound of my voice...'

Krasinski walked up to Nathan's desk as calmly as he could. 'Good morning, Nathan. I'd like to make a deposit please.'

'Oh, Mr Ness... certainly Mr Ness, if... if you'll just follow me.'

He was led down to the vault. He watched the teller unlock the door whilst remembering to breathe calmly. Inside the cage, Krasinski turned the tape recorder on. Deep sonorous words filled the vault's thin air.

'At the sound of my voice you will fetch the spare key for Mr Jacko Ricci's safety deposit box. You will open the box and give its contents to Mr Ness. Then you will close the box, relock it and place it back. After that you will show Mr Ness to the exit and forget about everything that's happened during the last hour. Start now.'

It should have worked perfectly. But Krasinski was dismayed to see Nathan just stare at him. He hurriedly rewound the tape to play it again.

'Excuse me sir, but what are you doing? I thought you wanted to make a deposit.'

'Just do what the voice says!' Krasinski told him through clenched teeth as he pushed *play.* It wasn't having any effect on the guy. But that was impossible; the Great Mystereo had never failed them before.

'I can't...'

'Look, forget all that.' He switched off the tape. 'You help us and there's enough in it for you to forget this lousy job. All you have to do is open up Jacko Ricci's deposit box.'

'Is...is Mr Ricci one of you?' Nathan asked nervously.

'Now you're getting the picture. C'mon, don't dick around. Take the easy way.'

Nathan smiled and nodded as he slowly stepped backwards. When he reached the cage bars Krasinski saw with a start the teller's left-hand reaching upwards towards a red button.

'Don't be a damn fool...!'

The alarm bell split the air. Security guards rushed down the stairs. Krasinski was too dumbfounded to make a run for it as they grappled him to the floor.

'There's a tape recorder in his pocket.' Nathan told them.

'Okay mate, let's go,' one of them told Krasinski.

When everyone had left, Nathan, hands still shaking, switched off the security cameras then went to a safe in the far wall. He took out sets of keys and selected two. Back inside the cage he pulled out two of the boxes and opened them, then he took a bulky package out of Mr Ricci's box and put it into Mr Ness's one. Then he slid them back into the shelves.

He would take the money out bit by bit. He knew exactly how much there was, of course. It would be nice to buy himself a new car, to start with. Nothing extravagant, mind. And there would be a donation in due course to his old alma mater, the St. Albans School for the Deaf.

It really was the least he could do.

THE 'STACK 'EM UP' MEN

Katharine Riordan

A story based on real life characters and events in St Albans and its environs, 1823.

The Red House Inn[1], St Peter's Street, November
He arrived without acknowledgment. Their contact dissolved into a large and rowdy crowd of market stall holders who eagerly stamped life into their bones after a poor day's trading in mucky weather. Stooping his tall, gaunt frame under the tavern's beams he sidled up to their table. Eyes too close together in a weaselly face; his black shabby frockcoat shining at the elbows.

'Ready to go a-wooing again, boys?' he taunted as he pulled up a stool.

John Jerome looked around furtively. 'How much this time?'

'Yer in luck, lads,' he replied in a sibilant whisper. 'He's offering eleven a long, eight a short-long and four for a small. Seems like the school keep wanting more 'n we can keep up with, so the price is gone up.'

---

[1] The Red House Inn was demolished to make way for the turnpike road that is now Chequers St.

He sniffed away the large drop of mucous hovering from one nostril. 'Yer usual cut, of course.'

'By when?' John Holloway asked. He was a heavyset brute of a man with large jowls and a face ravaged by years of hard work. He squared his shoulders at the man confidently, but underneath the table his right leg jigged up and down to some unseen rhythm.

'Two, three days tops,' the undertaker's clerk replied. 'With all this rain it's nice and soft underfoot.' He gurned; a mouthful of stained and crooked teeth.

The partners exchanged a look. Two more nights and they can get out of St. Albans and home to the East End. Money in their pockets, food for the wives and starving young'uns. Medicine too. Winter is paltry pickings for a labourer and a gardener. Besides, they'd only rented the horse and cart for a week.

'All right,' John Jerome muttered. 'We'll make the necessary arrangements. Delivery no later than Friday noon.'

The go-between departed as furtively as he'd arrived. The men sat back and gulped at their ale. They would need many more—and stronger—before the week was through.

St. Nicholas Church, Harden[2], a day later
The winter rain fell in diagonal sheets across the pathetic mourners gathered in the churchyard. It was the kind of rain that stung like needles wherever it found flesh: the nape of the bent neck, the back of the hand holding an umbrella, stiff with cold and

---

[2] Harden was renamed Harpenden in the 20th Century.

grief. William Gilman, sixty-four years of age, long-term resident of the village but more recently alas of the St. Peter's Workhouse, St, Albans, was being interred into the claggy soil. A sole niece and nephew who'd travelled from Huntingdon had finally coughed up the funds to avoid the shame of the mass pauper's grave. The remaining attendees: those meddlesome members of the community who could be relied upon to make their presence known at any event, be it foul or fair.

Amongst the menacing yew trees, dark-limbed branches dripping, were two huddled forms, chins deep in their chests. They shuffled uneasily in the rain waiting for the signal. Eventually the sexton slyly nodded at them, then walked towards the vestry. Jerome scurried like a roach down the side of the church until he reached the vestry door.

'He'll be going in the far west corner, second row in,' the sexton stated without any preamble. 'There's another due tomorrow, but I don't know where yet. 'Ave to work that out for yerself.'

Jerome merely nodded, his light but sinewy frame blending as best it could into the church wall whilst his eyes darted frantically around as if plotting his escape.

The sexton sniffed loudly and appeared to wipe his nose on his sleeve, a deft movement that ended with his open palm proffered. A muffled chink as he palmed the requisite coins and he ducked inside the vestry, the door firmly shut in Jerome's face.

Now the waiting game began.

Harden, Two Days Later

The two Johns had been drinking all evening. Tankards of ale, but then as midnight neared and the adrenaline flowed, they moved onto the cheapest yet highly effective rum. The kind that numbed their gums and minds. It did not do to be too sober for this job and a man also required a cast iron stomach. Having soaked their livers sufficiently the two Johns rose unsteadily on their feet then fell out into the foul air.

The incessant rain had stopped; the mercury dropped as sharp as a stone. A thick fog the colour of rigid steel swirled around them. The result was a macabre effect—the fog cutting off buildings and objects at mid-height, so they appeared to float like spectres above the ground.

Thankfully, the old mare remembered her way to the church from the Old Red Lion Inn[3]. Holloway grasped her by the nose, his dark lanthorn hardly visible in the murk to Jerome who ostensibly functioned as look-out at the rear. In fact, he gripped grimly to the cart's side boards at the rear for fear he'd slip under the wheels onto the cobblestones slick with a crust of ice, mud, and excrement.

He was still very much the junior partner in these sojourns, Holloway having recruited him into the sinister machinations of the Borough Gang earlier that year. He loathed the work and had spent several dawns after the first few jobs vomiting up his guts until his insides were scoured. The reek of

---

[3] The Old Red Lion Inn was situated on the west side of the High Street, near the toll gate, just south of Sun Lane. Later moved to 72 High St until circa 1920.

decay seemed to have seeped into his pores and under his fingernails no matter how much carbolic soap he used. Ghosts and ghouls tormented his sleep. But tonight, he needed his wits about him—Harden was new territory since they'd exhausted St Albans.

The Norman tower of the church loomed like a half-strangled monolithic giant as they tethered the horse and cart to a tree in the long shadows of the lych-gate. Holloway checked his stolen pocket watch and raised his arm for Jerome to halt. Then he extinguished the lanthorn.

The dark night settled deeper around their shoulders as they waited, glaring into the inkiness, every fibre of them alert for the slightest sound above the keening wind. A lone crow screeched and dived overhead like a vengeful phantom.

The bell tolled the half hour causing the mare to whicker. Jerome jumped.

It was their signal to begin.

They pulled their neckerchiefs up around their faces, grabbed wooden spades and two long poles from the cart and set off into the heart of the graveyard.

Myriad branches overhead created shadows that moved across the crumbling gravestones like eerie fingers, reaching out to stop the men. Shapes shifted everywhere in the churning fog and without the lanthorn to guide them they frequently stumbled over contorted tree limbs, tangled vines, and markers to the long dead. A huge, baleful rat skittered across Holloway's boots, and he kicked out in disgust.

''Tis far too close to All Hallows Eve for my liking,' mumbled Jerome, that unearthly event just a few days hence. 'It don't sit easy with me tonight, John—'tis bound to bring bad luck.' He crossed himself.

Holloway chucked sourly. 'No point developing any kind of conscience now, man. Our souls are long since sold to Lucifer. Think of the money,' he added, keen to keep his younger colleague focused on the task. 'If this fella's a long that's you and the kids sorted for a few weeks. Another couple later in the week more 'n likely too if that sexton ain't double-crossing us.'

He's right, Jerome thought. This'll be the eleventh child on the way; three dead and buried and Marcy still yet young. Recalling his young family wedged into their paltry, verminous lodgings in Hackney, the walls alive with damp, he hardened his resolve.

Once at the approximate site of the burial, for in these labyrinthine grounds it was more than likely they'd miscounted, they split into different directions, backs doubled over, noses almost touching the rapidly freezing ground to find the freshly filled grave, its mound adorned with a single sparse stem to mark Mr Gillan's site of eternal rest. Jerome gave out a low successful whistle and Holloway lurched over.

'That's 'im all right. Well done, lad. Right, let's be having 'im.' But first he pulled a flagon from deep within his pockets and took a long, deep draught. Choking slightly on the cheap liquor he handed it to Jerome who took a larger but necessary share to enable him to continue.

Firstly, the spade, made from a soft wood to make as little sound as possible. Digging at a sharp right angle into where the top half of the coffin would be, Jerome's gardening experience ensured he made light work of it until the soft thud of the spade edge hit the wood below. They glanced at each other and grinned. After dropping in a hessian sack to muffle any sounds, Holloway got to work with the wooden pole, using the spiked end to work the newly hammered nails free, so separating the coffin body from its lid at the head. Then he deftly spun the pike at one hundred and eighty degrees exposing the other hooked end. With several swift movements he levered the pole in and upwards until a satisfying muffled crack told him he'd split the lid crossways, the weight of the soil on the rest of the coffin easing his task.

Then in silence, working one behind the other and each straddling the desecrated grave as if about to mount a horse, they squeezed their hands down inside the narrow coffin as far as they could, reached underneath the corpse's shoulders and heaved it back towards them then upwards in exhausting jerky moves. The corpse's head hit the back of the coffin several times. Despite the chill, sweat poured off both men as they tried to haul out the torso and legs, whilst the stench of days-old decomposing flesh assaulted their nostrils and made them gag. Once the body was a third of the way out it jammed; no amount of pulling or twisting would budge it further. Jerome looked to his partner in alarm.

'The bloody shroud must be too tight around 'im, or else it's caught on a nail further down. 'Appens sometimes, especially on these cheaper burials when the undertaker can't be arsed to secure the body in fully before hammering 'im shut,' Holloway stated, quite matter-of-fact.

'Let's swap. I'll hold 'im up an' you grab my knife, lad—it's 'ere on me belt.'

Jerome knelt at the graveside, thrusting the knife as best he could without any light down the sides of the corpse, trying to work the snagged shroud free whilst bloodying his knuckles against the cheap splintered wood.

'Come on, lad!' implored Holloway. 'Make haste. We're taking far too long. But mind yous don't mark the bugger or that'll lessen our fee.'

At last, the corpse came free, with a derisory sucking sound and a gust of putrefaction. They laid it briefly on the ground; fluids from some of the already decomposing organs dribbled feebly over the frosty earth. They forced open the mouth with a sickening crack to reveal, praise be, an intact set of teeth.

'That's another two pound there.' Holloway grinned, baring his own less than perfect set. A corpse with its own teeth was a bonus to sell onto the schools of anatomy and the profits belonged to the finder, the gang being none the wiser.

'He's good an' long, too,' said Jerome, pleased that despite the difficult extraction the extra length meant the maximum payment due. Now the priority was to get the body doubled over and shoved into a disused flour sack to lie amongst the other sacks in the back of the cart. Rigor mortis would have softened again now that several days were passed. Some of the other sacks were filled with flour to act as decoy should they be witnessed on their lengthy return.

They staggered and shuffled back towards the lych-gate, the heavy sack dangling low between them, this time caring not over what or whom they trod.

The clock was striking half-past one as they emerged from the shadowy, wooded lane back towards the Harden Road and St. Albans. They needed to be clear of both by dawn.

St Albans Road

It was in that strange lull just before daybreak, the last of the stars winking out one by one, that James and Thomas Finder made their way along Stakers Lane[4]. The uneven road was frozen and crunched under their hobnailed boots as they made their way along it before turning onto the wider St Albans Road. The winter sun threw down its watery shards but was losing its battle with the ghoul-grey, swollen clouds, and it was bitingly cold. The two young brothers leaned into the sharp wind, resigned to the long three-mile trudge to work. For the past two years the siblings, fifteen and eighteen, had been engaged at Fowler's Brickmakers at Bernard's Heath in St Albans. It was hot and gruelling work even in the depths of winter, but Joseph Fowler was a gentle giant of a boss, fair to his clients and generous to his employees, and so the boys were grateful.

They bowled along at a pace despite the treacherous conditions, shoving bread and cheese into their always-starving mouths as they went; the chance

---

[4] Stakers Lane was later renamed Station Lane.

for an extra ten minutes amidst their warm beds this morning had been too much of a pull. They were companionable in their silence, only passing comment if they felt the need.

As they approached the outskirts of St Albans, that venerable, populous town so richly steeped in history, they spotted a cart ahead of them, two men sat up front dressed head to toe in dark clothing. It was an odd sight, for the cart bore the insignia of an East London flour merchant, yet both Harden and St Albans were blessed with multiple providers. The cart appeared oddly laden and listed curiously to one side.

'Isn't that the same cart as we saw a couple weeks back?' asked Thomas.

'I'm certain you're right, brother. It's a curious sight in these parts.'

'Shall we catch it up and maybe hitch a lift? It's headed our way and—' Thomas was always keen to find ways of shortening their journey.

'Hold fast now, Tom. We don't know who or what they are. Something's not right, that's for sure. They could be armed, even.'

'But—'

'Let's try and catch them up at least but be prepared to flee sharpish if we need to, ok?'

The thinner of the two men had heard the lads approaching and leaned towards his bulky companion. Whatever had been said, he twisted in his seat and leaned back into the cart, shifting sacks and straw around frantically whilst the cart perceptibly picked up pace. This raised the boys' suspicions further. They quickened their speed and were soon within a few metres of the cart. Close enough to double-check the merchant's livery, they watched in horror when, due to the driver's increasingly erratic control of the horse, the cart's wheels hit a deep rut in the road, causing it to falter and then stop. A pale, grey yet obviously human arm flopped loose and free from one of the bulkier sacks; yellowed, curled nails seemingly beckoned the boys to come to its aid.

A foul stench filled the air around them, a thick, cloying smell that made them feel the air was like sewage water to breathe. They glanced at each other; two boys who lived in a small countryside village were no strangers to the stink of death. James shook his head slightly at his younger brother, whose eyes were wide with alarm. James gripped one of Thomas' arms tightly and hissed, 'Walk past and raise your cap in a friendly greeting. We must do nothing to arouse their suspicion. But listen, get a good look at 'em.'

Hearts hammering, sweat building around their collars despite the bite of the morning, they scurried past almost at a run, caps aloft and eyes firmly on the drivers' faces, acting as mannerly as their beloved mother had taught them.

Just two young lads on their way to work, minding their own business.

'Mornin' gentlemen!' said James, adopting as neutral but as cheery a tone as he could muster.

'Cold one today,' added Thomas

The silence that greeted them was deafening.

The brothers realised beyond any doubt these were 'stack 'em up men'; body snatchers, to give them their proper name. Ghouls of men that performed unspeakable actions to earn a cut of the lucre shared with a network of surgeons, undertakers, and sextons. Bodies sold on to London's more disreputable surgeons and anatomy schools for dissection, as the rules entitled them to no more than six a year.

They raced ahead, limbs burning, pulses racing, daring not so much as to even glance backwards, but focused now on the asylum that awaited them inside the brickworks, whose furnaces were already setting the early morning sky alight.

The cart followed menacingly at their heels.

St Albans House of Correction[5]

'It's a sorry state of affairs, Mr Porter.' The mayor, Mr Brown, both thumbs thrust deep in the pockets of his waistcoat, rocked to and fro on his heels. 'These fellas come up all the way from London. Seems that's how desperate they are for bodies these days.' He coughed and visibly straightened, chest puffed out—embarrassed that this had occurred undetected on his watch, but determined to show he was now in control again.

'I recognised him soon as I laid eyes on him, poor bugger,' said Mr Porter, master of the workhouse. He had crossed himself twice as if the horror he'd witnessed could be wiped from his memory with a double blessing.

---

[5] The House of Correction in St Albans was situated within St. Albans Gateway. It stopped being a gaol for St. Albans in December 1823.

'The two miscreants concerned are, as we speak, gentlemen, being held next door in the cells, and I've requested extra guards be put on duty to ensure their mob can't reach them and—' Mr Brown pontificated before the brickwork's owner Mr Fowler interrupted him.

The latter coughed to remind the mayor of his presence and signalled with his eyes towards his charges, James and Thomas, who stood awkwardly, staring at their shoes. They wished desperately to just return to their regular lives and forget this sorry, stomach-churning business.

'Of course,' Mr Brown spluttered. 'The witnesses' conduct should not go unrewarded. Let that be an end to it."

Inside the cells, the walls dripped with slime and excrement. The mangy rats nibbled audaciously at the prisoners' boot soles with yellowed razor-sharp teeth.

The two Johns sat side by side, knees hunched, manacled to the walls at their wrists. They'd spent a miserable twenty-four hours with only water and stale biscuit breaks to liven the monotony.

Hope had turned to desperation.

Desperation to fervent prayer.

'Can't understand why no bugger is come to release us,' Holloway groaned. That was an inherent part of their deal with the Borough Gang—bail, protection and any associated fees paid, and no questions asked.

The Abbey's bells, ear-splittingly loud at this proximity, pealed out their own verdict:

Sinners! Sinners! Sinners!

Hours passed before the screech of the large key in the un-oiled lock shook them from their torpor. Both Johns tried to sit up straighter, heads up, chins raised to greet freedom. The tiny amount of late afternoon light released by the opened door cast long shadows across the cell floor and doubled the perceived bulk of their gaoler.

'It's your lucky day, gentlemen.' He leered as his smell of stale sweat and beer breath fugged out towards them.

A moment of hope, a flicker of joy

'Yer to be committed for trial at the next quarter sessions—Epiphany Sessions that'll be, in January. Until then you're my last lucky guests.' With that he belched loudly and bent his huge frame back out of the door, chuckling to himself as they were plunged back into darkness and despair as black as an abyss.

January 1825 - Spitalfields, East London

'We'll pay nine a long, six a short long and two for a small. Take it or leave it.' The voice that delivered this was gruff; it spoke of years of hard living and money spinning. The man's features were almost impossible to make out in this thick yellow fog; a nose broken multiple times, eyes with more than a hint of menace even in the gloom. It was clear he wasn't a man to trifle with.

'It's less 'an I was hoping for, sir. I'd heard you paid more, and—'

'It's as good an offer as you'll get right now. Borough Gang's rates is the best and we looks after our boys an' all.'

The young lad weighed this information up. This was risky, repugnant business. But the thought of being looked after in case it all went awry; him and his family safe—that sealed the deal.

He spat on his hand and reached out in the murk to find his new master's palm.

'Just one more thing, son. You'll be needing to head out to St. Albans.'

SUZIE WITHAZEE

Howard Linskey

'Foreman of the jury, have you reached a verdict upon which you are all agreed?'

'We have.'

'Do you find the defendant guilty or not guilty?'

'Not guilty.'

No!

Detective Sergeant Paul Cassidy stared hard at the jury foreman to see if he could read corruption in the man's face, but he was impassive. The Judge had no choice but to let Tony Hannah leave St Albans Crown Court 'without a stain on his character.'

How many times had he been here before, standing impotently in the public gallery watching 'Teflon Tony' walk? One of the county's most notorious 'faces' had already successfully avoided conviction for fraud, blackmail, money laundering, supplying drugs, living off immoral earnings, GBH, actual bodily harm, kidnap, attempted murder and now, finally, murder. Most of those charges never even reached court. In Tony Hannah's world, witnesses suddenly forgot what they had seen and victims regularly changed their minds or had their credibility destroyed by expensive lawyers, while Tony's firm was busy threatening jurors' families.

This time, though, Cassidy had been convinced they'd got him, and just in time too, only weeks before the detective's retirement. It was his last case. Who else could have murdered Hannah's biggest rival? The jury didn't agree and outside court, Cassidy was confronted by the spectacle of a grinning Hannah, receiving pats on the back from followers and hangers-on.

'Oh dear, officer. Lost again, did you?' Hannah grinned. 'It's becoming a bit of a habit.'

'You got to them,' hissed Cassidy. 'You nobbled that jury.'

Tony smiled smugly back at him. 'There's a bunch of reporters outside who want to hear my story. I'll be sure to tell them all about you.'

As the two big men started to trade insults, they drew closer to one another and their voices became louder until others stepped in to separate them; court ushers, a uniformed police man, even Tony's solicitor got involved in the pushing and shoving.

'I'll finish you one day, Tony, bank on it!'

'Oh yeah?' sneered Hannah. 'Meanwhile, make sure you enjoy your daughter's wedding.'

That was it. The moment the gangster mentioned Linda, Cassidy felt the rage boil up inside him and he took a swing, which only missed because the uniformed PC hauled him back in time.

Back at HQ, Detective Superintendent Williams was unimpressed. 'I've been reading your file. There are almost as many commendations as official warnings,' he reminded Cassidy. 'But not quite.'

'Sir,' was all Cassidy could think to say in acknowledgement.

Williams sighed. 'What happened in court today?'

Christ, he'd heard about it. Of course he bloody had. Cassidy knew other detectives who got away with murder but he couldn't fart without the world knowing.

'It was just a bit of verbals,' Cassidy told him. 'From the prisoner.'

'Who had just been acquitted?'

'Wrongly, in my view, sir.'

'And you were understandably upset,' Williams said. 'But you made a scene and we can't have that.'

'No, sir.'

'You've only got a few weeks left, Cassidy. Keep your head down, your nose clean and your mouth shut until then. Chalk this one up to experience,' he advised. 'Men like Hannah always end up dead sooner or later.'

Thanks for the lecture in your cosy office about life on the streets.

'Yes sir,' said Cassidy, because it was expected of him.

He'd only had two Scotches when he called Janet, but his ex-wife still asked if he'd been drinking.

'No,' he told her firmly. 'I'm just ringing about the wedding, to see if you need me to do anything?'

There was a long silence from Janet.

'What's the matter?' he asked her.

Another silence until she finally said, 'Linda doesn't want you there.'

'What do you mean, she doesn't want me there? I'm giving her away!' And when there was another silence, 'I *am* giving her away?'

It all came out then. His daughter actually wanted her step dad to give her away, not him.

Worse, she was embarrassed by her father, had some crazy idea he would end up drinking too much and ruin her big day, which was ridiculous because he had the drinking under control these days, mostly.

His ex-wife ended the call abruptly after he shouted, 'I'm still her dad!'

Cassidy went for a drive to calm down. First, he thought about Janet and his daughter then he remembered Teflon Tony Hannah and the scathing words of the Detective Superintendent. He'd really thought this time they'd nailed the parasite and he'd go down for life. It would have been a little crowning glory for Cassidy at the end of his career but now here he was, just weeks from retirement, and it looked like everything he had spent his whole life doing had been a complete waste. He could feel the rage and frustration building in him again, fuelled by the unfairness of a system that allowed such injustice. Men like Tony should be snuffed out of the world, not freed to be courted by newspapers.

Cassidy still had a few weeks, though, and maybe there was one final, desperate dice to throw on this last case. He'd hoped it wouldn't be needed but he'd been cultivating one of Tony's girls for months. Almost without realising it, he had driven his car onto Suzie Withazee's patch. This was a world away from the quiet streets of St Albans. There were no houses here in this run-down part of a neglected town on the outskirts of London, just a handful of shabby shops with big metal shutters padlocked over their windows, behind which three tall tower blocks loomed. It wasn't quite a no-go area but a good many of Teflon Tony's punters lived here and a fair few of Suzie's.

Suzie wasn't her real name and, whatever her surname was, it wasn't Withazee. When Cassidy first encountered her, she'd told him her name was 'Suzie with a Z,' and she'd pronounced it the American way: 'Zee.' He'd found that amusing so the nickname stuck.

Cassidy often pulled over to talk to Tony's hookers. A lot of pimps liked to watch over their girls while they were working, but not Tony. He had better things to do and wanted to distance himself from their activities. But they were so scared of Tony they didn't usually tell Cassidy much. Suzie was different. She was young and cheeky and would stand up to the bulky detective in a way the older girls were disinclined to. Over time, he'd grown to appreciate her lack of bullshit when he asked her about one of the other girls or a dodgy punter he'd taken an interest in, and he could clearly see the intelligence in her eyes. It almost made him want to save her, except he knew that would be pointless. You could only be saved if you wanted to be and she never did.

Recently though, something had changed. Suzie had a friend and that friend had disappeared, which gave him an in.

Cassidy wound down his window. 'Get in,' he said. 'I'll buy you a cup of tea.'

'It'll cost you more than that.'

'Very funny, Suzie. Come on.'

'Can't,' she said. 'S'posed to be earning.'

'How much for an hour?' he asked and when her eyes widened, he said, 'Not with me. I mean how much do you usually charge?'

She told him and he said, 'Bullshit. I'll give you forty, plus the tea.'

She got in then. 'Ain't you bothered how this is going to look?'

'I don't really give a shit anymore,' he assured her.

They parked on an empty industrial estate and she drank the tea gratefully. He asked her a few questions about the estate then quizzed her on Tony.

'What you asking me about him for? You know I can't say nothing.'

Normally, he would have taken longer to get there, but Cassidy didn't have the time or the energy to avoid coming straight to the point. 'What did he do with Angel?'

'Angel?' That was her street name, the one she gave her clients. 'How should I know? She's gone, that's all.'

'She's your mate. You work the same stretch, but Angel hasn't been seen in a while. I heard she was holding out on Tony because she was using too much.'

'She never!' He'd made up the bit about using too much and, as he'd hoped, Suzie felt the need to defend her mate. 'She was trying to save some, that's all. She wanted to go home.'

'Can't say I blame her, Suzie. I mean this is no life, is it?' The girl did not contradict him; she looked worn out. 'Tony wouldn't like that though, a girl leaving, one who knew bad stuff about him. So I guess he did what he always does.'

'What do you mean?'

He shrugged, as if everybody knew what happened to girls who crossed Teflon Tony. 'Killed her,' he said. 'Dumped her body somewhere.' Suzie looked frightened then. 'Come on, Suzie, you must know how he operates. The girls never leave. He either turns them into skinny junkies no one wants to screw anymore or they disappear, like your mate.'

'I don't know anything about that.'

'You're a bright girl, Suzie. You're young. You could have a proper life. I bet you think about that sometimes when you're standing on a cold street waiting for your next punter. Angel thought about it too, so she decided to leave and he killed her. That's what I heard. Now if you were to tell me what happened to Angel, maybe I can help you to get away from him.'

Suzie thought about it for a long time before saying, 'Last time I saw her...' Cassidy held his breath. '...she was getting into his car. They drove away and she never came back.'

'Where did he take her, Suzie? If we can find her, I can put him away for life and get you out of here.'

'I don't know where he took her.'

'Then ask the other girls,' he said. 'They might let something slip. If I can nail him, I can bring in all the girls. That way he won't know who talked.'

'What about me?'

'Witness protection,' he said, even though he lacked the authority to promise her that. 'And I know journalists who'd pay good money for your story, but they wouldn't print your real name, so he'd never know.'

Suzie liked the sound of that. She liked it because she was desperate. She *wanted* to believe, and that was always half the battle.

For two weeks, Suzie kept up her irregular contact with Cassidy and told him everything she had learned from the girls who worked the streets near hers or crashed at the same doss house she used. She even casually asked the guys who came for her takings at the end of the night, masking her questions as concern for her friend. Little by little, Cassidy was able to learn more and more about the way Tony operated, but he still lacked one crucial thing. She couldn't tell him what really happened to Angel.

Cassidy had just two weeks left when he went back down to see Suzie Withazee again, to find she was no longer there. Frantic, he drove round the whole patch looking for her but there was no sign of Suzie. When he stopped, to ask made-up questions about a suspicious punter, the hooker he chose avoided eye contact. He asked her where Suzie Withazee was, as if he was merely curious, and her look gave it all away. 'Don't know,' was the mumbled response but she knew, all right, and so did he.

Cassidy's top grass was a man called Michael Maddox. He was strictly small time, but he did business with everyone, including Teflon Tony, and he was never going to help Cassidy bring the man down. Maddox could get stuff and fence more or less anything. Until now he had mostly given Cassidy intel on other criminals in the area, usually his rivals.

They met at a lock-up Maddox used, and the first thing Cassidy did was punch Maddox right in the gut. When he hauled the winded man to his feet, Cassidy barked, 'What's he done with her? Where's Suzie?'

Maddox knew everybody, but he feigned ignorance. 'Who?' he gasped.

His protestations lasted as long as it took Cassidy to brush everything from his work bench, haul Maddox up onto it and slam him down on his back. Cassidy grabbed one of Maddox's own screwdrivers and brought it right up to the terrified man's eyeball.

'I'm not messing about anymore,' he snarled at Maddox. 'You help me deal with Teflon Tony, or I deal with you.'

'I can't.' His voice trembled.

'Tony won't find out about this little chat, unless I want him to.' Maddox's eyes widened at that. 'But I already have enough to put you inside.' Maddox knew Cassidy could roll up his operation in minutes.

'So what? Most I'll get is a couple of years.' He meant he'd rather do that than grass up Tony. It wasn't loyalty, just simple fear.

'Then I'll put it about that you are a nonce as well as a thief.'

Maddox tried to protest his innocence.

'If I *say* you are a nonce, then you're a nonce. How long would you last inside then, eh?'

Maddox looked into Cassidy's eyes to see if he was bluffing and learned that he was not. 'He's got this cottage, hasn't he, in the country?' he blurted suddenly. 'There's miles of land round it. You can bury someone in the woods easy.'

'That's where he took her?'

'It's where he always takes them; a little place by a lake.'

'I know it.' Cassidy had been part of a raid there once. They were acting on a tip off, hoping to find drugs, maybe even a body. Instead, they found hiking boots and an Aga.

Cassidy locked eyes with Maddox. 'Are you saying he killed her?'

'It's what I heard. She'd been asking loads of questions and she was seen with you.'

Cassidy had to fight hard to banish the rage and the pain then. He wanted to stab Maddox in the eye, kill Teflon Tony, and scream in frustration for poor little Suzie.

Instead, he said, 'There's something else. Tell me!'

Maddox squirmed, but Cassidy tightened his grip. 'He's talking about doing you in after you retire. I don't think he would really do it.' Maddox said it quickly. 'But he's talking about it.'

'Is he there now?'

'Must be,' said Maddox. 'He's not back.'

'On his own?' Maddox nodded. 'When did he go?'

'Don't know. I just heard he'd lifted Suzie and not to ask about her again because she was gone.'

Cassidy thought for a moment, then he let go of Maddox. 'We never had this little chat.'

'You're bloody telling me.'

That was it; all bets were off. How could Cassidy play by the rules when Hannah never did? Time after time he had avoided justice. Now poor little Suzie was dead too, and all because she had been too careless with her questions, and why was that? She was desperate to get out and had believed Cassidy when he told her it would all be okay. Cassidy knew he'd have Suzie's death on his conscience forever. He hadn't been able to protect her, but maybe he could do something for her now that she was gone. And if he didn't, what was his alternative? Retire quietly and wait for the day when Teflon Tony felt safe enough to come looking for the ex-detective he wanted dead.

He made his decision then.

Cassidy parked three miles from the cottage by the lake and walked the rest of the way carrying a hold-all. He was dressed in an old coat, cap and dark glasses but it was off season and he saw no one along the way.

He watched the place for a while from a distance, but there were no signs of life. Maybe Hannah had gone out. Perhaps he hadn't even been here to start with. Maddox could have been misinformed, but Cassidy doubted it, and he wasn't turning back now. He took off his coat and tracksuit bottoms then shoved them in a plastic bag. He was wearing the right gear underneath. Cautiously he approached the cottage.

There was a steep incline down to the water's edge with the cottage at the bottom, space for Hannah's car at the top and not much room for anything else on this patch of land, except a small jetty that jutted out into the lake. Cassidy peered through a window but saw no sign of life.

'Silly bugger keeps a key under the mat,' one of the team had told him after they had already smashed the door down during the raid. Cassidy could easily have broken in but he lifted the mat and there it was. He let himself in, sat down on the stairs facing the door and waited.

It was nearly three hours later, and dark outside, before Cassidy heard the car. This was it. He was finally going to make Teflon Tony pay. He peered out through the window and watched an unsuspecting Hannah get out of his car, alone. Cassidy backed away into the shadows.

Hannah's key turned in the lock and he opened the door. He got a couple of feet inside his cottage before he howled in agony and dropped, writhing, to the floor.

Hannah probably didn't know what was going on at first. The Taser had put him on the ground with a combination of extreme pain and loss of muscle function, which enabled Cassidy to quickly subdue him. Soon he was sitting in a chair, with his hands and ankles bound with cable ties. Once he became fully aware of what was happening to him, he started swearing and threatening to sue Cassidy or kill him, possibly both. Cassidy said nothing. He was getting something out of his bag.

'Have you even got a warrant?' It was an obvious question, because Cassidy was wearing the gear SO-COs used to avoid contaminating a crime scene: a mask and latex gloves, over-shoes and a white Tyvek suit that had been hidden beneath the coat and tracksuit bottoms. The hood was over his hair now but enough of his face was still visible for Hannah to recognise him. Hannah's eyes darted around the room then. 'Where's everyone else?'

'There is no one else, Tony,' Cassidy explained.

Teflon Tony watched as Cassidy produced a clear plastic bag from his holdall, along with a roll of gaffer tape. 'All those expensive lawyers, the threats to jury members, the intimidation of witnesses, you never gave us a chance,' he explained calmly. 'So I've decided not to give you one.'

'What?' asked Tony, his voice wavering.

Cassidy looked him in the eye then. 'This is for Suzie.' He quickly placed the clear plastic bag over Teflon Tony's head and the man began to struggle. 'And all the others.' Cassidy unrolled the gaffer tape and started to wrap it tightly round the man's neck to keep the bag firmly in place there. The bag instantly inflated as Tony's breath came out. He was trying to shout something at Cassidy. The detective ignored the gangster's struggles. He watched as Tony pitched forward and fell to the ground, his hands and legs bound uselessly. He couldn't do anything now but squirm on the floor, gasping for air.

It took Teflon Tony almost five minutes to die.

Cassidy watched him intently until his final breath.

On his way out of the cottage, Cassidy saw the big, sporty Jaguar, the pride of Teflon Tony's useless life. It was parked at the top of the hill, pointing down towards the lake. He could have just left it, but it would take longer for people to investigate if they thought the cottage was empty. The car was unlocked. All he had to do was release the handbrake, give it a shove and let gravity do the rest.

Cassidy watched as the flashy, green car picked up speed and slid down the hill, missing the house by inches. It mounted the short wooden jetty, trundled along it then went right over the edge with a satisfying splash before disappearing beneath the water. It was only then that Cassidy felt the feeling of euphoria. He'd done it. He'd finished Teflon Tony.

Former Detective Sergeant Paul Cassidy had almost begun to stop dreading that he might one day be linked to the death of the murdered gangster. He was on the way back to his little flat when his old mate, DC Connors, pulled up alongside him in an unmarked car. Cassidy felt a surge of fear but his former colleague's grin told him he was okay.

'Left your car at home?'

'Went for a couple of pints at the Boot,' Cassidy explained. The ancient pub was a favourite and not too far from his flat.

'God, you've got the life of bloody Reilly, mate. Come on, we'll give you a lift home.'

Cassidy got in, feeling mightily relieved.

He really had only just drunk a couple of pints. He preferred that these days. Cassidy felt as if he was slowly sorting his life out. He'd even patched things up with his daughter. He'd been to see Linda and told her he respected her decision to let her step dad give her away. She had tearfully relented then and invited him to the wedding, if he promised to go easy on the booze, which wouldn't be a problem if he could just keep the black dog of depression at bay, and he was quietly confident of that now.

He often thought of Suzie and could never quite banish the thought that he had killed her, even if he hadn't been the one to actually pull the trigger. That had been Hannah, and Teflon Tony had got what was coming to him at least.

DC Connors' partner drove and let them have a catch up. Eventually Connors said, 'You must have heard about Teflon Tony?'

Even though he knew the question was coming, Cassidy's stomach flipped. 'It couldn't have happened to a nicer bloke. One of his rivals, presumably?'

'Had to be,' said Connors, and Cassidy experienced an immense feeling of relief. 'They tied him up then suffocated him with a plastic bag.'

'Not a nice way to go,' said Cassidy.

'He deserved it.'

'The world is a safer place now.' Cassidy was warming to his theme. 'Particularly if you are a woman.' And he realised it had all been worth it,the risk he had taken in bringing down Tony, for the girls he could no longer harm, for the ones he had already killed, for poor little Suzie whom he had been unable to save. It wasn't much when you offset it against a failed career, a broken marriage and a daughter who grew up not wanting to know him, but it was something; a small but important thread he could cling to. At least he had that.

'You wouldn't believe what they found in the lake,' Connors told him

'What?'

'That big, flash Jaguar car. They almost missed it at first, but someone walked down the jetty and saw it just beneath the surface, so they pulled it out to take a look, and you'll never guess what they found in the boot.'

There was something about the way Connors said that, which had the skin on Cassidy's face prickling. Was it a premonition?

'What?' he answered dumbly, though his heart was about ready to burst now because Cassidy had a terrible feeling he knew the answer already. He felt his whole world tilt alarmingly.

'That young girl, Suzie, the prostitute you used to tap for info. She was only in the boot, poor girl. He must have put her in there to drive her out to his cottage.' Connors shook his head sadly. 'And he hadn't killed her. She drowned. They reckon she was still alive when she went into the water.'

WHAT A RAT

Yvonne Moxley

He had always been a shooting man. It didn't matter what it was—rabbits, foxes, grouse, pigeons, rats. Fred had shot them all, mainly in Gustard Wood where he hoped he wouldn't be seen. It had made Maureen shudder. Fancy spending your life killing things. Who would want to kill a sweet little rabbit?

She hadn't minded so much about the rats. They had been infested with them in both the house and the garden, so it was good to see the back of those disgusting vermin. Fred and Maureen lived behind Snalbans Super Spuds, a take-away restaurant that was none too healthy and had been forced to close down. Evidently it wasn't just the customers taking away the food.

'I wanna be outside amongst nature,' Fred had told her once, in a sulky voice.

'Dead nature,' she had muttered under her breath and although he knew she hated his favourite pastime there had been no stopping him—until now.

He had fought and won against two heart attacks, but not the third.

The day that he died Maureen threw all The Shooting Times magazines into the recycling bin and she would have thrown away his air-rifle too, except that she couldn't find it.

'I want to be buried with my trusty gun,' he had said from his hospital bed and although Maureen was sure there were rules about what could and couldn't be buried, she hadn't been able to find the bloody awful thing, so that was that.

'What are you muttering about?' asked Sally, her neighbour, pushing open the kitchen door with her bottom as she juggled a pile of dirty crockery.

'Just talking to myself now that I haven't anyone else to talk to,' Maureen replied, knowing there wouldn't be much time for talking when she met her Tommy tomorrow.

'The last of the mourners have gone now,' Sally said, 'and I told them you were having a few quiet minutes to yourself, and they understood, of course. Said they'd be thinking of you, how the vicar at St Peter's had done you proud, and how sorry they were and all that sort of stuff. Now, come on, wipe your eyes. I'll wash this lot and you can dry.'

Maureen's eyes didn't need wiping but she said nothing.

'Where's your washing up liquid?' asked Sally, opening the cupboard door under the sink. 'Oh! Bloody hell! What's this?'

And there, right in front of the cupboard, was Fred's air-rifle.

'Who put it there?' demanded Maureen.

'Well, I'm sure I don't know. It wasn't me.'

'But I've been looking for that thing everywhere. I would have seen it this morning when I washed up after breakfast.'

Holding it at arm's length, Sally gingerly handed the rifle to Maureen as though it would go off just by looking at it and got on with the washing up.

Maureen put it on the kitchen table and studied it. There were tiny spots of rust on the metal bits but apart from that it looked in good condition as far as she could tell. 'Might get one or two hundred for it, I suppose,' she said out loud, thinking that it might at least pay for a romantic night away with Tommy. 'Funny how I didn't see it before, though.'

When Sally had gone, she phoned Tommy to tell him about her day. 'Yes, yes, it all went well. Lots of people turned up which was nice, except you, of course.' She giggled.

'What about me coming over tonight?' he said.

'I don't know. Best leave it for a day or two before you come here. You know how nosey Sally is. But I'm coming to your house tomorrow, aren't I, so see you then?'

'OK, my love,' whispered Tommy. 'See you tomorrow.'

After ending the call Maureen looked round the kitchen to make sure that everything had been turned off. She looked at the rifle again and shivered. She felt cold. Was it because of all that killing it had done, or had the house suddenly dropped a few degrees?

She climbed the stairs, got ready for bed, set her alarm clock and turned out the light.

The house was in total darkness. All was silent. Even the traffic along the High Street seemed to have stopped.

At the stroke of midnight, the bells at the Cathedral refused to ring.

A shadow fell across the house. The alarm clock stopped ticking. The fridge stopped humming. The electricity closed down.

Heavy, thick silence.

A faint, slow scraping noise could be heard from the kitchen. The rifle, left lying on its side, carefully righted itself. It lifted up and hovered a few inches from the surface of the table. Turning at right angles it purposefully pointed its barrel towards the doorway and floated out into the hallway.

Menacingly and deliberately, it climbed the stairs.

WAR ON THE STREETS
Tina Shaw

'Big Issue, Big Issue! Come on, madam, why not buy one?'

'You weren't here last week, young man. What's happened to the other fellow, used to stand outside Marks & Spencer?'

'It's a long story, madam; drink involved, I'm afraid.'

'Oh dear, such a shame. All right, let me have one.'

Kev handed over a copy and quickly pocketed the money, disappearing round the corner towards Russell Avenue before the woman noticed that it was last week's edition. Well, he thought, burying any residual feelings of guilt, it was every man for himself in this game. The other bloke had fallen asleep and Kev had nicked the bundle of magazines off him. There had been an empty can of lager strategically placed next to his bundle, so saying drink was involved probably wasn't an absolute lie.

Kev still had trouble with lying. Long ago, when he'd been a kid, his dad had drummed it into him that lying wasn't on, and the memory had stuck with him. It had made him even more angry when they had lied about his dad having cancer and stopped Kev visiting the hospital before he died. That memory had stuck too.

Stop living in the past, Kev told himself. *It's got you into enough trouble over the years.* He sat down in a shop doorway, out of the wind, and dozed off. A sharp kick in the ribs woke him up.

'Look at that old tramp,' the youngster yelled. 'Smelly, belly; bloody low life!'

Kev opened his eyes and rapidly assessed the situation. There were seven or eight of them, dancing about, clutching cans of lager, each trying to impress his mates. He was down a side street. It was getting dark. Cars were driving down Chequer Street and he could see people walking past the end of the side turning, but the odds were against him if he tried to defend himself.

'Piss off, lads,' he growled, but they just laughed at him.

He reached into his pocket, hoping that would make them think that he had a weapon, rather than the old, blunt penknife he had nicked from Wilko which he used to cut up his food. Unfortunately, it had the opposite effect. The biggest of the lads, who was making out he was 'top dog', suddenly produced a short blade, glinting in the orange streetlights which had come to life.

'Hey now.' Kev slowly raised his open palms in what he hoped was a gesture of submission. 'No need for that, lads. What harm have I ever done you?'

The big lad laughed. 'Harm,' he scoffed. 'You've done harm just by existing, mate. The likes of us, we have to support people like you.'

Kev shifted slowly into a sitting position, wondering whether to make a dash for it.

A couple walked by on the other side of the street and he considered shouting for help, but they hurried past, carefully looking the other way. He tried a different approach.

'Look lads, I wasn't always like this you know. I was a bit like you. I had mates, got a couple of GCSEs, you know, that sort of thing.'

'Bet you never had a girlfriend,' one of the other boys quipped. 'Who would want you?'

'You're wrong there,' Kev replied, hoping that by engaging their interest the danger would pass.

'So how did you end up in this bloody state?' asked one of the smaller boys.

'Long story…'

'We haven't got time for a long story,' said Top Dog, trying to reassert his authority.

'Boarding school,' said Kev, feeling the advantage slipping away again.

'What, like Eton?' said the smaller boy, whilst the rest of them started laughing.

Kev hastily shook his head, risking a smile along with the rest of them. 'Nah, course not! Bloody council boarding school, you know, where they send you if you don't fit in ordinary school.'

'Paedo castle,' murmured one of the quieter lads.

'What, is he a paedo?' someone asked, kicking Kev on the leg, as they all started laughing again.

Kev held up his hands and shouted 'No!' as the kicking subsided.

'What did you say it for, then?' asked one of the lads.

'I didn't,' Kev muttered, 'but you're right, it was full of paedo teachers like most of those places.'

Some of the boys looked interested and a couple even sat down on the pavement beside him. One of them got out his phone and scrolled down until he found some pictures to show Kev. 'Like this, you mean?' he asked, showing Kev a string of images of older men with boys and girls.

Kev shuddered. 'Where do you get that stuff? It's not nice.'

The boy grinned. 'Course it's not nice. It's all over the internet, innit? You got a phone? I can send you some if you want but it might cost you.'

Kev shook his head. 'Haven't got a phone,' he lied, 'and if I had, I wouldn't want that stuff. It's real kids, you know.'

'Doesn't hurt them if I just look, though, does it?' the boy countered.

'Bet you have got a phone,' one of the others said. 'Everybody has.'

'Let's search him,' said Top Dog, keen to take back control of the group.

'Yeah,' some of them agreed.

'Means touching him,' said one of the others. 'He might have some disease.'

The blade flashed again. 'Turn out your pockets,' Top Dog demanded, 'or you'll be sorry.'

Kev did as he was asked, his Pay as You Go Nokia making a dull thud as it landed on the pavement.

'Call that a phone?' they mocked. 'No bloody internet. It's like the one my little sister's got.'

'Told you,' said Kev. 'It's not worth bothering with.'

'Why do you keep it, then?' asked Top Dog, picking it up and lobbing it into a nearby rubbish bin.

Kev had just about had enough. He shuffled his position, considering his next move. It was almost dark now but there were still people about. He could sense that some of the lads were getting restive, wanting to move on to their next bit of evening excitement, and a couple of them had almost seemed sympathetic when he mentioned boarding school.

'Look lads,' he ventured. 'Time to move on, eh? I'm sure you've got better things to do with your evening than sit here talking to me.'

A couple of the boys nodded. 'Yeah, I want some chips,' the young one announced. They began to shuffle away but Top Dog wasn't satisfied with letting Kev off the hook so easily. 'Go on then,' he challenged Kev. 'You get up and make a run for it, and we'll have a bit of fun running after you, and we'll see who's fastest, eh lads?'

There seemed to be general agreement with the idea and Kev got slowly to his feet, picking up his bundle and trying to ease the stiffness out of his legs.

'On your marks, get set, go!' shouted Top Dog.

Kev raced towards the main road. Passers-by turned to look and hastily moved out of the way as Kev tripped over a paving stone and landed back down on the ground in front of the museum. He heard the boys' laughter as they ran off into the distance. He felt the pain in his side and reached round to assess the damage. As he brought his hand back round, the blood trickled slowly onto the pavement.

TYING UP THE MILDENHALL TREASURE

John Spencer

The small road off Victoria Square was old and narrow. Robert Samuels walked down it, realising that it was a part of St Albans that he had never explored. He found the house he had been directed to and knocked on the door, but as he did so the door swung open. Apparently, he was expected.

As he walked in, he saw that it was dark, and it made him think that outside, although still early in the evening, it was darker there too. He walked through the empty room and saw that the corridor through the house was also empty; the house looked unattended. There was one room to his right and he opened the door to check it out. It was also dark, completely black in fact and he assumed it too was empty. He'd started to close the door when he heard the voice.

'Come in.'

He walked into the room, and instinctively felt for a light switch, but the voice sounded again. 'Leave it. I want the lights off.'

'I can't see a thing,' Samuels offered.

'There's nothing to see,' the voice said. 'And I want to remain anonymous for reasons I will explain. There is a chair behind you; sit down please.'

Samuels sat down. The small amount of light creeping in from outside the room gave him enough to see the general geography. He could see a desk in front of him and someone behind it sitting in a chair that was completely obscure. In fact, he thought, there seemed to be a screen between him and the other person.

Samuels slipped a small envelope out of his breast pocket and waved it towards the desk. 'I received this one night. One thousand pounds. And an invitation to this meeting.'

'Yes. It is yours to keep. I have a job for you.'

'You don't sound like a job agency.' There was no laughter.

'This job is not one for an agency. But it is one for you. I have a copy of your record; your criminal record. A few thefts, some violence. One or two special assignments you have done well. And one murder.'

Samuels said nothing,

'One murder that you got away with very cleverly. You're not a school educated man, but you are streetwise. That is what I want from you.'

Samuels still said nothing.

'I want you to kill someone for me. Fifty thousand pounds. Very little risk if you do the job well. And by well, I mean keep it simple.'

Samuels put the envelope back in his pocket. 'Who? And why?'

'His name is Martin Dudley. Why do you need to know why?'

'I guess I don't. But the more I know will make it easier to get the details right. It's not like I'm likely to grass on you; I'm the one doing the job.'

'That is true.'

Samuels waited to hear what he would be told. One thing he already knew though; he knew Martin Dudley. One of the biggest assignments he had taken on was for him. He had helped him steal something very valuable which, he understood, Dudley had sold for a significant chunk of money. But probably Dudley had a string of deals he didn't know about and presumably this was going to be something to do with one of those.

'Do you know what the Mildenhall Treasure is?'

Christ, thought Samuels. That was exactly what he had helped Dudley steal. So, what did this guy know about it? He nodded, and then realised he probably could not be seen and added 'Yes.'

'It is probably the most valuable Roman collection ever amassed,' the voice said. 'It is a large group of 34 pieces of tableware from fourth century Rome. Almost certainly the most valuable single group of Roman artefacts ever discovered. It was found at West Row, near Mildenhall in Suffolk. During the Second World War, I think. Probably the most well-known item in it is the Great Dish, which weighs eighteen pounds alone. It was stored in the British Museum which was deemed to have the security to protect it, though replicas were on show in several locations including, obviously, the Mildenhall museum.'

Samuels waited again.

'For a one-month period it was moved from the British Museum to the Roman museum in St Albans.

St Albans was the third largest Roman town after London and Colchester, and very important to history, and to those who study Rome. When it was there, Dudley stole it. About a month ago. And he sold it to me. Why I wanted it is no concern of yours. But now I'm getting concerned and I want Dudley killed. It'll take the attention away from me.'

Samuels thought it through, and more quickly than he might have been expected to, because he knew more about it than this man apparently knew.

'Are the details up to me?'

'More or less. When you do it is your choice, but don't take too long, and where you do it is your choice. However, I want him shot because I don't want any mistakes. Soft-tipped bullet in the head; there will be almost nothing left of him, and that is how I want it. It will also make it less easy to identify Dudley which would suit me very well.'

Samuels felt rather than heard the rustle on the table, and he leaned forward and picked up the envelope thrown there.

'Half now,' the voice said. 'And half on completion. And there are details there about Dudley. Address. Places he will likely be.'

Samuels sat in his armchair, in his home, and thought through the details of how to kill Dudley.

It was clear from the details he had been offered that the 'where' part of the decision was obvious. Dudley would be at the Cathedral on a given day, at a given time. That would not be the place to try for a kill; too crowded and too confined. Samuels would need to be too close to make an easy getaway if he shot him there. But whenever Dudley visited the

Cathedral he stayed at the White Hart in the main part of the town, and there were several locations behind there where Samuels could operate from. In particular, he knew that Dudley never parked in the car park of the pub but had a parking place reserved in Samuel Square behind it.

Samuels had taken a short lease on a house behind the pub, in Hart Lane off Pageant Road, and from there, there were several possible target areas he could use.

He visited the area several times, measuring angles and distances to possible locations, sometimes spending hours there, sitting casually on low walls, eating his sandwiches and drinking cans of drink like a hundred other people every day. Watching the flag flying gently off the Abbey Church of St Alban. No one noticed him.

But he noticed her.

She was sitting down a little further away, on a small wall at the edge of the London Road car park next to the one he was looking at, huge sunglasses obscuring a lot of her face, reading a book, and sometimes a magazine, and apparently enjoying the dry and warm weather of the day. Samuels would never have noticed her if he hadn't been cautiously aware of his own reason for being there. The more he looked at her, the more she looked like him. Casual, not to be noticed, reading casually, chewing on something every now and again. Did she not look exactly like he did? It first raised an almost humorous question in his mind. As the hours wore on it raised a slightly more interesting question. Gradually, it raised a real question.

He thought about it, and was wondering what to do about it, and decided he should confront her and find out what was happening. But at that moment she stood up, straightened her dress, and walked off down the road, away from where he was sitting.

He sat and thought about it for a while, and as time passed, he calmed down, and quickly began to realise that he was over-worrying, and that probably she was just one of many casual people that day, and now she was gone. After a half hour or so more, he was also finished and he walked back onto Holywell Hill, around the corner to Albert Street and back to his car.

It was two days later that he revisited the site. He dressed differently, he had a baseball cap on his head and a loose scarf, all of which changed the way he looked, but as he looked around, he could see that no-one was paying attention to him. He sat back, munched on a sandwich, and examined the likely area he would use as a target when Dudley arrived.

He also looked for the woman he had seen before but smiled to himself when he realised that she was not there. There were a couple of youngsters playing on the street, a few elderly people sitting or walking nearby, and no-one else.

As time passed, they left, and others joined. He jotted down a few notes from the newspaper he was reading onto a scrap of paper. They were his calculations of angles and distances to where he planned to shoot, but no-one would have guessed that. He looked around. Youngsters had left but been replaced by others making a nuisance of themselves on skateboards, and a couple of elderly women were just down the road.

Both were elderly, perhaps sixty or even seventy years old. One was limited in her movements it seemed, but still mobile enough to move sharply when she needed to. Her hair was grey, but pleasantly tinted he assumed rather than just naturally grey. And her face, behind the oversized plain glasses, was quite fit looking.

It was the oversized plain glasses that alerted him. They reminded him of the oversized sunglasses that the woman had worn on that day earlier. And whenever she was looking away, he looked at her carefully, and became sure, at first, that she was younger than she looked probably by quite a few years. And soon after he became convinced this was the same woman he had seen before.

But if she was, she was clearly in disguise. If she was twenty or thirty years younger than she looked, and if she was the same person he had seen earlier, then she was in disguise. It came back to him in a rush that she was disguised to hide not from everyone, but from him.

Who the hell was she?

It concerned him too much to leave, and without his usual care he stood up and walked straight towards her. He would ask her directly who she was and what she was doing. And why she seemed to be watching him.

But she was ahead of him; she stood up and started to walk away. He picked up speed and so did she, and as he gathered even more speed, she ran away from him and around a corner, leaving the Samuel Square car park and into Ryder Seed Mews. He lost her. Around that corner were several ways she could have gone. Out to the left or straight down, past Café Rouge, and out onto Holywell Hill. He stood still for a while, hoping to spot her movements, but she didn't reappear and, reluctantly, he left.

He planned it to be his last visit. A few days later he was back on the street to confirm his angles and distances.

He leaned on a different wall and drank from a can he had with him. Another man was standing not far from him. They stood quietly together. After a while Samuels took a few casual looks at the man, but he seemed of no interest. Youngish, dressed scruffily but not in any way out of fashion for a thousand other youths. He just leaned back, looked around; bored it would seem.

Samuels could not see the woman anywhere. But that did give him the time to think more about her. She seemed to be on some assignment, and she also seemed to be monitoring the same area that he was. Could she be on a connected assignment? Clearly, she could not be there to kill Dudley—you wouldn't need two assassins for one job. He thought a bit about the rumours of the assassination of President Kennedy; it appeared there were two assassins on that job at least. But if that was true, they were working in harmony. Whoever this woman was, she was not working with Samuels. So, could she be working against him? Could she be keeping an eye on Dudley and where he was in order to protect him? Maybe Dudley had her, or her and others, constantly looking out for him and checking wherever he went. If so, then possibly the woman was keeping an eye on him too, if she knew he had been assigned.

Another thought occurred to him when he thought that through. If the man who had engaged him to kill Dudley wanted to protect himself more, perhaps she had been hired to kill him. To let him kill Dudley and then kill him so that the trail would go cold. But how cold would that be? There would still be her. Did someone then have to kill her? That was absurd; you could go on with that paranoia until you'd killed hundreds of people. That couldn't be the case. But somewhere in there he felt he had the clues to an answer.

'I want to know who you are,' the man said.

Samuels turned slightly towards him, disturbed in his thinking. 'Who I am? What's it to you?' Samuels wasn't rude or unpleasant, but he did want to end the conversation quickly because he didn't want to discuss it.

'I think you know who I am,' the man said.

That gave Samuels the opportunity to look directly at him. But he didn't recognise him, or place him anywhere. He shook his head. 'I don't know who you are. Why should I?'

'Because you've spent long enough looking at me. Checking me over. And I want to know why.'

Samuels almost squinted to see if he could see him more clearly, which was pointless of course. Again, he shook his head.

The man turned to look more directly at Samuels. The lack of connection drove him further: he ripped off his hat and tossed his head to reveal a mass of long hair. In one second the man had become a woman. That woman!

Samuels was taken aback. Firstly, because he had expected to be the one to confront her, and he hadn't thought it would happen this way round. Also, because he felt that she had something to hide that he needed to discover, but now she was challenging him to reveal his secret. He had been sure that he needed to catch her off guard to find out what she was up to, and now she had caught him off guard.

'I've seen you here apparently doing the same as I'm doing,' Samuels started. 'I wondered why.'

'What are you doing?'

Samuels shook his head. 'I can't say.'

'Neither can I,' she said. But he could hear a question in her tone. The subject was still open.

'I've got a job to do. It's not something I want to talk about.'

She nodded. 'So have I. And I feel the same about it.'

They said nothing for a while.

'But it sounds like we need to share,' she added.

Samuels wondered where they could go. If her job was to kill him, she was hardly going to explain it to him. In which case whatever she said, he couldn't trust her. And whatever he said to her, she couldn't trust him.

'There's a man going to be staying at that hotel soon,' she offered.

'Dudley. Martin Dudley.'

She nodded. 'So...we're on the same assignment.'

He nodded. But this time she said nothing.

'Given my job, I don't think I need you here. My job stands alone.'

'Perhaps,' she said.

'Go on.'

'I'll put it bluntly. I'm here in case you fail.'

'Fail to do what?'

'To kill him.'

Women can be blunt, he thought. He just nodded.

She smiled. 'You're here to kill him,' she confirmed again.

'Yes,' he said, unbending, 'And I assumed that you were here to kill me afterwards. Perhaps to protect him.'

'Pointless, and you should have worked that out. Someone would then have to kill me. That's not it.'

'So, what's your job?'

She was equally blunt. 'Firstly, to back you up with any assistance I think you need.'

'And secondly?'

'Secondly, to kill him if you fail to do so.'

'He must want to protect the job. One of us would get him, I guess. I have a job like it behind me,' Samuels said with a sense of pride.

That pride didn't last long. 'I have eight assassinations behind me; all successful. And this is relatively simple. But I guess we have a choice to make.'

Before he could answer she spoke again. 'One question I have is why you decided to kill Dudley in this way. I assume rifle assassination at night from one of three locations behind us is your plan?'

Samuels nodded, though he had only two options. She had obviously worked out something he hadn't.

'So, we both decided that was the way to kill him. We could have used a bomb. I did consider a knife attack to look like it was done as a robbery, or a teenage thug. But it seemed to me that only a rifle assassination would work cleanly...'

'And I agree that is the right choice.' She thought quietly for a moment. 'Who gave you this assignment?'

'Actually, I don't know. It was kept anonymous. Whoever it was, was the person who bought some stolen goods from Dudley, and wanted to keep it secret.'

'James Franklin,' she offered.

'I don't know the name.'

'I assume you are the guy who, probably alone, stole the Mildenhall for Dudley?'

Samuels nodded.

'He sold that for a huge chunk of money to Franklin. I was the broker. It's what I do when I'm not on a sanction.'

'Sanction?'

She smiled. 'A killing. It's what I do. Franklin was the guy he sold it to. I put them together. My name is Gordon, Serena Gordon.'

'And it was Franklin that hired you to kill Dudley? Or at least to back me up killing him?'

'Yes. He was scared that Dudley was going to cough up if chased. He wanted him dead.'

'Then I guess it was him who hired me. But why was he secretive to me?'

'He was secretive to me too. I'd helped do the deal, but I didn't meet him. Then. Or now.'

Samuels thought about that. It seemed to him at least possible that Gordon was there to kill him. He would keep an eye on that; he was confident he could head that off if it looked likely.

They thought on that for a while but decided to drop it. Gordon flicked her head behind her. 'Take me to your Texas Book Depository,' she said, smiling.

They both walked across the road, and Samuels took out a key from his pocket and opened a door in the house in Hart Road, directly over from the hotel. He had rented the place on a six-month let, but it would be used for very much less.

Gordon was clearly not impressed, but neither was she critical. She looked, coldly and professionally, around the room and over to the hotel. 'I would have thought the block over the road would have provided a better site. From the roof you have a clearer spread of range, there is almost no way to be seen up there, and you have a quick route down to an escape area.'

'I agree. But this provides a place to stay and hide if anything goes wrong.' He pointed to the room outside the one they were in. 'Back there is a panic room. It was easy to build and I set it up a while back. If anything goes wrong, police will swarm over the area. But I can get into the panic room and they can search this place with a toothbrush; they won't find anyone here. Then I can get away.'

She looked around the place and came back nodding. Samuels was pleased that she found the plan acceptable.

The day of the sanction, as she put it, had arrived. They would probably have two days but Samuels had decided to go ahead immediately. He arrived at the flat and let himself in. About an hour later there was a knock on the door and he opened it to an unknown, rather shabbily dressed old lady. By now, he was getting used to it. He let her in and watched as she stripped back to the simple clothes she usually wore outside of her disguises.

They discussed the plan briefly, and coldly.

While she made coffee, he took the rifle from where it was concealed, assembled it, and loaded it. 'Soft tipped bullet,' he muttered and she nodded. He attached the scope and laser, and pointed it across the road towards the hotel, checking all seemed to be working.

'Are the sights tested?' she asked.

He nodded. 'If I shoot accurately, and I will, if the sight is on his forehead the bullet will enter within millimetres of the area. And with this bullet any reasonable shot will take out most of his head.'

Gordon nodded quietly. Samuels opened the window slightly, as much as was needed, made himself comfortable on the chair, and took aim. She sat quietly to the side, out of sight of the window.

Gordon thought about her job. Her job to kill Samuels. She thought he would have guessed that but he seemed oblivious to it. Even she found it strange that Franklin had sought to put the two of them together when that wasn't necessary.

But once Dudley was dead, Franklin's instructions were clear. Using the small Ruger SR-40C she had in her pocket, she would fire one shot into Samuels which would take him out immediately. Near the back of the house they were in was her motorbike, and within two minutes of the sanction she would be roaring away through St Albans and into the countryside nearby, and onto the M1.

In the hotel, Dudley was just arriving after his meetings at the Cathedral. His car turned off Hollywell

Hill, and drove round through Albert Street, to the car park behind the White Hart pub, as always. He stepped out of the car, and walked through, and towards the hotel doors. His closest, life-long, associate—mostly in crime—walked with him.

'I spoke to Franklin again the other day,' the colleague said.

Dudley nodded. 'He is happy. And safely out of any danger.'

'What about the people you used, in particular the thief and the broker?'

'The anonymous Mr Franklin assisted with that. Though he will never know it,' Dudley replied.

It seemed to Dudley that he heard a massive explosion. He turned, calmly, to look at it and watched the black smoke billowing out of the flat over the road opposite. He tried not to smile, but he knew neither of them would have survived that.

THE PRIEST AND THE COOK
Clare Lehovsky

My name is Felix, and I was Alban's slave. I was not a slave for Alban for long. I do not want to say my true name here; for the purposes of this story, I am Felix, and I will remain that way in a land occupied by Romans. The story that I want to tell is that of my master, a retired soldier. He was a wealthy but generous man who could have had an easy life. He fell so spectacularly because of a priest, a priest that told him to think differently overnight. Thoughts dangerous for a Roman.

The priest came under the cloak of darkness. I was just going inside the house when I heard hurried footsteps. I had been listening to the sounds of raucous shouting from across the street; the voices were not far from the theatre where Alban had gone to see a play not too long ago. I prepared myself for a fight, but one did not appear. Instead, a man staggered towards me. I could not have guessed that he was a priest from what he was wearing: a big and heavy but extremely ragged cloak.

'I seek shelter!' the man gasped. He was talking in perfect Latin.

I answered in a faltering reply. 'I am not the master of the house. The master is this way.'

I wanted to tell him to clear off, but that was not my decision to make. Every instinct of mine was telling me to do this. The man was older than Alban; his white hairs and beard were matted from travel. His face showed the wrinkles of a man used to hardship. His eyes had a faraway gaze like the religious leaders of my tribe. As I spoke, he looked right through my eyes and into my soul, despite that he was clearly suffering from fatigue. He was beginning to remind me of who I was before I had been enslaved—a memory that I could not contend with. I looked down at his feet. He was wearing sandals and his toes were bruised and bloody.

I did not want to show that he unnerved me. I took him into the kitchen, the *culina,* I welcomed the warmth from the clay ovens on my brown skin. The locals of Verulamium seemed hardly bothered by the cold that pervaded everything. Perhaps it was because this month was one of their summer months.

'Felix, what is the meaning of this?' The cook, a rotund Greek slave named Proserpina, squealed in shock at what appeared to be a beggar entering her pristine territory. I wanted to remind her that the Greeks should expect visits from *their* gods in the guise of beggars, a fact that Alban had told me, yet at that moment the man leaned heavily on my shoulder.

I practically had to carry him past the summer dining room, or *triclinium* (this guest would not be eating there) and led him past the garden and towards the *tablinium*, the study, where I knew that Alban would be attending to his letters before he turned in for the night. That had been his routine the past few months. The man lived a quiet life.

I knocked on the door and opened it slightly.

'What is it?' Alban's voice came through the crack. His voice was deep, sonorous, a reminder of the battlefield he had built his career on. I shivered.

'I have a... man for you, *Domine*. He wishes shelter.' I was ashamed of my Latin and was only too glad when Alban came to open the door fully and survey the fugitive in front of him.

'Who is he?'

The man behind me was now breathing heavily. I felt a huge weight come upon me from behind and I realised that the man had collapsed. I turned around to support him.

'Felix, what is the meaning of this?' Alban ushered the man into his study. 'Come, my dear fellow, let me offer you a drink...'

He shut the door in my face. He did not emerge that evening and did not come out for dinner. One time I saw the stranger emerge; he was alone while Alban was in the study. The man had a peaceful expression on his face and was looking up towards the sky, smiling at something I could not see. I hurried away, fearing I had interrupted something private. I laid a tray outside Alban's door in case he and his guest needed refreshment. Alban did not even come out to respect his god-statues in the evening.

When my master finally emerged, he was taking down his Roman god-statues and talking with the man I had let in the house. I noticed a shawl had been draped over the bust of his emperor, a leader he had previously held in great reverence. They were discussing subjects passionately together, using words that I could not even begin to understand.

Soon enough, Alban noticed me watching them. He glanced to the man and then back at me.

'Felix, this is Amphibalus. He is hiding here in this house. He is a Christian priest. You must not tell anyone outside that he is here.'

I nodded and resumed my duties without a thought.

I went back to the culina and felt Proserpina eyeing me.

'What were you doing?'

'Nothing.' I said. I picked up a knife and began to carve the freshly cooked unidentifiable meat that was stretched out on the table.

'Hmm.' She sniffed at the meat. 'I just hope *he* knows what *he's* doing, bringing in *that* man. He's probably on the run.'

I nodded. She nodded too and went towards the door.

'I'm just going out to the forum,' she said, and left.

It was only then I realised that I had made a mistake. Proserpina had not disguised the look in her eye.

I did not know how to tell Alban. Even though he was my master, and I his slave, I didn't want to strike fear into that calm expression of his. It would remind me too much of my father when he realised that the soldiers were coming to our village. I brought the men's evening meal to them in Alban's study; they had been eating there frequently of late. It was sunset—golden light streamed through the open courtyard and landed brightly on the stone floors.

'Felix, wait a moment.'

I waited; had he found out what would happen to him? That it was my fault?

'Amphibalus has taught me a new way of thinking.' His eyes found the other man's; they smiled at each other.

'A single Father, a Son, no multiple gods to worship. Eternal salvation.'

I did not understand what these words meant, neither did I want to. I knew what was coming for him.

'*Domine*, I...'

But I could not form the words.

There was a loud knocking on the front door. I knew exactly what Proserpina had done. We would be the ones left in an empty house now.

'They've come for me.' Amphibalus rose to his feet. Alban stopped him, his pristine toga sweeping up to meet the priest's ragged clothing.

'No, they will come for me. Give me your cloak.'

I hesitated. I should have been opening the door. Yet I watched as Alban transformed himself into the priest, wrapping the heavy cloak around his shoulders. Alban looked at me. It would not work; the soldiers knew him too well. Why was he doing this? Why would he sacrifice himself for a man he barely knew? I glanced towards where the now covered bust of the emperor was. There was clearly no turning back for Alban.

'Felix, take Amphibalus with you through the culina. I will buy him some time to escape.'

The priest grasped Alban's shoulder. 'The Lord will reward you.'

Alban smiled briefly at the priest.

'I look forward to seeing you again in paradise.'

I wordlessly took Amphibalus to the back of the house, where the soldiers would not be able to see him leave. He glanced at me; I knew he knew that I was disapproving of his actions.

'I suppose you think me a coward,' the old priest said to me. 'No matter. I need to spread the word of the Lord before my Time comes, which will be arriving shortly, I feel.'

The priest was right, they would catch up with him later. Alban's sacrifice would be in vain; if the priest had survived it would have been worth it.

Proserpina was not where she should have been, by the clay ovens ready to gossip over what may or may not have happened in the forum that day. I suppose she would return sometime, triumphant, having disposed of her master in one successful evening. She did not know that we had been lucky with this one. I could already hear Alban opening his main doors to his old comrades who would find him guilty of a crime.

I watched the priest disappear into the coming night.

THE OTHER MAN

Dave Weaver

Michael awoke in the half-light, sweating and shaking. Gwen turned on the bedside light, her worried face looking down at him.

'What is it, what's the matter?'

'I…it must have been a dream.'

'You were kicking, muttering things…'

'Sorry. I'm sorry.' He stumbled the words out, trying to rearrange his thoughts, place himself. As breathing became easier and sense returned, he rolled away onto his side so she couldn't see his face. 'It won't happen again.'

He was walking the dog over the railway bridge on Station Road when he noticed the man's figure through the early morning mist. He looked drunk, maybe sick, wrapped up in ragged clothes like a bundle of rubbish put out for collection. Michael stopped to look. A leg slowly raised itself until it was parallel with the top of the bridge. The man shuffled awkwardly as if trying to pull himself up. Michael realized what he was trying to do.

He shouted, surprised at the unbalanced edge to his voice. 'Hey! Don't do that!'

The man hesitated. Surely another passer-by would take control of the situation. A car's diffused headlights loomed up the slope, catching Michael full in the face so that he automatically held up a hand. When it passed, he stared back. The hump on the top of the bridge had flattened itself more, as if it intended to roll over onto the tracks below. In the middle distance, Michael sensed a train approaching out of the mist.

Michael felt his feet move as if they were somehow bidden. He crossed the road to grab the figure. There was a terrible rotten stink of unwashed flesh and bad whisky, amplified by the breeze off the river. A blackened visage turned to him; it stared in dull-eyed incomprehension.

No words passed. The brief struggle ended with both slumped on the pavement as the train swept past below. A young couple fastidiously picked their way around them. The dog waited patiently a few feet away, incurious of its master's actions.

Michael stood up, shaking, then pulled the other to his feet and pushed him against the bridge's metal side. The straggly hair parted to show a face not dissimilar to his own, if you discounted the scars and bruises. The body was thin and undernourished but would have been roughly his height. Even the face, if you wiped away the blood and grime...

Blackened hands reached out to grip Michael's shoulders. No longer opaque, the pupils stared back into his, black diamonds spinning in wild eyes. Something unbidden seemed to pass between the two men. The other man blinked heavily and the dullness was back. He found enough strength from somewhere to shove Michael away then turned and staggered off into the spreading sunrise. Michael let him go. There was something in that stare he didn't want to confront. He hoped he would never see the man again. He began to shiver; cold or delayed shock, he didn't know. The dog was back around his feet. It gave a sniff then a strange little whimpering sound he'd never heard it make before.

A few weeks later, Gwen told him over dinner that the clothes had gone.

'What clothes?' He was barely listening, trying to read the Herts Advertiser. His response was automatic, uninterested.

'Your old clothes, for Oxfam. I put them in the garage. Now they're gone.'

'What are you talking about?'

'Someone's been into our garage and stolen your old clothes.'

'Don't be ridiculous. Who'd want to do that?' Her logic irritated him. 'And if you were throwing them out anyway, what does it matter?'

'I don't want some old tramp coming onto our property and taking things. And it's strange anyway, who'd know they were even there in the first place?'

He made no reply.

'Well, don't you think it strange?'

Michael lowered his head to the paper. Gwen didn't notice the small shudder he gave.

The office was busy doing forthcoming tax returns; usual last-minute panic. Michael's boss motioned him to step into his office.

'We've taken on some temporary people to cope, just for the basic day to day stuff. Make them feel at home, will you? Show them the ropes.'

Michael looked out through the distorting frosted glass; there were three or four new faces he didn't recognize. And one he did. It was different; changed, but not so much that he couldn't see the likeness. It was more pronounced this time. He walked out quickly to his desk.

'Who was that guy standing there just now?' he asked Jenny.

'What guy?' She looked at him strangely.

'What did he say his name was?' he snapped, more than he'd meant to.

He saw the familiar figure exit the room, blurred under the white-blue strip-light. Michael waited, poised for it to return. It settled at a laptop on the farthest desk. The man seemed to be wearing his old clothes. He was clean-shaven now, with a hacked short-back-and-sides. Michael felt a draining of energy and willpower. He sat down heavily to begin his work but the figures jumped before his eyes. He hadn't had a migraine in years. His numbed brain refused to focus as the pain intensified. He stuck it out until lunchtime then staggered from the room, sensing the other watch him leave.

He didn't go back into work for a while after that. When he finally plucked up the courage, he saw the other man seated at his desk, dictating a letter to Jenny. No one acknowledged Michael's presence; his boss walked straight past him. The only available desk was the one at the back of the room. Early in the afternoon Michael decided to go home again. And not come back.

But he did wait outside the office a week later to catch a glimpse of his replacement. The man's clothes were different now, as was his grooming. He sported a neat tailor-made suit, expensive leather shoes and a slick, razor-sharp haircut. Jenny was with him, as if they'd both come from somewhere together. Michael caught his own reflection in a shop window's reflection. He had the ruffled and slightly seedy look of someone who'd been wearing the same clothes for days. He threw some cold water on his face in the public toilets. He hadn't showered for a while. For the first time he felt a little self-disgust and resolved to do better.

He phoned in sick to put off the finality of quitting but didn't tell Gwen, preferring to spend his days hanging around the town and local park. No-one had responded to his message or called him back. If was as if, as far as the company were concerned, he'd ceased to exist.

It was Saturday night and Gwen was very late home. When her key finally turned in the latch, he sat waiting in the armchair with a large whisky grasped in his shaking hand.

'Where the hell have you been?'

'Oh, you made me jump!' She peered at him through the gloom as if trying to see a phantom. 'Why are you sitting in the dark like that?' She moved a hand to the light-switch.

'Leave it off please. I asked where you'd been.'

Her voice was suddenly prickly. 'I might ask you the same thing. I've hardly seen you all week. Anyway, I was with a friend.'

'What's her name?'

'None of your business.' She swept past him and up the stairs. 'I suggest you turn in and get a good night's sleep. You're starting to look a real mess.'

Michael hadn't meant to follow Gwen, but still found himself in the car park of their local pub. Her car was in the corner. He watched the two of them talking animatedly to each other in the lounge bar window. When they came out, he hid in the rose garden until they drove off.

He meant to go straight home and have it out with her, but instead he walked into town. He hung around the Maltings shopping centre with an opened bottle of whisky then sat on the concrete and drank. As skateboarders shouted at him, he gestured drunkenly back at them. In the end he was moved on after the policeman had taken down his address and given a half-hearted warning. It sobered him up enough to confront Gwen.

When he finally returned home, he saw all the lights were out, apart from the one in their bedroom. Gwen's car was in the driveway. Michael watched from across the road as two silhouettes were thrown against closed curtains. They disappeared then returned in shrunken form as if they'd moved backwards or lain down. He slowly crossed over and put his key in the latch, trying to slide it in and turn it as quietly as he could. He froze at its final click, paused, then pushed the front door open. He was still drunk, nearly toppling on the first stairs before grabbing the banister and hauling himself up as if ascending a mountain. His footfall creaked on the wooden stairs, but that giveaway noise was camouflaged by another steadily growing one of bedsprings. A knocking noise joined that, and he imagined their headboard making regular contact with the wall. He crept along the landing. Now he was out of the cool night air in the fug of the central heating he could smell himself, a rotten stink of unwashed flesh. He'd pretended not to notice until then but there could be no denying it. A creamy-blue light escaped from beneath their bedroom door. Michael unconsciously licked his lips in anticipation then cautiously turned the knob and pushed. There didn't appear to be any reaction, so he inched his head around the door. The man was on his back, sweaty and spreadeagled beneath her. Gwen was turned away from Michael as she moved above him in careful rhymical movements. She swayed forward, engulfing him, then arched backwards with a long deep grunt of satisfaction. As she moved out of Michael's sightline, her lover looked up at him. Their eyes met as an understanding passed between them. Michael closed the door and left the house. He wouldn't be going back.

He bought his old clothes back from the Oxfam shop on Holywell Hill once he recognized them. The woman behind the counter shook her head at all the small change. After he'd changed in an alleyway he felt more at ease, as if the strain of pretending to be someone else had finally left him. He hadn't been home for weeks now.

Individual days began to run into one another like oil swirling in water. He felt light-headed; it was becoming difficult to keep food down and there was only enough money left for crisps and cheap cider; the supermarkets had begun to bar him.

The fact that he smelled was plainly written on the faces of passers-by and most crossed the road to avoid him. He'd attempted to wash in the Clarence Park toilets until moved on by the park-keeper. The local fast-food outlets refused to serve him. His long hair had grown straggly and knotted and there was sick on the torn pullover and piss down the muddied trousers. Through a fog of bewilderment, he sensed an end was coming.

The man who used to be Michael found himself standing on top of the railway bridge in Station Road. He leant over to look down on the tracks below then, without seeming to make any effort, he raised a leg up and shifted his weight until he clung on sideways. The night breeze blew in his face, cold and misty.

In the faint moon glow a figure hurried across the road then laid a firm hand on his shoulder. Suddenly, realising what the other man was about to do, he reached out to grasp the hand, staring through straggly hair into a face he recognized.

The face stared back. There was a sort of pity in its eyes. 'I'm sorry...not this time.' The expression hardened and the hand pushed.

Michael awoke in the half-light, sweating and shaking. Gwen turned on the bedside light, her worried face looking down at him.

'What is it, what's the matter?'

'I...it must have been a dream.'

'You were kicking, muttering things...'

'Yes...' He tried to rearrange his thoughts, place himself. As breathing became easier and sense returned, he rolled away onto his side so she couldn't see his face. He sensed her bewilderment. 'It's okay, I've fixed it now. It won't happen again. I swear.'

But the creature inside his head knew different.

THE BODY IN THE THEATRE

Joan Crooks

The Chinese tourists and their local guide found the body in the Roman Theatre of St Albans at 10am. It was lying quite neatly on the round plateau, slightly hidden from casual view, waiting for the cue of an audience to quieten, a drum beat to rumble and a spotlight to illuminate the start of action. Instead, there was the gasp and chatter of shrill voices and a scream of, 'Oh my God!' from the guide.

By the time the police arrived the tourists were encircling the body from a distance having been told firmly by the guide to keep to the barely perceptible boundary wall. They had taken many photographs of this addition to their sightseeing schedule and were still quite excited by the scene. The guide, looking rather green, was in the small hut with the ticket collector, having a reviving cup of tea and chatting nervously. 'These tourist groups know the UK from television programmes, and this looks like an episode of Midsummer Murders to them. I think they're expecting Barnaby and his most recent side kick to turn up.'

The police inspector took the guide's phone number but realised he would get nothing of interest about the crime from him or the group. The ticket collector had arrived at the kiosk at 9.45am ready for his first customers. He had left the day before at 5pm and seen nothing unusual. In between those times a dead body had turned up with a particularly efficient knife wound through the heart.

Inspector James Ward sighed to himself. He had a bad feeling about this crime. This was a very well thought out murder which had been staged to perfection. Clumsy murders done in the heat of passion and anger left clues and DNA material that moved the police on nicely with their enquiries. This body had been cleaned and spruced up ready for his dramatic moment. Here there were no bushes or trees for clothes to brush against, no sign of footsteps or traces of vehicles.

The ticket collector apologised for a lack of CCTV cameras and rather unnecessarily pointed out that they were in an isolated spot with no houses close by. It was possible someone driving along the main road would have seen a vehicle turn off and been curious, so Ward would set up a media interview. Meanwhile, he needed to find out who the corpse was and why someone had wanted him dead.

The police data base recognised the corpse's face and fingerprints and Ward began to learn something of his rather murky story. Trevor Smith, aged sixty-five, had lived in a small pleasant two-bedroom flat in Finchley with a woman called Jane Trent.

She was in floods of tears when interviewed by Ward and had no idea who would want to kill Trevor.

She said, 'Trevor's been dating a lady in St Albans; that's why he was over there last night. Trevor and me have a platonic relationship, more like brother and sister. We are still very fond of each other, you know, just good friends.'

Ward nodded. 'I'd like to look at Trevor's bedroom now.'

Jane gave him a filthy look when he stopped her from coming in with him. He could not help but notice that Trevor and Jane shared the room and the double bed, judging by the extent of male and female clothes, cosmetics and cologne that was on show. He felt a bit cynical about Jane's story that she and Trevor were not in a relationship. He thought she would need to be investigated more closely. He also took Trevor's laptop, much to Jane's fury.

Trevor had been quite prolific on dating sites for older people and his most recent conquest had been 68-year-old Kitty from St Albans. He had seen her on the day of the murder for lunch. A booking for two had been made at The St Albans Waffle House for 1.30pm.

James found the interview with Kitty excruciatingly difficult. He was very relieved to have PC Mary Curtis with him to offer tissues and make comforting tea. Kitty had also wept when told of Trevor's death and had started to tremble in an alarming way. Mary helped her into a chair and asked how she knew Trevor.

'I met him five months ago. I felt we were really hitting it off. Trevor was so charming and behaved beautifully, often bringing me flowers.' Kitty blushed as she explained, 'It felt like old fashioned courting; nothing too pushy or frightening.'

Mary suggested Kitty give them some background to the relationship. Kitty nodded.

'I was widowed five years ago when my husband Bill was on the point of retirement. Bill was a partner in a London firm of solicitors and we used to live in large house in Harpenden. Bill felt it would be good to downsize before retirement and we bought this sweet little cottage in Fishpool Street, St Albans. It's convenient to the Verulamium Park, St Michael's Manor Hotel, lovely pubs and shops. We were very happy.' Kitty became overcome with tears and struggled with the next words.

'Bill had a heart attack just a year after we moved.'

Mary gave Kitty more tea and asked gently, 'What happened next?'

'I felt very lost and disorientated without Bill. A couple of my friends eventually suggested I should try a dating site. They said it was about time to pick life up again. I talked it through with my daughter Liz and she said as long as I was very careful and she was given an oversight of anyone I dated, then to go ahead.'

Kitty looked at the police inspector and Mary and smiled. 'I had some really funny dates. I'd spend long lunches with my friends giggling about them. One man turned up at St Michaels Manor in dirty trousers and a scruffy old jumper. I thought they could be his gardening clothes. I asked him why he hadn't made more of an effort to dress nicely on a first date, as I was sure most women would try and look good. He said he expected the right woman to take him as he was. I said, 'fair enough' and got up and walked out.'

Kitty sighed, lost in her thoughts. 'Most older men are only interested in talking about themselves and want someone to fit into their homes and life-styles. After a really tiring hour and a half with one man I asked what he had learnt about me. He looked surprised and said I was a good listener.'

James and Mary smiled sympathetically. 'Tell us about Trevor.'

'He was different, good looking, well dressed and charming. We had a lot in common. He liked walking in the parks, and we would walk around the lake and go up to the abbey for coffee. We went to a couple of lovely concerts at the abbey too and had just booked another one. We often ate at St Michaels Manor and I was proud to be seen with him. He wasn't pushy but made it clear he thought we had a future together. He said I was everything he had been looking for in a partner and his search was over. He even talked about marriage, and that we needed to realise at our time in life we should grab happiness when it was offered.' Kitty paused and drank more tea.

'I was more cautious. It had been true love with Bill and I really wanted a companion now, not a husband. We were beginning to talk about going on holiday for a couple of weeks in Greece to test out whether we could get on when we were together in an intimate way. Liz said she would want to meet Trevor before the holiday was booked but also said he sounded very nice, showing respect and consideration to me. My daughter often asked who paid for our outings and I told her on the whole Trevor did although occasionally I insisted that I picked up the bill.'

Kitty looked shocked when Ward told her about the probable partner Jane and even more so to hear that they shared a home and bedroom. She had not heard about the dozen women he had dated in the last five years either. She looked very upset and confused and Mary asked if there was anyone she could call to come over and stay with her.

Kitty phoned a friend and then her daughter. Ward talked briefly to Liz and asked if he could visit her to get some more information. He learnt that Liz was a solicitor, like her father, and she could give him time the next day.

In the police car Ward said, 'Kitty is rather a dear, isn't she?'

Mary nodded. 'I'd have her as my mum any day.'

Ward met a smiling receptionist at Liz's St Albans office and was taken up to her room, which had 'Senior Partner' on the door. Liz was a tall, attractive, smartly dressed woman with shrewd eyes and a calm manner. Ward thought she probably took after her father rather than mother, but there was a hint of Kitty in the smile she gave him.

Ward started, 'I am afraid we have discovered Trevor was a serial dater.'

Liz looked surprised. 'My mother really liked him, and it all sounded promising and quite safe. I googled him and didn't find anything untoward; just a few details about a couple of work journals he had contributed to. I had said I wanted to meet him before they went on holiday together and he told mum that he would like that.' Liz smiled and said, 'It's a bit like having a third teenager when your elderly mum starts dating. I know I'm lucky that she is willing to accept my support, and we both felt it was good that her dates knew she wasn't on her own.'

Ward continued, 'There is something else about Trevor that you should know. He took four of his dates on holiday and strangely, each time the women lost their bank cards and several thousands of pounds were stolen before the women realised and got the bank to freeze their account.'

Liz looked Ward in the eye and said, 'How did he do it?'

'We're not sure, because the money was stolen while Trevor and his date were in each other's company. The thief managed to buy thousands of pounds' worth of expensive gifts or, in some cases, was able to move money straight out of the bank account to another untraceable one.'

Liz looked thoughtful. 'Surely these days the banks text or phone their customer to check unusual purchases?'

Ward explained. 'These women all said their mobile phones stopped working and they were messaging their family at home on Trevor's phone. We believe the sim card was removed and must have been given to an accomplice who was able to reassure the banks that the transactions were legitimate. We also think Trevor picked up security codes and pin numbers from watching these women closely when they used their cards.'

Liz got up and walked to the window. She turned and said quietly, 'My mother has had a narrow escape. She would have been devastated to lose my father's money to a scam. She often says she was looking after it for me and the grandchildren.'

'The police were not able to make a strong enough case against Trevor Smith for the Prosecution Service to take him to Court. I know some of the families were very upset about that and felt it was giving him carte blanche to continue.'

Liz asked, 'Do you think that this was the motive for his murder?'

'We have to take it seriously into consideration. However, in my opinion Mr Smith's murder was very professionally carried out, so it is possible he fell out with some fellow villains. I need to tell you that we are looking into the bank accounts of everyone who had dealings with Mr Smith just to see if we pick up a money trail. We may then need to follow up with searching computers and phones.'

Liz nodded slowly. 'I understand. My mother and myself will give you access to anything you need. I would be very grateful if you communicate with me rather than my mother if you have any information about the murder to impart.'

Ward left Kitty's daughter feeling pleased that Kitty had good loving support and would be taken care of in a kindly way. He was also glad Trevor Smith had died before taking Kitty on holiday.

About six months later, Ward got in touch with Liz to update her about the murder of Trevor Smith. Over the phone he said, 'The case has gone cold and any lead we followed went nowhere. There was a remarkable lack of forensic evidence connected to the body, and the knife had been wiped very clean. We are fairly sure that Trevor's accomplice in the fraud had been Jane, who seemed to mysteriously be away from home whenever Trevor went on his holidays. We believe she used aliases and had false passports, but we cannot discover where she went, and her family gave her alibis. We cannot find evidence Jane had anything to do with Trevor's murder and she was unhelpful about possible criminal connections.'

Liz asked, 'Was there no other evidence?'

Ward continued, 'I interviewed the families of the women who had been robbed.' There was a smile in his voice when he said, 'All of the family members said they were pleased Trevor was dead. He had caused a lot of grief and upset to their elderly mothers. One middle aged son said he would like to shake the hand of the person who did it. However, most also said they would rather he had gone to prison and murder was a bit extreme. They were decent people and we are not expecting that there is any purpose in investigating them any further.'

'Is my mother under investigation?'

'We do not feel your mother was involved in any way, apart from it being convenient for the murderer to pick Trevor up after he had lunch with your mother. It could be it was someone he knew, as there was no sign of a struggle, and quite possibly he willingly went into the murderer's car. I believe the car park at The Waffle House is always full and overlooked by the restaurant, so a commotion would have been noticed.'

Liz said, 'Thank you for the update. The whole experience with Trevor has knocked the confidence out of my mother. She's decided dating is too risky and she will just socialise with friends and family from now on. I suppose our mothers have to learn to be streetwise about relationships just like our teenagers do. It was a hard lesson for her, but she knows it could have been a whole lot worse.'

Three months after this, Liz received a handwritten letter at home. The writer suggested they meet in St Albans Park at the bench overlooking the lake. There was a temporary phone number Liz could respond to. Liz sat on the bench with a bag of bird seed which she knew was healthier for birds and ducks than the bread she and her mum used to bring. A woman about her age sat down next to her and the two of them contemplated the crowd of birds for a while.

'It seems to have gone according to plan,' said the woman. 'The police aren't continuing to investigate the case.'

Liz agreed. 'Inspector Ward has been in touch and said the same thing to me.'

'How did your mother take the news of Trevor's murder?'

'She was very upset,' Liz replied, 'but also relieved that she hadn't been robbed of money my father left her. I am so sorry about your mother. She was the real casualty in this whole affair.'

The woman nodded. 'I know the police couldn't make a link between my mother's depression and death so soon after the scam, but I have no doubt the shock of losing fifteen thousand pounds just broke her. She lost the will to live and we discovered she had stopped eating, and although the death certificate said heart attack, we felt the real cause was Trevor Smith.'

'Are the other women getting over it now?'

'Their sons and daughters say they are not the same confident women that they were before meeting Trevor. One other woman became very depressed, stopped going out, and could not manage to eat. She died in a very frail state about six months after Trevor Smith stole thirty thousand pounds from her bank account. It was all her savings as she would not let her family put the money into safer places. However, the other two are moving on with their families' support. I know we won't meet again but I felt it would be good just to touch base so we could have closure.'

Liz continued to feed the birds as she watched the woman walk away.

She remembered meeting her about six months ago when a note was popped through her door. *I have some information about a man who is calling himself Trevor Smith. I will meet you tomorrow at one of the benches by the lake in St Albans Park. Bring a bag of bird seed and I will look for a single woman feeding the birds. My name is Jenny.*

Jenny had spoken bluntly. 'There are four elderly women who have dated Trevor, gone on holiday with him and had significant amounts of money stolen from their bank accounts. All of the women have been affected very badly and their families are upset and angry that the police could not prosecute him. In my case the devastation was even worse because my mother died just a few months after the robbery. I have a plan which would involve the families of the four victims and you, daughter of the potential fifth victim. We are either all involved in this scenario or it will not happen.'

Liz said, 'Go on, tell me about your plan.'

'My ex-husband Steve was extremely fond of his mother-in-law and continued to pop round to see her after our divorce. He is also an ex-copper and still has all sorts of contacts both in the police but also with a more shadowy criminal crowd, some of whom feel they owe him favours. He has come up with an idea of bumping Trevor off but in a way that will not lead back to the families. He said the police would be looking for an individual who has taken out about £25,000 in cash to pay a hit man. Steve is willing to be the guy in the middle, but his suggestion is that five members of the elderly victims' families take out five thousand pounds each. They will need a backup story to say what they want the money for. The other family members are willing, but it needs a fifth. Would you be willing to lay out that sort of money?'

Liz said, 'I need to think about it.' After a pause she asked, 'How did you find me?'

Jenny looked a little embarrassed. 'Steve knew where Trevor lived and started following him. He saw Trevor meet Kitty and then that led to you.'

Liz had responded to the stories about Trevor as she would if she heard someone was planning to harm one of her children. She felt outrage but also that sense of being a protective lioness who would stand in the way of a predator who was out to destroy her vulnerable cub. Her mother had protected her daughter in childhood and kept her safe. Now it was Liz's turn. Liz would never have expected she would take this type of risk or actually consider ending someone's life but looking at what could have happened to her mother if she had gone on holiday with Trevor made her blood run cold. Kitty could have ended up like Jenny's mother; ashamed, guilt ridden and feeling she had let down her daughter, grandchildren, and the memory of her beloved husband. The question Liz asked herself was, could she live with herself if she got involved in this plot to murder? She was surprised to find the answer was she could.

Ward put the phone down after talking to Liz and sighed heavily. He had really liked this woman. She was smart, straight talking and looked at him directly in a way that felt to him like they had a connection. She was also extremely attractive, slim, and feminine with a hint of ruthlessness which he found exciting. He knew she was divorced and there was no record of her being in a relationship at the moment. Ward had wanted to visit her at her office again, perhaps even suggest he see her at her home to bring her up to date on his enquiries. However, he knew he could not allow anything to develop between them. It could be a signal to an up-and-coming officer to look more closely at Liz. She would never know that he was protecting her.

He had looked at the bank accounts of the sons and daughters of the elderly women who had been robbed by Trevor Smith. He had been searching for a large cash withdrawal of approximately twenty-five thousand pounds which was, he believed, the asking price for a murder. He did not find it. However, what he found was that four family members had taken five thousand pounds out of their banks within a couple of days of each other. He had a good look at Jenny's ex-husband Steve's bank account but found no unexpected withdrawals there. He had a very strong hunch that ex Police Sergeant Steve Jones was involved in this murder. He had a record of being a brilliant copper at times but also of mixing too deeply with the underworld of criminals at other times. Ward knew Steve Jones had been given early retirement before his exploits became a public embarrassment to the force.

Ward had looked into Liz's eyes and wondered if he had found the fifth contributor to the killer's fee. The five had not hidden their cash withdrawals, and it had been easy for Ward to find and guess the reason the money had been put towards. He had not written this part of his investigation down in his report. This was not just because he really liked Liz but was also because he had liked Jenny and the other sons and daughters. Hand on heart he could not say he would not have wanted vengeance if someone had scammed his elderly mother out of her life savings His mum was very proud of being independent and paying her way. She often said she could not bear to be a burden on anyone and hoped someone would find a way to finish her off before that happened.

Ward's Chief Inspector accepted his report that it was likely a criminal contact of Trevor Smith, with some grudge against him, who was the probable murderer. Ward suggested Jane Trent was a strong suspect but had expertly covered her tracks and there was no criminal trail they could uncover. The fuss over the murder died down and the only people left remembering it were the Chinese tourists, who often wondered what the story was behind the body in the Roman Theatre.

REGULAR SERVICE (OR CRIMES AGAINST HUMANITY)

Judith Foster

Rained nice and hard last night. Should be plenty of puddles. Fewer people at the market, though. Never mind. Make do with what's there. Be a bit inventive. Usual route. Boundary and first stop coming up. 30 sign.

Bin lorry ahead. That's a chance. Slow down gently, then stamp the brake. What did I get? Just a grunt. Don't think I can count that. I'll keep it in reserve. I can get past now, just. Move out fast, swerve back in. Don't want to hit my mate in the other green one. I heard a squeal. One of them hit his head on the window. That counts. One blood point[*]. Scribble it down.

There's a van with its door open. How close can I get? Raised his fist at me. Cheeky sod. That counts too. One point[*].

Couple of old codgers at the stop, sticks and all. Let them in all unsuspecting. 'Get your card out. Can't wait all day. Can't find it? Sorry, rules is rules. That's £2.10. Ta. Take your ticket. There, where it shows.' I'll get her again later. Next one's glaring nicely. Pity he's got his card. Still, there's another, nearly two[*].

Next stop's that college place. Let them off here. Stop a bit quick. Made them stagger. Bitchy kid swore at the one in front. Cor, hurts my ears. Kill my daughter if she talked like that. There's a few trying to cross in front. Quick, catch 'em. One made it, others jumped back. Two more points[**]. Though I think the swearing might be worth more.

Nice little bit of double parking at those shops. And a deep gutter. I'll stop here. I can flash them to come through it to me. She's wearing sandals. She'll get her feet wet. Hah. And I've blocked the road in both directions. I can give myself three for that[***].

Someone coming downstairs? Stop sharpish at the next. And I can shout to hurry them up. Nice, high squeal. And she thinks he pushed her. He'll come down first next time. Then he'll get it for bad manners. Two points[**]. Mark it down.

Lots of people at Murchisons, always. 'No, I can't change a tenner. I'm not the Bank of England. Well, get off then.' Old bloke paid for her, and had his card ready. Only one[*]. 'Make room for them at the back there...'

Now the cemetery. Oh good, funeral. And solid parking both sides. This is a treat. Four horns blaring. Shouldn't do that for a funeral. No respect. Shake my fist at them. Creep a car-length at a time. Stop, start, stop, start, little jerks to unsettle them. Couple of points[**], I think. My respects to the corpse.

Pity, straight through the lights first time, and race up the hill. Shall I let that man running catch me? Yeah. Then I can squeal the brakes and stop that car behind. Oh, tut-tut. What a rude gesture! One point[*].

Man wants to know if I'm going to Lumpstead. 'It says St. Albans, dunnit?' Does that count? I don't think so. I want to be fair. Well, hell. Why should I tell him we stop at the same stop? Yes, one point*.

Sharp corner into the station road. Whoops-a-daisy! Bumped its hip, I think. 'You all right, love?' And another sharp one. Hah, she dropped her stick. Have a job getting into the train without that. Two points**.

Back into the road and left at the lights. I'm in luck. Cyclist on the hump bridge, right in the middle of the road. Long hoot. Obstinate blighter. But I'll get him with the puddle at the lights. One point*. Good one, that. And a raised fist. 'Keep your hands on the handlebars, matey. You're a danger to road users.' Another point*.

Tricky little roundabout. Can't see what's on the right. 'Course it was her fault. Couldn't she see a great green bus? Sorry, folks, she just came at me. You all OK?' One point*.

Crossing with lights. I hate these. People take advantage. There, did you see that? Right up to the last second. What chance do I have? And another roundabout. You'd think I was on the minor road. 'Well, this is a bus! Where's the priority for old people?'

'All change. You want to complain? There's my inspector, over there, shirt sleeves and tattoos. See where it gets you.' Final flourish, two good points**.

Lock the bus. Shan't bother with the rubbish yet. Ten minutes break? It's raining again. I'll take fifteen.

Unlock the bus. 'No, not yet. I've got to clear the rubbish now.' One*.

'You're dripping, Missus. Close your umbrella before you get on. Well, if you haven't got one, you should get one.' Flustered nicely. 'Move along, now. They're getting wet. That's not a return. £2.10. No, I can't wait while you find it. £2.10. And what about the kid? Doesn't look under five to me. And why isn't he in school? Don't you cry over me. Not my rules. Full up, sorry. Sorry, mate. What's that? Not very? Keep your opinions to yourself.' That must be three***.

St. Peter's is always fun. Crossings, jaywalkers, buses, market stalls, then that grand corner by the old town hall. I can swing round there like Hamilton. Stop. Nearly got that bumper. One*.

Two buses at the stop. I make three. My tail's well back in St. Peter's. And there's that car stopped at the clinic. I love it when the others have to drive round him. What a row! Another point*.

No passengers on and none off. Free run down over two sets of lights and two stops. I can make 45 miles an hour down here. Catch up on my break, bit longer next time. Two**.

Another hump bridge. Listen to that. Someone's oranges and onions all over the floor, and a can rolling around. 'Oy, careful there with your bags, and keep 'em out of the gangway.' Old biddy can't reach her fruit, old feller can't either. They'll have to wait until the station. She's giving up on the last one. It's gone to the back. 'Isn't anyone going to help her?' I don't know. People's manners. 'Come on, let 'em along now.' Kicked the can. What a racket. Three***.

Traffic lights, right turn. Tight corner. Made that pedestrian on the pavement jump. One*.

Sharp stop at the next lights, and again. Grunt and a squeal. One*.

'Come on, get the buggy in. Can't you fold it up? No, I can't wait for ever. I'm behind time.' One*.

Stop with no points! Huh. But there's someone in a disabled chair. What luck. I'll wait till they ask. 'What? Can't you manage? Oh, all right, I'll drop it. Now, hurry up. Special pass? Get it out. Let me do it. You don't want my hand in your purse? Get on with it then.' Two**.

Kid's got a skipping rope caught in mum's trolley. Kid squeals, mum shouts, wet passengers grumble. One*.

Students upstairs. Pretend they rang the bell too late. Shouting down. I'll keep on to the next stop. Stamp the brakes. One of 'em tripped. Ooh, bad language; but that's students for you. Two**.

Road works ahead with lights. Bit of luck. I'm a long way back. If I dawdle, I could be the last to get along. Nearly, just one behind me. Yeah, nice big gap. Someone's coming straight on! 'Hey, you don't expect me to back this bus all that way, do you? You'll have to go back. Shouldn't be so impatient. I've got old folks in here to look after.' Two good ones**.

Yellow bus stopped there, and a different one in front of it. That one's going off. If I go tight round the yellow one, I can squeeze in front, and stop him moving. Haven't had that chance for weeks. One point, and one extra because he's a yellow one**.

There's the boundary. Let's count up. 45 blood points. Not bad, but not a record. I'll jot it down at the depot.

UNCLE DAVID'S LAST PRANK

Ben Bergonzi

Mary-Lou Garic looked admiringly across the auction room at her husband. Gene was standing with his feet apart, his jacket open to reveal his seersucker waistcoat. There he was, tanned and fit and braced for action. Her fighting Kentuckian. He wasn't even bothering to lower his hand between bids. These little skinny English fellows would have no chance. She liked to see him win but she wished he didn't get such bees in his bonnet. Like insisting on stopping off here in another 'sweet little cathedral town' when they could have been back in London in another twenty miles. Instead of their suite at Claridges, she would have to spend another night in another black and white 'coaching inn' with a freezing bedroom and the bathroom a chilly walk along the corridor. But no, he wouldn't have missed this auction in St Albans. Yet another place that pesky David Garrick had happened to visit.

'One hundred and ten pounds, one hundred and twenty pounds, thank you, sir. Any more, yes, one hundred and thirty, one hundred and forty, bidding sir? One hundred and fifty...' The auctioneer had an Edwardian air to him, with his grey hair parted in the middle and a wing collar. Here in England, Mary-Lou had noticed, those famous days of fifty years ago seemed a much more recent memory than they were back home. This country had fought two wars and beggared themselves in the effort to come out on the winning side. And now it was 1954 but meat was still rationed and the towns were peppered with empty bombed sites. And as for the hotels!

This afternoon's sale of Fine Vintage Wines and Brandies was nearly over, but Gene had had to wait until the very end for the one lot that had drawn them here. She irritably glanced again at the page in the auction catalogue, the entry he had circled so emphatically with a red pencil: *A bottle of old Cognac, with label reading 'Duke Humfrey's finest Vintage for you, Mr Quinn, from Mr Garrick, the Christopher Inn, St Albans, 1765.' Signed by David Garrick as a present to his friend the actor James Quinn. Handblown bottle. Cork and wax seal in good condition. This is a unique lot recently discovered during renovations of this old coaching Inn, known to have been visited by the famous actor manager. C.W. letter of authentication. Estimate £30- £80.'*

The bottle had easily doubled its estimate and was comfortably cruising upwards. There were about seventy-five people in the room and when this lot had come up as many as twenty of them had tried to have a go, optimistically waving their paddles in the air. But the auctioneer had speedily seen off the no-hopers, raising the price by ten-pound increments. Now more and more of the bidders were sadly shaking their heads and retiring from the fray. Gene had dragged her along to quite a few auctions on this trip and she knew the contest was about to come down to just two competitors. Apart from Gene, the one man left here with funds to keep in the game was massive-shouldered with a contented broad Irish face and curly red hair. He was wearing a baggy old suit with frayed cuffs. Now he hardly seemed to be listening to the bidding, but still mechanically raising his arm like a semaphore signal.

When the auctioneer reached five hundred pounds there was a tentative handclap from the back of the hall, which soon spread to a rolling burst of applause that almost everyone joined. The rich were being applauded for spending their money. The Irishman's smile just widened slightly. Gene remained tight-lipped, ignoring the crowd noise just as Joe Di Maggio would as he stood waiting for the pitch in a packed Yankee Stadium.

Within a few moments, the auctioneer raised another fifty pounds. At this, the Irishman finally kept his hand down. Mary-Lou noticed that he still looked satisfied.

'Going once. Going twice. Any more? I will sell, for five – hundred – and – fifty - pounds.' Conversations started all around the room. 'Quiet please.' The auctioneer gave a perfunctory last look around and then raised the gavel high into the air. Then at last there was the time-honoured impact of old woods. 'Sold to you, sir.' Gene lifted his paddle – no-one here knew his face – but turned to Mary-Lou, grinning broadly. He looked as happy as a boy with a new bicycle. The underbidder came across the room and put out his hand. The auctioneer said, 'Now sir, Mr O'Shaughnessy is one of our most sporting gentlemen, so if you would kindly shake him by the hand?'

'Yes indeedy,' said Gene, and they shook hands like tennis players meeting over the net.

The auction room burst into a round of applause, much louder than anything heard before.

Two hours later, Gene and Mary-Lou were finishing a thick pudding accompanied by the usual undrinkable English coffee. They were in a chilly dining room, the huge fireplace cold and empty, and with a suit of armour, a grandfather clock, and a gilded throne-like chair looming from dark corners. The few other diners were either silent or whispering to one as other as if they were in church. Gene felt a strong glow of pride. He knew his voice was clearly audible to the whole room, but he didn't mind.

'It's so great, honey,' he boomed. 'It's like I said to the clerk when we booked in here. Garic without a K is my name, which is the original French Hu-gon-aut name.'

'Hu-go-on-oh, dear.' She seemed weary. Had he perhaps told her this story before?

'Whatever you say. David's father put the K in, to sound more English. But his brother stayed in France, and his side o' the family kept it the French way. Even after they'd come through Ellis Island. But still, David Garrick is my great, great, great, however many greats, uncle. My uncle. The greatest actor of his time. A writer and poet. Buried in Westminster Abbey.' He remembered the time he'd spent a weekend's leave in London and nearly missed his train back to Lakenheath. 'When I was here in the War, I saw that grave and I thought, uh huh. If I get through this alive, I'll get something of his. And now I've done it. I've darn well done it.'

'You've got quite a lot of things of his.'

'Yeah, but this is the best.'

'I'm glad you're happy.'

Now he wanted to drink a toast to his illustrious ancestor. He raised his hand for the waiter. 'Wait till you try it, eh? What say we have a little nightcap upstairs?' He reached across and stroked her knee.

She smiled indulgently.

The elderly waiter padded over. 'We've finished dinner, so that will go on our slate, room 12, and can I get two shot glasses to take out?'

For some reason the man did not look so pleased to receive these instructions. But he was back soon enough with the glasses.

'Here you are, sir, but it's a rule of the house, no drinking in the bedrooms. You'll find the residents' lounge up the stairs on your left, there.'

'The rules you people have. What the hell is the harm in a married couple having a nightcap in …'

'Never mind, Gene,' said Mary-Lou, then turned to the waiter. 'Okay, sir, we will surely sit in your lounge.' She gave him a sweet smile. Always so damn nice. Gene felt a mixture of admiration and exasperation.

'Thank you, ma'am.'

The waiter discreetly withdrew while they stood up. Gene looked at the table. No, half a crown was too much. He carefully picked up the coin he had originally intended as a tip, and replaced it with a shilling, then strode off towards the stairs, leaving his wife to pick up the glasses and follow him.

Halfway up there was a narrow door on the left. Gene pushed it open. The room was in darkness but at its far end was a diamond-leaded window that gave a view out to the glistening cobbles of the road-way leading to the Cathedral. The huge medieval tower loomed down, casting a black shadow. When he turned on the light, he saw wood panelled walls and a long shiny table with upright chairs around it. The only attempt at decoration was a pair of typical English sporting prints of men in red coats gallop-ing their horses over fields. A small bookcase stood by the door, holding a few maps and guidebooks.

'So they call this their lounge,' he said. 'I've been to board meetings in more comfort. OK, hon, sit down, I'll get David's bottle.'

Mary-Lou sat down next to another dark fire-place. Gene climbed the creaking stairs to their room and retrieved the precious bottle. When he re-joined her, she had a book open in front of her. She looked up for a moment then went back to her read-ing.

'What's so interesting to read?'

'Oh, just some history.' She lifted the book and he saw an old leather spine embossed with the title *Antiquities of St Albans*.

'So here goes,' said Gene, disappointed not to have her full attention. He removed the bottle from the wooden case in which it had been packed, placed it on the table, and carefully untied the string at-taching David Garrick's label. Who had last tied this, he wondered? Then he took out his penknife and neatly cut the old, blackened foil around the cork, and then pulled out the penknife's corkscrew. He in-serted it into the cork and turned. There was a satis-fying pop, and the little cork came out strong and intact, giving little sign it was nearly 200 years old. This seemed promising.

'Sir David Garrick,' said Gene, as he poured two glasses, 'we drink your health.' He raised his glass, but before he put it to his lips, he caught a sour smell. The liquid was brown and opaque, leaving an inky smear inside of the glass.

Mary-Lou was still reading, for some reason. Still, Gene was a Garrick. He was going to go on and drink. There was a taste of brandy but something else, something rather foul. As he swallowed, a lump seemed to form in his throat and breathing became difficult. He found himself coughing several times, almost retching. At last, she looked up.

'Don't try *drinking* it. Oh God, you have.'

'All right, I admit it, it's horrible.' He coughed some more.

'Gene. Do you feel all right?'

'I did not buy that for the taste, put it that way.'

'I wonder if you need a doctor.'

He reached into his pocket for his hip flask and took a swig of the bourbon that had been such a good companion on this trip.

'That's better. But why a doctor?'

'You need to hear what that is you just drank.'

'Old brandy. But we can't be too surprised, even the finest liquor can spoil at such an age.'

'You seem OK.' She tapped the book in front of her. 'But listen to this and then tell me if you feel OK.' She read, '*Humphrey, Duke of Gloucester (1391-1447) was the son of King Henry IV, and brother of King Henry V. A man with a great love of learning, he often visited St Albans and became friends with the learned abbot. His death may have been as a result of poisoning, as he had been accused of treason against the young Henry VI, his own nephew. At these times the Wars of the Roses were raging through the land. He was buried in St Albans Abbey. After the Dissolution of the Monasteries his tomb was lost, but in 1703 it was rediscovered. Duke Humphrey's body was found to be amazingly well preserved, steeped in a brown fluid. His remains went on open display, and such was the fascination of the find and the fluid's preserving properties that visitors began taking it, rubbing it on their faces to retain their youth, and even drinking it.'*

She was always interested in the damnedest things. He said, 'So some Dook died. Some people were crazy. So what?'

She read on. *'In 1765 the famous actor David Garrick visited Humphrey's tomb and was shocked at this practice, known as 'Dining with Duke Humphrey.' Later at supper in the old Christopher Inn in French Row, Garrick composed a poem saying it would be better to be in a pickle of Burgundy while alive than to waste good liquor on a corpse. It was even said that, as a prank on a friend, he had some of the miraculous fluid bottled, but it has never been found.'* She put the book down. 'So, what did you just drink? Embalming fluid? The blood of an old corpse? Huh?'

He took another swig of Bourbon. 'Why the hell didn't you tell me?'

'I tried to. You didn't wait. You never do wait. I only hope you're going to be OK.'

'If I take enough medicine, I should be OK.' He drained the hip flask, then re-stoppered the old bottle. 'There, I'm putting the cork back.' He carefully retied its label. 'Right, I need a top up. I will just take these glasses back to our friend downstairs and get two more with a bottle of bourbon to go with them.'

He stood up and started down the stairs to the bar. Yes, he guessed he would live to fight another day. It was the foulest thing he'd ever tasted, though. He wondered if they would keep any bourbon here, or would it just be Scotch whisky? Never mind, anything would be better than that.

The next morning Mary Lou was relieved to find her husband was in his usual health. A bit quieter than last night, with a headache for sure, but mercifully only the usual whisky hangover. As they started out of town, at the top of Holywell Hill he turned left. 'You wanted to go right, dear,' she said, looking at the map on her knee. 'That's London Road. But if you turn now, you can go back on yourself. Take that little alleyway by that big clock tower.'

As they drove into the narrow road, she saw the name of the alleyway on a sign. *French Row.* Up ahead was an ancient overhanging building, shrouded in scaffolding. A large painted hoarding protected it from the sidewalk. As the car slowly passed, she saw bold lettering stencilled onto the hoarding. *Renovation of the Christopher Inn on behalf of St Albans City Council. Main Contractor, Malachi O'Shaughnessy and Sons.*

'Oh look, hon,' she said, 'this is the Christopher Inn under that scaffolding.' The moment she said it, she wished she'd not told him.

'But look at that name. Mr O'Shaughnessy. Hang on.' He stopped the car and rubbed his cheeks and eyes. 'Uh oh. *Now* I get it. He found the bottle in his building site, took it to the auction, but then he heard I was here, so he went there himself to shill me up.' Mary-Lou reflected that people working in a hotel might possibly know people in an auction room down the street, and tell them about the boasts of an American guest, but decided to say nothing about that. 'My God, these English, shysters and crooks the lot of 'em. I'll see you in court, you no-good Irishman, have the last cent off you. So help me, I will.'

'OK, but we need to get back to London. We're on the Queen Mary on Thursday, remember.'

'Not till I've sorted this out. They're not getting around me so easily. Hell, it wasn't even a nice drink.'

'Gene, what is fifteen hundred dollars to us? Come on, don't they need the money? And maybe,' added Mary-Lou, whose maiden name had been Kelly, 'there's an Irishman even better at practical jokes than your old English uncle.'

He ignored her smile, but at least he looked at her. She went on, 'Listen. You weren't really paying for the liquor. Forget fifteen hundred, no brandy is worth a hundred and fifty dollars. Right?'

'Ok.'

'You were paying for the label and the signature.'

'Yeah, OK. But shill bidding is a crime.'

'Very hard to prove. And where else were you going to get David Garrick's signature?'

Gene leaned back in his car seat, looked up at the roof, and she realised that once again she'd managed to tame his temper. His laughter came in a deep rumble. 'You've tricked us nicely, David. By Jiminy, it's only fair I should be the one caught out. Ha. My old uncle David has played his last joke on me. Me.' He banged his broad chest.

'So we're going home then. No more auctions.'

'You said it. No more auctions.' He let in the clutch and the car moved off.

Mary-Lou and Gene Garic never visited St Albans again, but some of the people there remembered them for a long time afterwards.

***

This story was partly inspired by real incidents. The practice of 'dining with Duke Humfrey' and the visit of David Garrick are described in Wendy Turner's book A-Z of St Albans *(Amberley Press, 2019).*

THE THIEVERY OF TIME

Cécile Keen

On the 32nd February 1581, Time disappeared.

The clock face on St Albans' clock tower[6] had been stolen overnight. Only its two hands remained. Without guides, they had no idea where to go and took to running backwards and forwards at the speed they pleased, devoid of any thoughts for the world. They made their own entertainment by racing round and round, crossing one another's path or hiding behind each other. Lethargic seconds lasted hours, obstinate minutes refused to tick and hours opted to stay idle. The Sun took his one and

---

[6] St Albans' Clock Tower is the only surviving medieval town belfry in England and is designated as a Scheduled Ancient Monument. The people of St Albans built the tower, which was completed by 1405 as a symbol of their resistance against the power of the abbot of St Albans. The Tower allowed the town to sound its own hours and, until 1863, the curfew. (http://www.stalbansmuseums.org.uk/visit/clock-tower)

Right from the start, the tower had a mechanical clock, which would have been a very rare and expensive piece of machinery at the time.
(https://www.britainexpress.com/counties/herts/properties/st-albans-clock-tower.htm)

only opportunity to elongate his romantic date with the Moon. Their lovemaking was so intricately intimate that it became impossible for Mortal Men to distinguish which one was destined to illuminate their day or light their night. In the confusion of the strange dimness, the cockerel did not crow causing a great number of townspeople to be late for their usual morning affairs. Time had been stolen. And it was about to disappear completely.

For a populace that had never been ruled by time but by the completion and succession of tasks, the thievery of the town clock should have been of no great consequence. Most folks paid no attention to the hour, let alone the precise minute. One would eat to quieten the stomach's growl. One would stop working the field when tired and one would shoe horses before their hooves were worn down. If the harvest was early, folks would sing openly, aware that the Wind Spirits would carry their thanks far beyond the Chiltern Hills to Mother Nature. But in the event of a meagre crop, they only dared to mouth their discontentment and refrained from demanding recompense from the Witch in fear of her aggravated wrath. Why would the absence of a clock make any difference? That is why the chain of events to follow the inconspicuous robbery was to be most unforeseen.

The first person to notice the theft was the town's idiot, Adalbert.

Adalbert shared his name and birthday with the town Lord's son. Adalbert's mother, Letecia, had known right from her labour bed that her beloved son was not quite as all mothers would hope. She

174

looked at his flattened face and almond-shaped eyes that slanted up and held him close:

'My dear boy, I will love you whatever the Witch has placed upon you.'

If Lord and Lady Lockey were first to name their new-born Adalbert for its meaning, 'noble and bright', Letecia chose the same name on the same day so it would bring greater auspiciousness to her son than his already ill-fated beginning: if the name was good for the young Lord, so it would be for her precious little one.

Nonetheless, for greater help than a name might give, Letecia walked south of the town, as soon as she was able, to bathe the baby in the river Ver. There, she called out for the Water Fairies, who appeared one by one from up and down the river, from its banks as well as its depth. At six inches, the Queen was slightly taller than her companions, though that was the only difference. All fairies wore their pure white long wavy hair as their garment. Split in several ways from the neck down, the velvety curls covered their modesty. None were in the way of the delicate lace-like wings when flying, for the curls would dance gracefully round the body with each movement as if alive.

'Could you bless him with some good fortune, please, Queen Oriana?' asked Letecia.

At a sign from their Queen, the magical creatures took off elegantly in an orchestrated ballet and landed all around Adalbert. Together, they carried the baby to the water, letting him mystically float.

'Won't he be cold?' worried Letecia.

'With each droplet of water that cleanses him, Adalbert will be warm and bring warmth to those who accept him for who he is,' reassured the Queen. 'With each touch from our hands, Adalbert will find happiness in the simplest of things.'

When the bathing ceremony ended, the Fairies brought Adalbert back into his mother's arms. Just as Letecia mentally remarked that Adalbert was inexplicably dry, two sisters, Maryell and Olyffe, landed softly on the baby's ears.

'As my name means *Drop of the Bright Sea*, you will grow to be bright in ways your birth did not pledge,' vowed Maryell.

'As my name refers to the Olive Tree, a symbol of friendship, you will never be alone and will have a great many friends throughout your life,' promised Olyffe.

While they simultaneously kissed Adalbert on his cheeks, Queen Oriana spoke:

'Have no fear, we will always respond to Adalbert should he call for our help.'

Before Letecia could thank them, all Fairies had disappeared, leaving just a glittering flutter on the water surface. Letecia looked at her son and saw that two enchanting dimples had appeared exactly where Maryell and Olyffe had kissed him.

Life for Letecia, her husband Thomas and little Adalbert was blessed. Destiny had bound intentionally Adalbert-the-clever and Adalbert-the-half-witted from birth. Since Letecia was minder to one and mother to the other, the boys developed the type of close friendship that views difference as a strength.

Young Lockey, much kinder than his father, showed compassion for the less fortunate. When young, he watched and played with little Adalbert.

When older he gifted food and blankets from his belongings to tenants in need. Now, sixteen years old, he endeavoured to persuade his father to forsake the extravagant plans that had already led to unforgivable destruction.

As for little Adalbert, he was a contented young man, who walked daily in the quietness of early dawn to enjoy freely the natural world and all magical wonders. Illiterate, he never used the town clock for its intended purpose but could nevertheless observe its absence despite the odd murkiness of the light.

'Wake up, something's happened,' shouted Adalbert whilst knocking on the door of the clock tower's shop keeper[7]. Unexpectedly, the cobbler opened the door almost immediately.

'Shush, halfwit!' he scolded.

Behind him, a woman was hiding. Adalbert recognised her for the wife of the clock master, who lived on the second floor. 'Why is she downstairs in her nightgown?' Adalbert was wondering when the cobbler pushed him. 'Go away, fool!' he said, and closed the door.

The insult was no surprise for Adalbert. Many folks rejected him, copying their Lord Lockey. Many others, though, followed the young Lord's lead and befriended Adalbert's merry nature. They trusted him to pick wild carrots from poisonous hemlock

---

[7] There are 5 floors within the tower; the bottom floor was let as a shop premises, with the shopkeeper's residence above. The second floor was where the clock keeper and his family lived from 1412-1866.
(https://www.britainexpress.com/counties/herts/properties/st-albans-clock-tower.htm)

water-dropwort, confident in Adalbert's botanical expertise. They listened in awe to his stories of the magical world, recognising that Adalbert's uncomplicated mind allowed him to connect intuitively with all creatures in a way they could never do. And so, they rejoiced and thanked Mother Nature for granting such a gift to Adalbert. Evidently the cobbler was not one of these people. Unbothered, Adalbert shrugged it off, resuming his way to the river Ver.

He often walked, following the gentle regular flow of the water, whose purity reflected the virtue of his own soul. Alongside, he met with his friends, natural or magical, who populated riverbanks, woods and meadows and who shared with him the marvels Mother Nature had conceived. Adalbert conversed with Her and them all as they conversed with him: in the richest universal language that only speaks from noble hearts.

On this fateful February morning, his stroll took him up to the Do-Little-Mill in Redbourn. Adalbert noticed how the scenery had changed more again. Where there used to be tall beech trees with beautiful leafy canopies, a desolate cemetery counted thousands of stumps. Where fields had been bright with colourful wildflowers and grass, stones walls and buildings were being erected to house fighting men. Birds would have nowhere to nest and bees no pollen to collect. There was no life left, not even a flicker of a butterfly. The magic, too, was no more.

Adalbert, distressed by the disappearance of his many friends and not knowing where Mother Nature was, questioned the Fairies instead:

'Do not worry, Adalbert. All creatures, natural or magical, have sought refuge in the enchanted forest of Ashridge. Mother Nature herself is protecting the bees to safeguard future seasons for us all,' Queen Oriana reassured him, concealing her own concerns.

But the Queen's words did not quiet Adalbert's unusual worry, for his innocent mind was distraught. If Lord Lockey could deny the forest its trees, could he also deny the river its water? If so, where would the Water Fairies go?

Two weeks after the clock burglary, two journeymen were resting at the King's Inn[8], on top of the hill at the crossroads of Radelet, Hemlamstede and St Albans[9]. Busy with hucksters[10], the tavern was a popular place to stop when markets were touring.

'I hope for long employment despite the low pay,' said the stone carver.

'Lord Lockey is known more for his ambitions than his generosity. He wrecked the countryside and cut the forest down for his grand new manor and fortress walls. Those who opposed him found themselves locked up,' replied the carpenter.

'I just want to earn my money without quarrel.'

Hearing them, a pedlar joined in and warned: 'I wouldn't go near St Albans nor Lord Lockey! Avoid them like the black death. Of my needles, knives and

---

[8] The King's Inn is fictional; the A414 and North Orbital were built much later, in the 20th century.

[9] Now: Radlett, Hemel Hempstead and St Albans.

[10] Hucksters were medieval mobile vendors.

ribbons, nothing sold at market. All folks have gone berserk.'

'Please explain,' encouraged the carpenter.

'Look through the window and see how, right here and now, the sun has retired for us so the candles have to light our supper,' indicated the pedlar. 'Yet, over St Albans only, the sky is this ambiguous mix of odd light and darkness.'

The journeymen nodded when two brothers sitting nearby offered: 'We concur,' stated the older, 'Our father is the potter in Tring. We sell his pots, plates and cups, and were in St Albans today. What a peculiar and gloomy place!'

'We waited for Prime[11] but no bell rang! No one could sell for risk of being taken to the gatehouse[12],' said the younger. 'Many St Albans shop keepers failed to turn up altogether.'

'Folks were most confused,' the elder added. 'One man asked me what we're all doing here at night. And another shouted: didn't we know it wasn't market day?!'

'I heard a woman complaining her husband demanded supper when he should break his fast,' said his brother. 'Only to hear another whining about the opposite.'

Other traders started to talk:

---

[11] 'Forestalling' is buying goods before the market opens for business officially when the bells ring for Prime, the first hour of the day, at 6am.

[12] In 1553 the Lady chapel was used as a school, the Great Gatehouse as a town jail, some other buildings passed to the Crown, and the Abbey Church was sold to the town for £400 in 1553 by King Edward VI to be the church of the parish.

'The Lord is demanding his rent but tenants are adamant it's not due for another moon. They're forced to pay and anger is spreading,' said one.

'A man sought my advice: should he be ploughing or harvesting?' laughed someone. 'I am a linen tradesman but I know March is no time for either!'

'That's another befuddled farmer, not alone in his ignorance of seasons,' responded someone else. 'St Albans folks shall go hungry with such foolishness.'

'I'm glad to have taken leave from this doomed town,' concluded the older potter's son. 'The longer we stayed, the faster we were losing our wits ourselves!'

'We're indebted to you all. I won't waste time in St Albans,' concluded the carver, and then asked: 'What is this treachery though when folks here are well but St Albans ones are taken by madness?'

'It began when the clock face was stolen,' answered the innkeeper who had kept his counsel so far. 'Since then, days and nights are indistinguishable over there; ordinary things are upside down, back to front, folks' wits included. It's getting worse every day from what we hear.'

The carpenter dared: 'Is this a folly of the Witch?'

'Who else can magic out time cognizance?' asked the carver quietly.

'St Albans folks say just so,' whispered the pedlar.

'Hush!' demanded the innkeeper's wife 'or you'll bring us her rage for repeating ill of her. My children are sleeping upstairs; I want them safe.'

No more was said but St Albans was erased from anyone's road plan.

Their efforts to talk quietly were futile. The Witch was listening. As the innkeeper's wife had feared, her anger grew greater at St Albans' people for the rumours they were spreading about her.

When yet another two weeks passed without harmony in the order of things, the atmosphere in St Albans reached boiling point. Enraged folks congregated on the marketplace. Poor sleep, anger, persistent confusion and constant muddy light formed weak ground for rational discussion. Complaints and demands were shouted at Lord Lockey in a commotion hard to contain:

'Why haven't the church bells rung?'

'I'm not paying more rent!'

'When will we see the night from the day?'

'Isn't the baker baking no more?'

'How come there's no market anymore?'

However, one question was heard over the others:

'Will you speak to the Witch?'

All fell silent as the response was a loud thunder and a sudden cold enveloping them tightly. Folks gathered closer to each another, for they knew who could talk whilst remaining unseen. In her commanding voice, she declared:

'Hearken me, people of St Albans or be deceased

If you now find the north where was the east

And the west where the south used to exist

Be warned, your lives will depart and not persist

If Time is no more at its right place

You must wonder why it no longer has its face

Its disappearance is not a plain displace

You shall know, it reflects Men's disgrace

Think back to when the tower
Proudly could reveal the minute and the hour
From the natural order of things and its master
You shall find your answer
Of Mortal Men's ugly traits, the foulest is your greed
Above all others, you grade your needs
To the simpleton amongst you this must lead
From the one with innocence, help you must plead
Of your crimes you are guilty
To the Nature of things, you should go to humbly
Caution, Men, no more accuse me wrongly
Or my fury, you will suffer badly'

A Witch does not linger. At once, she left.

Now certain the clock's disappearance was the source of recent troubles, suspicious eyes fell on the clock keeper, who swiftly relocated accusations before they were phrased: 'Who is this simpleton who knows what happened?'

'I saw Adalbert-the-half-witted the morning of the theft,' interjected the cobbler, keen to avert correlated suspicions on his lover, the clock keeper's wife.

'That's true, I saw him too,' she validated and went on lying, eager to protect her husband but equally keen to conceal her amorous secret with the cobbler: 'Strange noise woke me. I ran downstairs and saw him just outside looking devilish. Luckily the cobbler, already awake, kept us safe.'

In their hurry to condemn, men failed to challenge the claim's validity and ignored the Witch's guidance. Instead of pleading help from the one with innocence, they seized Adalbert. Powerless,

Letecia and Thomas watched their son being kicked, punched and brought before Lord Lockey.

The crowd went from: '*Cretin!* to '*Make him talk!* and vilely, '*Put him in the stocks!*

Young Lockey, horrified at the treatment of his childhood friend, pleaded: 'Upon my oath as your son, I pledge myself on the behalf of Adalbert-the-half-witted. Father, I beg of you, release him!'

That was to no avail; too many needed someone to blame. Lord Lockey was willing to oblige. *Who cares if the imbecile is innocent, as long as things go back to normal?* he thought, whilst Adalbert was locked into the stocks.

Letecia quickly grabbed young Lockey: 'Go to the river Ver promptly and call for Queen Oriana. Tell her my son needs her. Make haste!'

When young Lockey reached the Ver, the Fairies listened intently. Queen Oriana responded reassuringly:

'Thank you, young Lord, for reaching out to us. Maryell and Olyffe will attend you and free our friend. You must keep him safe from Men's evils till we join you with higher authority than ours. You are equal to the task, but do not be distracted in your pursuit, and leave immediately.'

Upon their departure, Queen Oriana began to blow gently into the river. A few small bubbles formed at first. Once all fairies joined their Queen, a mesmeric medley of emerald and indigo lights rolled and tumbled sparkling in the water currents carrying Queen Oriana's message through Hertfordshire and faraway Shires' rivers, lakes and wells to reach the only one who the Queen knew to be capable of ending this terrible unfairness.

Maryell, Olyffe and young Lockey found the marketplace as busy as earlier. Half of the townspeople were trying to protect Adalbert from the other half. Civilities were forgotten and fights had started to spur. Maryell wasted no time in singing her magic into the air. Once the musical notes reached the clouds, they fell back down as snowflakes that melted on mortal men, subliming them with such sleepiness that they immediately retreated to their beds, leaving the square deserted. Olyffe approached the stocks. At her light touch, wood and chains shifted into water, whose flow vanished between the cobbles, letting one crying and exhausted Adalbert fall into the protective arms of the other. All took refuge in the manor's stables where Letecia nursed her weakened son, whilst Thomas and young Lockey readied horses, food and ale in case flight should be necessary.

But hours passed uneventfully. When the clock tower's bell rang the next morning, St Albans folks woke, stunned by the sound unheard for weeks. They gathered at the feet of the tower, astounded to witness that the clock face had returned but the stocks and Adalbert had gone. The whole town was there; children had even climbed on the Eleanor Cross[13]! All heads were up, for beyond the clock,

---

[13] The Eleanor Cross was completed in 1294 at a cost of £100. The master mason was John Battle who was also responsible for the crosses at Northampton, Stony Stratford, Woburn and Dunstable. https://www.stalbanshistory.org/buildings/historical-buildings/the-eleanor-cross-in-the-market-place-st-albans

occupying the whole sky, was glowing the majestically beautiful visage of Mother Nature. Her hair was floating above the dwellings' roofs, displaying in subtle waves the colours of the four seasons from shiny white to auburn shades. When Mother Nature spoke, her voice was kind and warm:

'I have received sad tidings from Oriana, Queen of the Fairies. Who will explain?'

'Yes, it's Adalbert the-half-witted who stole...' started Lord Lockey, but he stopped when his son arrived with the accused and then shouted instead, 'Here's the turd!' endorsed by half a vindicated crowd.

Mother Nature was hurt by the hateful words. Wasn't it obvious from Adalbert's sweet full moon face that he was incapable of treachery?

'He is innocent, Dear Mother,' asserted young Lockey confidently.

Mother Nature observed the way the young Lord cared for his friend and how numerous good people stepped forward to stand for the truth. Was this enough to restore her faith in Mortal Men?

'This is true. Adalbert is innocent. I, and I alone, took the clock,' she decided to reveal causing a gasp amongst the townsfolks.

'You are altogether mistaken in the nature of the crime which led you to commit yet another in the

---

For centuries the St Albans 'Eleanor Cross' stood outside the Abbey entrance, but in 1703 the town government pulled down the cross and replaced it with a town pump. The pump was replaced by a water fountain in 1874. The water fountain was later moved, so the only reminder of the Eleanor Cross is a small plaque on the side of the Clock Tower. https://www.britainexpress.com/counties/herts/properties/st-albans-clock-tower.htm

shape of injustice. Follow the Witch's advice and hear the one you failed to listen to,' she continued as she gently cupped Adalbert in her two hands, holding him securely above everyone.

'*Tell us Adalbert, tell us about the countryside.*'

When Adalbert started speaking, he did so candidly: his happiness by the river Ver; the magical sounds of the wind high in the leaves or low in the grass; how flowers paint each season with a forever renewed palette of colours; how each and every creature brings its own unique beauty to the world.

'It's nearly all gone. All the trees are cut down. Little ones fled or died. My friends have no home!' cried Adalbert. 'The river isn't pure anymore; it's full of men's dross.'

The crowd grew quieter, not so quick to cheer at the plain revelation of the truth.

'St Albans needed to expand and prosper. Folks are wealthier now!' defended Lord Lockey 'In any case, you're the one who took Time from us,' he accused, in a last attempt to shift the blame.

'*Yes, and of all the punishments I could inflict, I only took Time away. But beware of Water Fairies, Fire Verves, Wind Spirits and Earth's Hands. The Four Mistresses of Life are kind-hearted but also capable of terrible omens,*' she reminded everyone. '*Who is the criminal here, may I query?*' Mother Nature put gravely. '*Nature who steals Time from Men, or Men who by stealing Nature, steal Nature and Time all together from themselves and from all others?*'

Lord Lockey remained silent, his shame defensible no longer.

'I have heard nothing propitious and seen less from you, Lord Lockey. Knowing your son will be Lord in your stead gives me hope and is my unquestionable condition to return the Time permanently. He and Adalbert know how Men and Nature can live in harmony'

St Albans folks all knelt down in respectful agreement.

And so it was that Mother Nature reinstated time. Without its return, St Albans would perish and all men with it. She did so willingly but not without a final word:

'I am here as a Mother to see a better future for all my children. Mortal Men that you are, be advised to look after me, as Nature does not need Mortal Men, but Mortal Men need Nature.'

In her benevolence, Mother Nature chose to forgive Men and believe them in their promise to do better and look after Her. In her gentle ways, she forgot that each generation of Men breeds another, each one a bit less resolved to keep the pledges of its elders, each one a bit more driven to broaden their own fortune and each one gradually more blind to its ancestors' learning.

Yes, Mother Nature forgot.

She forgot that Mortal Men are not Mothers: they do not think of their children before themselves.

A GENERATION LATE

Robert Paterson

My name is Julian Forsyth and I'm a normal guy.

Mostly.

Well, I am pretty average, as is my life. I'm 43, a bachelor, pencil thin, with thick, dark grey hair and smart dress sense. I'm a laboratory technician at the University of Sussex (my alma mater), I like books and movies of all kinds and I volunteer at a dog shelter. My great love is strolling along Brighton seafront at sunset, watching the starlings wheeling in the sky.

But the day my cousin Peter told me my mother had cancer, I *didn't* want to rush back home to comfort her. Not very normal at all, right? But you'll soon discover why.

My big brother Gerald was the first person I talked to about it, via a Zoom call to his villa near Palma De Majorca.

'Pete emailed me about it,' said Gerald. 'You'd think he was writing to Hitler.'

'He drove all the way from Reading to tell me,' I groaned. 'He's insisting I see her or he'll stop having me over for Christmas, even after they've been some of our best Christmases ever, not to mention all the help I've given him getting over Alison!'

I was referring to Peter's late wife, who died four years ago, falling out of a hotel balcony.

'Pete says 'That Selfish Bastard', as he calls you, lives 700 miles away,' I continued. 'But I've no excuse when I only live 90 minutes' train ride away.'

'He just doesn't see her right, J,' Gerald said plainly. 'Mum was always toxic, even before Dad died.'

'I guess,' I nodded, 'And yet …'

'What, Julian?'

I took a deep breath first. 'Somehow, Gerry, I keep hoping this cancer has *changed* her. Maybe it's mellowed her, made her kinder now she has so little time left.'

'You know what, Julian?' Gerald grinned, 'I was hoping the same thing.'

'So, we're going?'

'I know what, J.' Gerald was perking up. 'Why not take a friend with you? Mum might not fly off the handle with guests around.'

'Good idea!' I said cheerfully. 'I'll ask Violet. She's ever so nice and Mum might appreciate having another woman there.'

'And I'll bring my friend Julio,' Gerald grinned. 'He's really sweet and charming. You're sure to like him and he'll mellow Mum out.'

'OK, it looks like we're doing this.' I shrugged. 'But I tell you, Gerry, if Mum turns out to be as toxic as ever, we're never going back again, Christmas at Pete's or not. Agreed?'

'Agreed.' Gerald nodded. We said goodbye and rang off.

I met Violet at Harry Ramsden's the following evening, since she knows I'm at my best with a good meal inside me. We both ordered cod, chips, mushy peas, bread and butter and some soft drinks before we got chatting.

'So what's so wrong about your Mum?' Violet asked as she speared a chip with her wooden fork.

Violet is short and rotund, and pretty in her own way, with glowing cheeks, a bright smile, short auburn hair, innocent blue eyes and a dainty nose. Suzie, Violet's Pomeranian, is the apple of her eye, and we've been fast friends ever since Suzie went missing in Preston Park and I found her under a rhododendron bush.

'It all started going wrong in 1990,' I told her. 'The year I went to Verulam. That's the local comprehensive. Gerald had been there four years. Unlike me, he was a real social butterfly, very musical and a proper ladies' man. He's even got me some dates over the years.'

I didn't tell Violet I had lost my virginity during my only ever casual fling, which was with a stunning young woman named Carmen, whom Gerry had introduced me to during a party at his villa. I once felt a thrill when I thought of her hourglass profile silhouetted against the rising Mediterranean sun in the bed we had shared. Back then, I couldn't listen to the song *Oh What a Night* without thinking of Carmen.

'One night that summer, Mum got mad at Gerry because she thought he'd been screwing around with some girl,' I went on. 'Whoever she was, the argument was so loud I heard it through the floorboards. Mum was convinced of his guilt, but Gerry stood his ground. 'I never had sex with her, Mum!' he screamed. 'Ask her *yourself* unless you're too chicken!' When Dad came home, he dismissed her beliefs out of hand. 'Women *know* these things, Jasper,' she yelled. 'No, Sharon,' he yelled back; 'Women *suspect* these things! It isn't fact!'

'Then, in August, after weeks of coldness, Mum perks up and suggests she and Dad go to a Rod Stewart gig in Leicester. They dropped me and Gerry off with Great Aunt Stephanie. While Mum and Dad are going up the M1, the car gets a puncture. Dad jumps out to inspect the damage on the hard shoulder, but steps too far out. A lorry hits him and kills him instantly.'

'Oh, Julian!' Violet gasped.

'Gerry kind of took Dad's place after that,' I continued. 'Getting me to school, cooking dinner, sorting out bullies and that. Then, in 1992, Gerry was expelled for having sex with a career consultant in the boys' toilets. One shouting match later, Gerry marched down to the Kiss club, talked to a DJ named Kid Conqueror and became his roadie. He left that night and never came back. One thing led to another and Gerry became a club promoter and DJ in Ibiza, raking in millions.

'Mum really got bitter and twisted after that. She compared me to Dad or Gerald whenever I was in trouble. She lost her job. She kept forgetting to make dinner, check my homework, or clean the house. In summer 1997, Gerry sent me a letter with a cheque enclosed, large enough to cover all my expenses for university. He even supported me financially as I sought work. I went to Sussex Uni, got my job and then my flat. I only ever saw Mum on family occasions, never at the house. Funny; Gerry actually predicted the future when he ran off.'

'How?' asked Violet, her food forgotten as she listened intently.

'He yelled at Mum, 'I'm leaving and I'm never coming back! And when J's old enough to know you better, neither will he!"

'I know how... I'm genuinely sorry, Julian,' said Violet. 'I've got Auntie Holly to look after me and Suzie to care for. You've got... nobody.'

'Are you sure you want to come, Vi?' I said earnestly, breaking the silence. 'It could get bad. And you might not get time away from the shop.'

Violet worked as a shop assistant and bookkeeper at her Aunt Holly's aromatherapy store in the Lanes. She lodged in the upstairs flat too.

'Don't worry, Julian, I can handle it,' said Violet. 'Auntie Holly can look after Suzie and once I do the inventory and clear this week's order, I'm a free agent. And as long as we don't actually stay over at your Mum's, we'll be fine.'

How wrong she was.

Violet and I agreed to spend three full days in St Albans, so I booked two rooms for two nights at the town's newly built Premier Inn. Not long after we checked in, Gerald told me via WhatsApp that he and Julio were staying at St Michael's Manor, arguably St Albans' best hotel. Julio was in bed recovering from a stomach bug the previous night, so wouldn't be joining us, but Gerald himself was OK and would take us to Mum's house at 10 o'clock tomorrow morning.

As we stood outside the Premier Inn the following morning, Violet gave a girlish squeal when she saw Gerald slanting towards us in a dark blue Mercedes. My brother slid down the electronic window and smiled like a movie star. His swarthy, square-jawed face and slick brown hair shot with grey were unmistakeable. He beckoned with his hand.

'Hop in, love birds.'

'Gerry, she's…'

'Yeah, yeah, just a friend, as *usual*,' he quipped, rolling his eyes. 'Never even the bridesmaid, let alone the bride. Now, you in good? Let's get this over with.'

Gerald's driving is of Formula One quality and we were pulling up in the driveway beside Mum's old VW Golf before we knew it.

The Forsyth household is on Clarence Road, which faces the verdant idyll of Clarence Park. Sadly, our childhood home was not half so idyllic. It had a kind of… miasma hanging over it. Ivy grew all over the walls. The paintwork was flaking and the windows seemed dark even in broad daylight. It was a house, but it didn't feel like a home.

Gerald took a deep breath as we got out. 'No turning back now, J.'

'Is she *really* as bad as you say?' Violet said apprehensively.

'You're not family, you know, Vi,' I said. 'You needn't stay.'

'No!' Violet protested. 'I'd do any… I *want* to do this with you, Julian.'

'Thank you,' I smiled.

I knocked, and the heavy brown front door eased open. I gasped. Sharon Forsyth, our mother, was now 71, but she looked 100. Her eyes were sunken and empty, her smile was wan and her 'hello' was croaky as she beckoned us all inside.

'Well!' she rasped. 'Hasn't the world gone topsy-turvy? Julian's bringing a girlfriend and *you're* not!'

'Violet isn't...' But she chivvied us all inside before I could finish.

The house felt even less of a home indoors. There was so little furniture and so few ornaments it felt like a half-empty warehouse. The big dresser from the hallway and Dad's old grandfather clock were gone, as were the coal scuttle and tongs from the hearth. There weren't even as many photos on the mantelpiece. Mum must have sold it all to make ends meet. She had left the house with a body, but no heart.

Thankfully, there were still easy chairs and a sofa to sit on, and we three sat on them while Mum took tea and coffee requests. When she returned with them, she decided to stand instead.

For a time, things were almost congenial. Mum never smiled strongly, but Gerald and I stuck to nostalgic subjects like holidays and weddings and Violet's positive attitude kept spirits up.

Sadly, it was too good to last.

The tension reignited when I mentioned Dad's great nephew, Warwick.

'Cousin Terry tells me Warwick's won a special award for maths three years running, Mum,' I said. 'He might take over from me as the genius in the family!'

'Perhaps,' Mum sighed, turning towards Gerald. 'Too bad I won't have any *real* grandchildren to tell it to.'

Gerald gripped his cup so hard I feared he'd crush it. He looked daggers at Mum.

'Oh yes, *Gerald*,' Mum hissed. 'The thirty-year-old elephant in the room can be addressed now. You've kept it hidden very well, but now I've seen proof with my own eyes.'

'Proof of what, Mum?' I asked.

She whipped out an iPhone she could somehow afford and opened a photo she had stored on it.

'I came out of Tesco's with my shopping yesterday and saw... *this*!'

All three of us looked at the screen on Mum's phone and gasped. Gerald stood in the middle of St Albans high street embracing a good-looking young man of about 30; tan skinned, probably Spanish, his hair thick, dark and curly with a reddish tinge. Gerald was kissing him on the forehead.

'Decades of never knowing the truth,' Mum went on, 'And finally, there in front of me, was proof of *years* of disgusting betrayal!'

'Mrs Forsyth!' Violet shrieked.

'Shut up, you lardy little bitch!' screamed Mum. 'I haven't finished!'

'Don't you dare you speak to Violet like that!' I roared, leaping to my feet.

'Mum,' Gerald added savagely. 'Take out your anger on me but leave Julian and Violet out of this! As for Julio, he's as innocent as they are and I *love* him.'

Mum's face creased and uncreased, her face running through a thousand different emotions as she stared in mute shock at her elder son.

'Mrs Forsyth,' said Violet, fighting to keep calm, 'Homosexual love is just as valid as heterosexual love. If Gerald loves this man, then...'

Mum drowned her out with a hideous, scornful bray of a laugh.

'You *really* think that's why I'm angry with him, you stupid girl?' she sneered. 'Why don't you tell them, Mister Superstar DJ? Tell them who this Julio *really* is.'

Gerald stiffened, took in a deep breath. A tough smile appeared on his face. 'Josephina is dead, Mum.'

Mum's look of triumph melted away like rainwater down a window pane. She gave a choking noise, wheeled around and ran upstairs. We heard her weeping and banging on the walls a good while.

Gerald promised to watch Mum while Violet and I took a walk in Clarence Park. He told us he'd settle things with Mum and then explain what he meant about Josephina later. It was a pleasant walk past the bowls club and cricket pitch, but Violet was far from cheerful.

'Your Mum would be lynched in Brighton with her kind of attitudes,' she said, scowling.

Compelled to set her straight, I argued Gerald had only kissed the young man chastely, on the forehead. It might have been cultural. Besides, Gerry had charmed any number of women over the years and never spoke of men suggestively. As for Mum, insufferable as she was, she had never spoken ill of gay people.

And yet, there was still doubt in my heart. When did Mum actually *praise* gay people? Didn't they say women were often drawn to gay men? And Gerald had never married, for all the women he'd bedded. Could *this* be the reason?

We agreed we would put the question to Gerald later. Clarence Park was too nice a place for an argument. Walks in the park had been cathartic for me when things were tense at home, and they still were today.

'I hope Mum didn't hurt you too badly when she called you fat,' I sighed as we passed the cricket pavilion. 'Even having the cancer doesn't give her the right to. I don't care what size you are, Violet Humphries. You're an angel at heart and I... I really care for you.'

'And so do I,' she replied, slipping her hands into mine. 'But isn't it time we both say the words we really feel?'

And so we did.

Of course, we loved each other. What else could it be when we gave each other such powerful moral support, or I was the hero who brought little lost Suzie back to her? And why else would Violet, so innocent and yet so wise, find a grey old beanpole like me handsome?

We kissed deeply, then I put an arm around her shoulder and took her round the rest of the park.

'I never told you why I live with Auntie Holly, did I?'

Violet had decided that as two people in love, she must be as honest with me as I was with her. She began by telling me she had originally lived in Surrey with her severely alcoholic mother. Her father walked out, disgusted, then threatened to sue for custody. Mrs Humphries was so frightened she went on a huge bender, then shoved Violet into the back seat of the car with the child locks on and said they were going down to Southampton to jump a ship out of the country. Three miles down the road, a police siren went off behind the car; she panicked, hit the accelerator and drove into a tree. Mrs Humphries lived the last eight months of her life paralysed, unable to move anything but her head. Although Mr. Humphries sold the house, there were too many nightmares for Violet to continue living in Surrey, so Aunt Holly took her in and gave her a job.

'I guess that's why I was drawn to you, Julian,' she sighed. 'We're both from broken homes, but *we're* unbroken.'

'Let's make hope we never go that way,' I smiled.

For a long time, we walked round Clarence Park simply enjoying one another's company. Then, on the way back to the house, Violet asked; 'Who's Josephina?'

'Oh yes, I never said,' I replied. 'She was our babysitter when I was in junior school. Spanish, from Barcelona. We played hide-and-seek all the time in the park. We even had mini-discos in the living room, like the time we all danced like mad to Gerry's single of *La Bamba*!'

'She sounds like she was great fun!'

'She was,' I said. 'Really pretty too, especially her hair. It was an unusual colour for a Spaniard. A kind of dark maple red. And her skin was a bit like coffee... Are you OK, Violet? Hang on! Don't tell me you're jealous!'

Violet held up a hand. 'Did you say she had...*red hair*?'

'Yes.'

'What other Spaniards do we personally know who have red hair?'

We both went deadly quiet as an earth-shaking thought struck us.

'Julian, when did this lady *stop* working for your family?'

We raced back to the house to find Mum's Volkswagen gone from the driveway and Gerald in one of the best moods I'd ever seen him in.

'J! Vi! Great news! I've patched things up with Mum! She came out of her bedroom and apologised. You'd have thought she was a toddler from the way she grovelled. She told me it was pointless having a feud between us when I'd come to say goodbye, just like she did with Dad. She's accepted Julio as one of the Forsyths and she's going over to St Michael's Manor now to take him for shopping and a coffee at the Atria Centre.'

'You *idiot*, Gerry,' I growled.

'What?'

'Come over here.'

I manhandled him into the living room and pointed out the photos on the mantlepiece.

'Look,' I snarled. 'There's none of Dad. There's me and you, Mum, all our relatives and yet... not *one* of Dad. That's why there are fewer.'

'So?'

'*So*, Josephina left the month after Dad died,' I said coldly. 'Two months after you fought with Mum over a girl you'd been with. Dad dismissed it, then he died on the motorway. Stepped in front of a lorry, killed instantly. Instantly, Gerry. Mum's changed her story. Dad had no time to say goodbye.'

My ordinarily rock-solid brother started to look very ill.

'I don't think Dad's death was accidental, Gerry,' I hissed. 'Mum suspected Josephina was being a bit too loving as a nanny, didn't she? She might not have been able to prove it but she suspected it strongly enough. Why else would Dad cover for you? So, Mum faked a breakdown on the motorway and shoved Dad just as that lorry passed. The perfect murder. But she suspected Dad wasn't the only one getting it off Josephina. Gerald... did both of you have her?'

Gerald was now quivering with fear and remorse.

'And Julio was the result, wasn't he?'

'Yes.'

'And you just told Mum that for thirty years, you've played her for a fool. You waited for Julio's mother to die, just to rub it in her face that she could never seek redress.'

'But it isn't too late, Gerry,' Violet said in leaden tones. 'Sharon Forsyth is dying. She's vengeful and has nothing left to lose. *And there's still Julio.*'

If Gerald had driven like a racing driver before, he drove like Roadrunner now. There was still a chance to reach St Michael's Manor ahead of Mum because the high street was often congested. Gerald took us north instead, driving in the direction of Marshalswick until we reached Beech Road and the Ancient Briton Junction. Across the junction was Batchwood Drive, which led almost as far as Fishpool Street. A red light held us up, which gave us a chance to talk.

'You really do love that kid, didn't you, Gerry?' Violet muttered.

'He's the reason I pushed myself to make all that money,' Gerald said, with smarting eyes. 'Him and Julian. It's also why I never married. I wanted to prove my commitment to his mother and leave Julio with a nest egg. And I won't lose him if I have to...'

'MUM!'

I screamed the word as I saw, much to my surprise, Mum's Golf coming round the corner of Batchwood Drive, heading straight towards the junction at breakneck speed. I could just make out Julio's reddish curly hair in the back seat.

'But the lights are red,' Violet gasped. 'She must be crazy!'

'Why go this way?' I wondered aloud. 'There's no motorways in this direction. How come she didn't ... *Oh no!*'

Before our disbelieving eyes, Mum's Golf zigzagged around the cars just pulling out of the opposite side of the junction. It's a three-way stop, so the traffic joining Beech Road from Batchwood Drive got a green light before we did.

My voice rose to fever pitch. 'NO!!!'

Violet behind me shrieked in dismay. Instead of following the road, Mum was now veering off it, turning slightly to her left and jumping the kerb. Stunned pedestrians leapt back in terror. Trapped behind stalled traffic, the three of us sat helpless as we now realised Mum had never been heading for the motorway after all.

You see, the Ancient Briton junction also marks the start of Devil's Dyke, a long, tree-lined defensive ditch dating back to Saxon times. Now it became the perfect target for a kamikaze run by a dying, vengeful woman driven to end the life of her bastard grandson.

'NO! JULIO!!!'

Gerald's scream was in vain. The Golf plunged into the Devil's Dyke and disappeared from view. There was a horrible sound of crunching metal and splintering glass. Heedless of the lights, we tore the doors open and raced towards the trench.

Three months later, and I was back in the spare bedroom in Gerry's villa. The warm Majorca sun was rising, yet it had not been that which roused me, but a pained groan from the other room.

Julio's ribs had still not quite healed and he was calling for his father to bring his *analgésicos*, or painkillers. Luckily, his seatbelt had saved him from fatal injury and he had been rushed to casualty once the fire brigade had cut him loose. As for Mum, a snapped-off tree limb had gone right through the windscreen and impaled her, bringing death much sooner than cancer ever could.

The fiery orange sunrise was once again silhouetting the curves of a beautiful woman who had given herself to me. But the days of sharing my bed with women Gerry chose and seduced on my behalf were past. This was a woman I loved as much as life itself and she found me just as special.

I slid my thin, grey-haired arm around Violet's tantalizing belly. I nestled into the small of her back and rested my head against her shoulder. She smiled and squeezed my hand, speaking volumes without saying a word.

Violet, Gerald, Julio and I now guarded a secret that bound us together and had to remain unspoken. None of us felt wonderful about it, but a man has to accept the things he can't change, like my parents not being there, or Julio's far from normal parentage.

Would the four of us remain bound together in love and friendship, or would our devastating secret tear us apart? We didn't know. All we knew for sure was that we must go on living, taking every day as it came and looking out for one another, whether near or far. Time might not heal the wounds of the past, but we could still shape the best future we could provide for each other together. Perhaps, one day, I would feel normal again.

Crimes Times

The Voice of the Crime Industry
St Albans Edition
Ken Osborne – Editor-in-chief

News Section

Freak Storm to Devastate Warehouse

In a freak storm tomorrow, lightning will strike the warehouse of the Picts Furniture Store. Despite valiant efforts by staff members, the fire will take hold and they will be driven back.

The same freak storm will bring down a tree across the entrance road, delaying the fire brigade. When they get to the scene, the warehouse should be a burnt-out wreck.

The owner of Picts will be summoned from somewhere very far away and will say, 'I am absolutely devasted by the fire. We had only just taken a delivery of some very expensive three-piece suites and now they are gone. We are fully insured but that's not the point. Picts has a name for quality products and good service renowned throughout Hertfordshire. We will continue trading from our Hatfield Road store with the limited stock we have and ask our loyal customers to bear with us while this excellent business is rebuilt.'

When asked for further details the owner will explain he can say no more while waiting for the insurance loss adjustors' investigation.

No one will be injured in the incident.

Local Opportunity for Crime of the Year Award
Nobley Bullion and Safety Deposits is opening a temporary premises in St Peters Street while rebuilding their North London branch. The vault will have one of the new Eisen and Stein Mark 6 doors. Totally state of the art. Anyone cracking this would be a strong contender for Crime of the Year Award. Cracker Mahone got a highly commended a couple of years ago for getting to the last level with a Mark 5 before getting caught.

Schemer Jones of Crime Data and Planning Consultants (CDPC) said they only had outline specifications of the Mark 6 as the E&S design security was very tight. He added, 'Our contact says a large sum will be required to liberate the detailed drawings and specifications. We have an outline scheme available for coming through the adjoining basements and the 12-inch spiral reinforced vault walls, but for the prestige of West Hertfordshire we are holding back on this to give the opportunity to our local talent.'

Who will step forward to put St Albans on the map and show we have still got it?

Marriage Links Two Local Families
The heads of the Capone and Moran families are delighted to announce the wedding of Al and Lucille. In a joint statement the two families say this marriage was made in heaven and will unite the North Side and South Side Gangs as one enterprise. The happy couple have recently celebrated their 16th birthdays.

Fishy Story

In a recent nab, a couple of part timers were seen on CCTV making off with two boxes of koi carp. When apprehended a week after the event they said that if they had known how valuable they were they would not have eaten them. They later added that they were absolutely delicious, cooked in butter with a sprig of tarragon and washed down with a reasonable Chardonnay.

Editorial

Threat to Crime Industry

The recent arrest of over 140 of our fellow crime workers by Hertfordshire Constabulary in co-operation with adjoining authorities shows the need for constant innovation. The recent standards of Continuous Professional Development for registered crime operatives will go in some measure to raise industry standards.

With CCTV cameras everywhere and these wretched Ring doorbells, some are considering whether the time has come to seek new employment. Smash Perkins the respected jewel thief commented, 'At my time of life, a newspaper shop looks a viable career change. I would miss the thrill and chase, but the pacemaker slows me down. Might get a sub-post office too. Got a friend in head office who can add a few extra lines of computer code. Keep the hand in so to speak.'

Our industry has a long and illustrious history. Hope rests that the rising talent of new blood will protect that heritage for future generations.

Classified
This Week's Releases
Weasel Bloggs: Out on good behaviour after 3 years. Interviewed by our reporter, he said that he hoped Mad Man Smith and Axe Jones were not miffed that he had shopped them and that they had been in chokey for 2 years.

Alex Smart-Mann: Weasel's accomplice was also released. He went straight to the airport to an unknown destination. Anyone interested in where this is should send an SAE and £500 to the editorial team.

Gordon Naïve: Out in fresh air for the first time in 12 years. He was pleased to see the many new children he had and that they all looked different. 'My wife and I share our love of families,' he beamed.

This Week's Lock-ups
Lock up Johnny: In for armed robbery of a police station. 'It's getting cold at this time of year and I wanted to be somewhere warm,' he said when cautioned.

Deaths, Marriages, and Births
Weasel Bloggs: Died mysteriously in Drovers Way multi-storey only 2 hours after being released from prison. The funeral is going to be a very quiet affair, said his friends Smith and Jones in a statement.

Employment

Hit Man: Minimum 2 years' experience. Preferably services trained. Interesting work with an equal-opportunities employer. Permanent position. Good pension.

Moll: Light duties mainly lolling and being cool. However, occasional messy work, so some medical experience useful. LGBT and minority candidates welcomed. Annual bonus.

Snitch wanted: Must be discreetly nosey. Weaselly demeanour preferred. No guarantee of safety offered.

Services

Financial services: Money laundering a speciality. Year-end accounts drawn up. Income and VAT returns filed. Prompt, friendly service.

Cleaner: Things gone messy? Cleaning services offered to remove all traces of an event. Quick response to problems. Unwanted bodies securely disposed. Wet cleaning services also available. Premium rates charged for night and weekend work. Family business for over 30 years.

Collection service: In the protection business? Free up time to expand your enterprise. Enthusiastic freelance collector offers services on a payment-by-results basis. References available.

Hardware: Specialist in Austrian and Italian made hardware with serial identities removed.

Handmade bullets available for the budget conscious. Range of hunting knives, coshes and knuckle dusters. Five star rated.

Documents: Need your identity changed? Specialist offers documents for your new life. Passports and driving licences to highest standards. Valid tax references and NHS numbers supplied. Credit rating set up. Start with the best—don't try the rest

Training: Badlands College offers short courses of 1, 2 or 5 days in car theft, lock picking and safe cracking. Preparatory course for Institute of Crime and Thuggery exams. Small classes.

Garage Services: Specialist in souping up Transit vans. You supply the van. No questions asked. We offer a 2-day tuning-up service. Stick on trade labels to your choice. Cloned number plates fitted. Vans may be prepared for explosion after use. Drop-off service available.

Escort Services. Discreet service provided by tactically trained men and women for your night out in town. Refund if you are wiped out.

THE HANGMAN, THE BARMAID AND THE CHURCH WARDEN

Jane Palmer

Back-in-the-day in the 1200s, there was a hillock called the Ayott Magna standing near the river Maran. 'Twas where I espied my secret sweetheart, Christabel. Where the cows stood through long summer days in the murmuring of the stream, ruddy cheeked Christabel sat astride the tri-legg'd stool in the cowpats and pulled udders full of milk, her blonde curls bobbing from a white bonnet, and dimpled smile imprinted forevermore in my imagination. She'd be a beauty for future artists and photographers. For me, sworn to chastity, she was forbidden fruit.

My monastic vows forbade me to know Christabel. I could only watch her silently from the Ayott every morning. Then, reluctantly, I would return to the epinard and cress beds of the monastery to await the creak and groan of the trap and the 'umph of the 'orse comin' up the hill, bringing the blessèd churns of milk, drawn by Christabel's fair hand.

How innocent and naive I'd been, when I made those vows at eleven years old and became a novice, learning my letters and Latin, gardening and brick-laying for the monastic quarters and the church consecrated to St Lawrence of Brindisi.

I had not yet experienced the allure of the feminine form, and in my brown cowl, Christabel would not distinguish me from other monks processing and chanting at the tall-upstanding church of the Normans. Here Anglo-Saxon labourers shuffled into vespers, standing bowed and uncomprehending of Latin, fatigued by long days of earthy toil.

Ah, Christabel, she stirred me so. I gazed upon her.

The haggard abbot, you'd call him the 'thought police' today, noticed my averted eyes, and summoned me to confess. There would be punishment for such sin of thought. And of deed too: a theft of honey from the monastic kitchen for my beautiful milkmaid. A sweet and simple gift from God, to declare my forbidden love, caught by the abbot before it was given; such a petty theft could be punished by a severed arm, but the abbot perceived my straying desire, accusing me of broken vows, with fatal punishment. 'Go to your maker, for breaking your holy vow,' he bellowed with jealous, bloodthirsty glee.

The hangman's mad eyes were as deep pools which stared into mine, as he wrapped the noose tight around my neck.

I shouted aloud to the empty sky, 'I borrowed honey for my love. 'Tis now a gift turned into a deathly sentence. The guilt is yours, not mine!'

The deep pools blinked, and the hangman pulled the wooden scaffold from under my sprinting feet and splaying arms. Lurching forward, I saw again a vision of my belovéd among the cows—that land of milk and honey forever barred from me; and I relived all my great labours cutting and lifting stone, building that monumental Ayott church. I saw again my well-tended spinach plants glistening with dew in rows near this brick house scaffold. I remembered my mother bending over the firepot behind the smithy, down the dip, and my smiling baby sister, now dead from pox. My strong, young gullet drew in a last, deep inhalation of warm air and uttered a fish-like gasp, with the sharp crack of my windpipe, sounding like a necked chicken, in a cruel and sorry end.

Cheated of life, love, marriage, children and old age, I patrol the lanes of the Ayots, which is a pretty purgatory for minor sinners such as I.

And sometimes there are reasons to reveal myself!

That awful Sir Lionel Lyde, the vain tobacco merchant, and his wife, always at loud, verbal odds! He wanted to show off his status with a grand house of gracious living to lord it over the calm and rural life of Ayott Magna. The old St Lawrence church, which we had built in the Lord's strength stone by stone with bare hands and nothing more than old-fashioned horse-drawn power, would be dismantled.

Our monkish lives were dedicated to the memory of St Lawrence of Brindisi, not to the pleasures of parks and grandeur—we knew the toll of martyrdom. St Lawrence was burnt to death in 258 A.D. in Roman Emperor Valerian's time, his heart roasted on a gridiron for defending Christ. Our Lawrence, now patron saint of comedians, mockingly told his Roman executioners, 'This side is done. Turn me over and take a bite.'

Why should our church of Lawrence, saint of school children, the poor, and cooks as well as comedians be decimated for a manorial view? Why must it be replaced by Sir Lionel's and Revett's 'Palladian' folly, a Grecian revivalist imitation of the stone portico and pompous Doric columns of the Temple of Isis in Delos? From that Greek ruin of pagan beliefs came a poor imitation and a sacrilegious demolition.

Altho' I grant you, now they adorn it with beautiful furnishings, the strong sound of a pipe-organ, and chequered flagstones, and it is become a pretty site.

Sir Lionel instructed masons to scale the walls of the old church to lift off the roof and knock out the very stones which I had placed, and which had stood the test of many hundred years. Ancient building blocks, which had heard the chanting and hymns of centuries, tumbled to the ground.

As a soul in purgatory, my supernatural powers incited the Bishop of London to issue an injunction to stop the desecration of our ancient and worthy church. But Sir Lionel, obsessed with his Greek temple of Isis, made no reparations to our past, and insisted, 'Our descendants cannot properly approach the twin mausoleums of our separated remains. The Church which united us in life, can make amends by separating us in death.'

After a sumptuous dinner, Sir Lionel stood hobnobbing with Revett, the Grecian expert, about how 'the Norman monstrosity' impeded his plan, how the new altar would face West and not East and there might be an avenue from the manor to the new church, if only the old church was not in the way.

I blew angrily in the wind and rolled the last stone I had laid centuries before from its great height, bouncing off the buttress, splitting in two and thumping at their feet. The men in their tight breeches ran home, while I chuckled in the branches of the oaks with all the mirth of our St Lawrence.

The ruin of our church stands to this day, open to the elements, overgrown, sometimes tended, and a sad landmark of the once proud and diligent monastery of Ayott Magna.

I hang around to keep watch. Just me. The other brothers rest in peace.

'Tis said the old scaffold, instrument of my murder, was used as a crossbeam in the timber-framed house which was added to our monastic rooms in the 1500s. No more punitive hangings here now. Had I wanted revenge for my execution, I would be glad for those gory hostilities of the Reformation... But I don't. We monks are in the business of forgiveness, and I use my powers compassionately.

The motto at the pilgrim stop, now the Brocket Arms, says *Felis demulcta mitis,* meaning 'a stroked cat is gentle', and today, the hopeful creature patters through the passageways of the kitchens and curls up in the inglenook of the heart-warming hostelry, frequented no longer by pilgrims, but by beer and wine-loving foodies.

The cats and I keep company after-hours.

Some years back, around the sixties–time doesn't matter—there was a Brocket barmaid who quite resembled Christabel. Blonde curls, dimpled cheeks, long lashes, brisk and smiling... She had a quick way of working-as if stroking the customers like the cat and soothing their stresses.

She cleaned the hearths and laid the fires every day; cooked and served full plates of good food; washed piles of dishes in the scullery until late, and then risked her life hurtling down Bride Hall Lane and through the woods towards Lemsford in a rusted, mint-green Ford Anglia with dodgy brakes.

I hovered around the lanes to see the lady home, keeping my face hidden in my brown cowl and robe among the trees. I enjoyed the magical chase, brushing branches, swooping over deer, scattering pheasant, which ended up on the Brocket plate on several occasions. Jilly was quick to scoop them up!

Usually I loiter, clacking my clogs, on the stairs near the old rooms of the monastery, now with the comfort of four-poster beds, remembering the 'slapping' punishments meted out there for small misdemeanours, such as lateness, greediness, laziness... But nothing worthy of capital punishment, such as stealing honey!

Sometimes, I hang around the vegetable beds, where the seasons do their work and mortal men sow and harvest food, or I float nearby in the pub garden, to enjoy the silly conversations.

One night, at closing, Jilly was turning the chairs up on the tables, for the floors to be cleaned the next morning. The last customer threw a newspaper into the fire with disgust at Page 3. The lady laughed and pushed her chair back carelessly near the fire, and they left with jovial words... Something about showing too much flesh demeaning women. I hear snippets.

Jilly hurried to pick up her keys to get away.

My apparition slowed her in her tracks, as flames flared, and embers spat.

'Who are you?' she asked in a trembling voice.

The folds of my brown cloak wrapped tight around my formless body, my hollowed eye-sockets stared up at the scaffold beam above, and the old sound of plainsong chanting came down the chimney with the wind.

She grabbed her keys.

I raised my loose, brown sleeve towards the blazing hearth, and vanished.

She stared at where I had been, for a few minutes. Then she picked up the fire tongs, lifted the spilt embers carefully back into the fire-basket, and moved the scorching chair where I had sat a moment before, safely away from the fire and beam.

Tho' no-one knows it, that scaffold beam is a lasting relic of the murderous, medieval acts that took place in the monastic dwellings at the Brocket Arms.

Jilly recklessly raced home to her cottage by the stream, while I flew above, protecting her.

My self-revelations are few, and only when necessary. Even more recently, in your lifetime, I had to show my ghostly self again.

It was the end of August, and festival sounds blew on the wind, from the doves at the Goat, up the old Ayott. Drums, guitars and high-volume speakers throbbed at the Goatfest on Charlie's field with 'We're the Kids of America' and the high whine of a wild female voice. The Brocket locals were dancing their hearts out beyond Codicote Bottom, without any heed to our Ayott.

Over at the 'Palladian' church of the late Sir Lionel Lyde and his wife, now firmly separated in death for centuries, a cyclist leant his bike down. He stood and listened and took a mobile phone from his roomy bomber jacket with many pockets. Soon a Mazda pick-up turned up.

Rose clouds scudded the sky above the temple-church before day quickly drained to night. The Milky Way seemed to reach right over the Goatfest revelry and the hedges and ditches of Ayott Magna and the old river Maran, now called the Mimram.

Beyond the western altar, three men worked with ropes, ladders and crampons, and were soon up on the lead roof with crow bars and pliers. I wafted behind them, in ironic laughter at the thought that Lyde's roof was being plundered, just as he had done ours! I might have thought it divine justice, but of course, Lyde has long gone. Perhaps it's just a slow nemesis of the past.

Sheets of lead were pitched down the ladder and loaded into the pick-up with experienced gloved hands; within an hour the thieving rascals took the metal. The contents of the church were exposed and open to the star-filled air and curious insects of the summer night.

It would have caused me mirth, except for the state of the good, old and pallid church warden, John, when he arrived on the next Sunday morning.

'My God, the roof has gone—we've had a lead theft!'

Palpitations of the heart struck John again. I appeared, brown-robed in the early morning sunshine, as his friendly guardian, and held his hand as he walked around the building, inspecting the crime scene, until others arrived, when I evaporated.

Holy Communion was put on hold. In my time, that would not take second place in any emergency—not that there were many back then. Life mostly had a patterned calm.

The vicar and congregation gathered and examined the remaining contents, according to the semi-updated church inventory. It seemed that nothing else was missing. The police came and opened a crime report. 'It's a planned job by an organised network, taking metal only. It's happening everywhere…lead from church roofs, copper from phone lines, heating panels.'

A hurriedly convened standing committee decided that someone must stay and camp in the church, until the roof was replaced, and the Greek folly secured. A tent was erected for the intrepid warden, meals were brought by hard-pressed commuters, barbecues lit, and the church was happily inhabited, as the monks had lived daily at the old Norman church.

I hung around keeping watch. Finally, they put cameras on the new roof, alarmed to the slightest movement, to alert patrols of Alsatian dogs, according to the signage.

I'd not be needed here in any ghostly shape or form.

The church which I had so disliked is thriving and the church I loved a ruin! The Lydes have long gone, and the Manor has beautiful gardens, with plants of special interest from around the world, and delicious produce. Their open-garden invites everyone to sample its delights.

At the Brocket Arms, I'm known as 'an affable chap,' but my appearances can disturb those I visit. I think, next time St Peter opens the gates to me, I will forgive all the misdemeanours and injustice of times past, hang up my clogs and take my rest.

'Farwel, for I ne may no lenger dwelle. The fires which that on min auter brenne, Shul thee declare, er that thou go henne, Thin aventure of love, as in this cas... And forth he wente, and made a vanis-sshinge.' *

*Chaucer, the Knight's Tale.

THE SIGN OF DEATH

Sam Ellis

'Will? Will! Come quickly. It's Carol. She's missing!'

Will was sitting in his usual seat at the Fighting Cocks pub, a pub so old that the wooden beams had their own smell of a thousand years of beer, wine and log fires. He'd been nursing half a shandy for the hour he had waited for his friend Lilly, his black and white border collie Maisie sitting restlessly at his feet. It was a warm day and Maisie didn't do well in the heat.

'Missing? What do you mean?'

'She's missing, Will! Just as she said she would be. She's gone out on a walk and not come back.'

Will and Lilly knew Carol from the local dog walking group where, once a week, owners and dogs would go for a woodland walk—and a gossip. Lilly was usually there with her retriever, but thanks to Carol's over enthusiastic bloodhound Biggles, Lilly's dog was nursing a sore foot and a bruised ego. Carol was a relative newcomer and had seemed distant, earning herself a reputation as an aloof millionairess, but in recent months she'd become closer to the group by actively organising events and being generous with gifts. She'd recently provided a donation to make the group an official charity, as well as gifting each member individual gift bags containing a dog lead, collapsible water bowl and treats especially chosen for being 'a favourite of Biggles—he's just mad about them.' Even the sight of the packet had made Biggles jump up with delight.

The more generous she was, though, the more paranoid she seemed to become. Upon giving Will his goody bag of gifts a couple of weeks ago she'd pulled him to one side and said in her hushed, raspy voice, 'Will, I want you to know that I'm going to be murdered. I don't know when, but it's true, and there's no way out of it. I wanted you to know because you seem to have a good head on your shoulders.' Will hadn't known how to react, but he'd tried to assure her it wasn't going to happen, to which Carol had turned on her heel, Biggles in tow, and marched off.

Now it seemed like an actual possibility. Will jumped up from his seat in the pub and followed Lilly out. Maisie's interest had been piqued; her ears stood on end and remained so as she trotted through the park with Will and Lilly.

'We'll head to her house. I've not met her husband, but maybe he can tell us where she was last seen and we can form a search party.'

Will and Lilly marched the few miles up to Carol's house, a thatched, sprawling mansion on a country lane on the outskirts of the city with smoke gently rising from the chimney. Carol had always said she'd lived in a little cottage. Typical understatement. Her family had made their money in printing hundreds of years ago, which had allowed her entry into upper-middle society where she met her husband, the newly OBE'd Raymond, who now appeared at the door. The silhouette of two forlorn young adults and a policeman lingered in the hallway, and Biggles idled into view. He immediately bounded up to Maisie, almost knocking a confused-looking Raymond to the floor, and got himself tangled up in her lead.

'Yes?'

'Raymond, my name is William, and this is my friend Lilly. We're friends of your wife—in the same dog walking group. We've just found out that she's missing and wondered if we could help.'

'Oh, er, thank you. That's very kind. The police are here now, as you can see, so everything is in hand. Thank you so much for your concern.'

'Of course, tha—'

'Oh! Do excuse me,' Lilly cut Will off. 'We completely understand, and we'll leave you to it. I just wondered if I could please trouble you for some water for Maisie here. You see we've walked a lot further than we thought and we're worried she's dehydrated.'

Raymond gave a quizzical look at Maisie who was happily wagging her tail as she played with Biggles, who was chewing at Maisie's lead.

'Er, yes, all right, if you must. You'll find a hose and a bowl just through the gate and around the corner. Thank you for your concern. Goodbye. Come on, Biggles.' He took the reluctant dog by the scruff of the neck and shut the door.

'You can't expect him to be in a mood for niceties, Lilly. And Maisie is fine. I just gave her some water.'

'I know, but it bought us a way in, didn't it? Come on.'

Will, Lilly and Maisie walked to the side gate of the house and opened it to reveal a magnificent garden. The smell of fresh-mown grass seemed out of place in the muggy day.

Without a word, Will bent down to the hose and filled a small bowl for an uninterested Maisie. Knowing full well what she would do, he watched as Lilly peered into the empty rooms of the house.

'Will!' she whispered. 'Come look.'

Will crept towards the sash window and looked through thick curtains into a dark room. Inside were perhaps a hundred old typewriters, many battered and broken, strewn across the floor. In the middle of the room was a camp bed, unmade.

'Very peculiar,' said Will. 'Looks like someone was sleeping in there.'

'AYYY, that she were!' boomed a voice from behind them, making Will and Lilly start. Maisie had clearly noticed the man before them: she was wagging her tail vigorously as he patted her on the head. The man was dirty with mud but the clothes looked neatly pressed and fresh. In one gloved hand he held a bag full of leaves.

'Carol had taken to sleepin' in there.'

'Oh!' exclaimed Lilly. 'We're so sorry, we were just getting some water for—'

'Ah, ay, I know, I know,' said the man with a wry smile. 'This is a strange day for us all.'

'Do you know why she was sleeping in there?' Will asked.

'The divorce, I'd say.'

Will and Lilly glanced at each other.

'Wasn't a week ago that she told old Raymond that's what she wanted, but she'd been sleepin' in there, ooh, a good long while now. Can't have been comfy.'

'And the typewriters? Why them?'

'Ohh, she started collecting them. I think she liked them. Reminded her of her family's past, I suppose. That's how they made their money, printin' things, so I guess she was always around those things. Made her feel at 'ome.'

'Did she say where she was going at all, when you last saw her?'

'Out for a walk. She'd taken to the woods over by Potters Crouch. Think your dog might've had enough water.'

Rather than drinking the water in the bowl, Maisie had upturned it and was happily yapping at her reflection in the pool.

'Thank you so much. She was our friend, you see, and we're concerned.'

'Well, 'ope you find her. Good luck to you.'

'Just one thing,' said Will. 'You don't know us at all. Why have you shared this information?'

The man snorted and smiled. 'Well, let's just say if you knew her recently, you'd know she was preparin'. She may have thought that you would come. And...' He hesitated. 'You both look like you've got a good 'ead on your shoulders.'

Will and Lilly walked back past the front door and ambled towards the woodland lane towards Potters Crouch. 'Well, that was...informative.'

'It was. If Carol was after a divorce, that would be bad news for Raymond. I happen to know that it's Carol who owns the business, so Raymond would've been left with nothing.'

225

Suddenly from behind them came the noise of rapid footsteps followed by an enormous burst of leaves as a rampant, salivating Biggles dived at Maisie. Maisie was unphased as Biggles, twice the size of Maisie, rolled about on top of her.

'Biggles! Come on! We need to take you home!' Will untangled Maisie's lead that Biggles was caught in once again, held him by the collar and turned towards the house. As they did, they spied Raymond standing at the open front door. Will expected him to be calling for Biggles as any dog owner would, but instead he stood motionless, his fist clenched as if locked up. After a moment he stepped out, shut the door and headed into the woods without following the path.

'What is he up to?' As she said it, Lilly's voice cracked.

Will clasped the dog lead. The last reminder of his old acquaintance. A tear came to his eye and he gripped the lead tighter as his anger and frustration spilled out and tears started to flow down his cheeks. Maisie sat up and licked his face. He put his hand to her ear and gave it a scratch.

'There, Maisie, it's OK.'

As he scratched, Maisie tilted her head. As she did so he noticed a drop of blood form on the end of her ear and drip down one of her patches of white fur.

Will sat up sharply, which made Maisie's ears prick up. He pulled her toward him and started feeling her fur to find the source of this blood. He felt around, but nothing. Then he realised it wasn't coming from Maisie. He turned his palm up, and there was a patch of blood. He wiped it away and to his surprise saw what looked like the letter 'M' cut into his palm.

As he stared at his palm in confusion, Biggles, by this time standing, was sniffing intently at the lead that Will had been holding a moment ago and started mouthing at it once more. Slowly he picked it up and ran his thumb across the single seam of the nylon lead. He felt nothing as he slid his thumb along until quite suddenly it hit something sharp. He recoiled, looked at his thumb and wiped away the drop of blood to momentarily reveal the letter 'T' before the flowing blood obscured it from sight.

Lilly had been observing this and watched as Will slowly stood up. 'Lilly,' he said. 'Call the police. We'll tell them where to meet us soon enough. Now, come on, Biggles.' At this Will prized open the seam of the lead he was holding and out fell a little brown lump that Biggles pounced on. 'That looks like one of Biggles' treats!'

'It is,' said Will. 'But it's so much more—it's also the key to unlock the whole thing. Now Biggles—lead on. And make it fast.' With that, Biggles sniffed at the floor for a moment, then bounded off, with Will, Lilly and Maisie behind him.

After a few minutes of following Biggles through the woods the trees began to thin out. Will took Biggles gently by the collar and whispered to Lilly, who had been on the phone to the police and explaining what had happened, that this was the spot. Lilly muttered into the phone. Together they strode out in to the clearing. There was Raymond, pacing around the ground.

'You can stop there, Raymond. The police are on the way.'

Raymond jumped at the sound of Will's suddenly commanding voice.

'You two! What are you doing?'

'Following you, Raymond. You can stop now. It's over.'

'What are you talking about? I'm here looking for my wife. I'd remembered she'd mentioned this spot as a place she'd come on her walks.'

Will put up a hand to silence him. Raymond's face started to redden, but Will spoke softly. 'Carol knew she was going to be murdered, but she wanted to do it on her own terms. She'd told her gardener to look out for strangers and to tell them everything. The treats were pungent, and a favourite of Biggles, a bloodhound—the dog with the best sense of smell of all dogs. But it was the lead. It was a gift from Carol a few weeks ago, so I should've known to look closer at it. It contained a message.' Will rummaged reached into his coat pocket and pulled out the lead. Quite deliberately he began to rip away at the seam, out of which fell small shards of steel.

'What's that? Looks like dirt,' said Lilly.

'Not dirt,' said Will as he picked one and held it up. It gleamed in the light as a perfect letter 'S'. 'Letters. Made of metal. From typewriters, to be exact. That's why she collected them—for the letters, as you discovered, Raymond.'

'Nonsense.'

'It was when you answered the door, you see. Smoke coming from a chimney on a warm day like this. Most unusual. You killed your wife by strangling her with the dog lead, and to get rid of the evidence you threw it onto a fire. In doing so the nylon burnt away, but the metal letters remained in the grate, didn't they? When you realised what that meant you came rushing out here, back to the scene of the crime, to cover up your error.'

Raymond's face grew redder. 'I have no idea… Honestly, the impertinence of you two!'

'Well, we shall see.' As he spoke, three police-women approached from the opposite side of the clearing. 'Officers, I recommend you start digging, starting at the spot where that dog is currently stood.' All eyes swivelled over to a patch in the middle of the field where Biggles was sniffing intently. Two of the officers headed over and began to dig while one, thinking better of it, stood close behind Raymond.

'You see, Carol removed the letters she needed from the typewriters, filed them down and sharpened up the edges before putting them very carefully in the dog leads to spell out any message she wanted. It must've been a painstaking task.'

'What was yours?' Lilly asked.

'I'm glad you asked.' Will bent down and tipped all the letters from his pocket onto the ground and started to arrange them. After a few moments he stood back to uncover 'WILL FIND OUT'.

'We've got something here!' called one of the officers. The other was holding Biggles back. The party approached the patch of mud that had been dug up and, sure enough, there was the lifeless body of Carol.

Lilly took a sharp intake of breath and turned away. 'Oh Carol!'

Without betraying any emotion, Will faced Raymond and looked him squarely in the eye. 'She left a message for me, Raymond. And she left one for you, didn't she?'

Will bent down to the body. One of the officers tried to stop him, but the other held her colleague's hand back to allow him closer. He reached down and very gently pulled the collar of Carol's coat down to reveal her neck. Everyone apart from Will gasped. There, on her neck in angry red letters lay the words 'MURDERED BY RAYMOND'.

PILL POPPING

Wendy Turner

I couldn't wait to gulp down the pills. You know, those new things that are supposed to open your 'third eye' and give you a quick film show of your previous lives before your very eyes. I have to say that most of mine were instantly forgettable, until that day in the café in St Albans Cathedral.

I'd popped in for a quick latte and had barely got my newspaper out when, amazingly, I viewed myself sizzling into a previous life among the black and white print. I saw that I had once been...could it really be true...Richard III? 'Ah!' I cried out in front of all and sundry, jumping up and clutching my back in case I'd grown a damn great hump. I upset my coffee in the process and people started giving me peculiar looks. I hastily left and legged it along French Row, musing on what I remembered of the life of Richard III as so darkly portrayed by Shakespeare.

I searched my palms like mad Lady Macbeth for signs of dripping blood but there were only a few latte stains which would have been a total mystery to Richard. I seemed to be attracting unwelcome attention again so I slipped into Smiths and purchased a copy of Shakespeare's *Richard III*. I planned to read it before I nodded off that night.

But I didn't nod off. In fact, I stayed roaringly awake. Did Richard really murder the little princes in the Tower? How was I supposed to feel about that? Was I really deformed, unfinished, sent before my time into this breathing world, scarce half made up? What evidence was there of my black and cunning heart? Had I once been the most-foul murderer of Edward's heirs? The whole thing was scandalous. By 5am my blood was up and I was almost spitting bones.

Next morning, I regarded the pills with a little caution. Should I pop one? What if I discovered I'd been Nero, Hitler or the mad axe-man of St Albans? However, the desire to merge with Richard again was irresistible so down the hatch it went.

It was Saturday and, craving more, I took a trip to the Library in The Maltings to pick up a biography of Richard III. I smiled at the librarian, who returned the courtesy and bent his head over his computer. But suddenly, a dazzling picture shimmered into life in the air above his head. An old-fashioned scholar came into view, sporting a high lacy collar and twinkling gold earring. He was surrounded by an adoring crowd and had evidently just cracked some witticism as everyone fell about laughing. The scholar looked pretty pleased with himself. He caught sight of his reflection and lifted his chin admiringly, smoothing his beard. In a flash, I knew for a certainty that this was Shakespeare.

Outraged, I strode back to the desk. 'You Shakespeare?' I yelled into his face.

He smirked. He actually smirked. He polished his fingernails gently on his shirt for a moment before meeting my eyes. 'Cor-rect,' he said in a superior voice.

That's when I smacked him right on the nose.

Well, needless to say, chaos ensued.

'How dare you blacken my name without a shred of evidence?' I shrieked, tugging at a handful of hair. 'What gives you the right to be judge, jury and executioner?'

'That's ripe, coming from you,' he bawled. 'What did you do with the bodies of the little pr....' His knuckles caught my chin dislodging a new and expensive filling.

Time suddenly stopped. Shakespeare and Richard III disintegrated into a kaleidoscope-like image. I closed my eyes and felt drawn backwards into a mad whirlpool of time and almost lost consciousness.

When I opened them again, the librarian and I were still brawling on the library floor. Books were scattered everywhere, and a decent cross-section of readers peered at us with great interest. His spectacles were cracked and his tie askew. My hand flew to my poor injured jaw. Slowly, I retrieved my library book.

The librarian staggered to his feet, straightened his tie, and cleared his throat. 'Would you like that date-stamped, sir?' He raised an eyebrow. I nodded and he duly performed the task. It read *Returnum prior ye 25 Mai 1483*. I met his eyes.

'You always were a clever bastard,' I whispered.

He whistled softly, polishing his fingernails on his shirt.

***

Richard III reigned from 1483 – 1485

GRAVE CONCERNS

Gerwin de Boer

The interview took place in this little old cottage just behind the gate of Hatfield Road cemetery in St Albans. It was all English quaint: a slate roof and cobblestone walls. The groundskeeping team used it as an office.

I spoke to Ben, the boss, a white-haired pasty-cheeked fifty-year-old, and Liam, a skinny forty-something bald bloke with a gaunt face and black dots tattooed on his knuckles. Both wore their uniforms. Moss green trousers and jackets.

'So why do you want the job, Ernan?' Ben asked me after I had introduced myself.

'Honestly…' I started.

'Wouldn't have it any other way.' Liam cut in.

I sighed and got on with it.

'Honestly, I spent fifteen years in the military and learned that whatever you do, you make it worse. I am done with it all. I understand this job mainly involves digging, mowing, trimming, weeding and the occasional stone working. I'd like that.'

Ben then asked me some other questions. Most I answered with yes or no. Then he asked me what size of clothing I wore. I said XL. It was for my uniform. I got the job.

Two weeks in as groundskeeper, and I noticed something was off.

That day the mini excavator had broken down. I offered to take a look, but Ben said they had to call in an official engineer. The cemetery was council owned. We were civil servants. There were rules. I understood. There had been rules in the army as well. I hadn't always followed them, but I'd sworn to myself to do things differently.

So, I had to dig a grave by hand. Ben guessed it would take me the entire afternoon. The sun was out. The air smelled like fresh cut grass. For three hours I stabbed my shovel in the black earth, kicked it in a few inches further, and then threw the dirt over my shoulder. Repetitive, mind clearing labour. I enjoyed it. Best exercise I'd had in months. I felt good afterwards. Better than good: healthy and clean. I also felt I'd contributed to something worthwhile for a change: a dignified end, and remembrance.

I walked back to the office. On the path to the door, I heard Ben and Liam talking inside.

'Isaac rang me. He needs us to do another nightshift. I already picked the spot.' Ben said.

We didn't do nightshifts, or any shift for that matter. I pushed the door open. My colleagues looked startled.

'You're back. You sure made quick work of that.' Ben said.

Liam took a hard look at me. He nudged Ben. 'He's going for Gravedigger of the Year.'

I shrugged and left it at that.

A week after that, Liam came to work in a new car. A BMW M5. Bright red. It looked new. Expensive.

'Nice car. Fast?' I asked.

'Yeah, I got family money. Some of us are born lucky.' Liam ignored my question. He must have heard an accusation instead of a compliment.

I met nightshift-Isaac the following week.

He pulled up in a white van with 'gardening supplies' written on the side. In the back he had sacks of compost, fertiliser, weed killer, and cement. Ben asked me to help Liam unload.

Isaac was a short man with thick black hair and a matching beard. He wore jeans and a black polo shirt. He had a smoke while Liam and I emptied his van. I saw the black dots on his knuckles.

'So, you are the new guy.' Isaac said, as I walked by with a bag of compost under each arm.

'Yeah.' I carried on to the maintenance shed where we were stacking the supplies.

When I came back for another batch, Isaac had another question. 'You getting along with Ben and Liam?'

'Ernan keeps to himself.' Liam had joined Isaac for a cigarette.

'That's fine too.' Isaac said. 'As long as everyone is happy.'

I carried on working.

A few days later Ben came up to me and invited me for a drink at the social club across the road. It would be impolite to decline, so I didn't.

We sat at the bar. Pints in front of us. Ben wanted to know whether I liked the job. I said I did. It was peaceful and there was a certain dignity to it. Ben agreed.

'Are you able to stretch your wages till the next salary slip?' Ben asked me then. 'Well, if you find yourself struggling, don't keep it under your hat. I can always throw you something extra.'

'The council lets you do that?'

'No, it will come out my own pocket. I won the lottery once, and we working stiffs need to look after each other in these times of austerity, don't you agree?'

I nodded. Ben talked about football and the royal wedding over the next pint. He called a cab for me afterwards and handed me money for a ride to work in the morning. A hundred pounds.

I didn't like how things were adding up. A nightshift, Isaac's weird involvement, identical prison tattoos, and an abundance of money.

The next day I was replacing some cracked pavement tiles. Around 4 o'clock, Ben walked up and told me I deserved to call it an early day. He'd finish up.

I left, but I didn't go home. I parked my car down the road, and jumped the cemetery fence. I made my way through the bushes towards the office. There I waited. I saw a pair of visitors leave. Then after an hour I saw Ben come back from the tiling job. He locked the cemetery gates and ducked into the office. Liam joined him there not much later. Ten minutes after that, they set out together. Ben was carrying a shovel and blue lifting straps. Liam walked to the shed and got the small excavator out. He drove off after Ben. It looked like they were going to dig a grave.

I followed them to an old part of the cemetery, where the leases on the graves had proven to be longer than the memory of the deceased's families. Unvisited. Hiding behind a stone angel, I saw where they were digging in front of a gravestone.

Liam and the excavator made quick work of the first three and a half feet. Then Ben carefully stepped into the grave, and I saw that final half foot of dirt come out of someone's final resting place. There would just be the coffin now. Liam tossed Ben the lifting straps. Not much later they used the excavator as a crane to lift a mouldy coffin out of the ground. They set it down next to the open grave. Liam then had a smoke and Ben checked his watch.

Ten minutes later, the shadow of the angel grew longer. Headlights appeared between the gravestones. Isaac's van was slowly making its way up the cemetery's main gravel path, drove past where I was hiding, and stopped as close to the freshly dug-up grave as possible. Isaac got out, opened the rear doors and jumped in the back. Liam came over. Together they carried out something wrapped in blue tarpaulin. About two meters long. On one end of the bundle, I saw a pair of white sneakers sticking out.

'Tall bastard.' Liam said.

'Will it fit?'

'We can fold over the legs.'

Liam and Isaac carried the bundled-up body over to the soon-to-be double-occupied grave. I waited.

Isaac came back to the van. His job was done. The driver's seat was on my side. Away from where Liam and Ben were working. Isaac walked around and got in. I sprinted towards the van and pulled the door open.

Isaac turned to see who was there. I grabbed him by the collar of his shirt and punched him in the face. Hard. Then again, and again. His head sagged, and I pushed him to the passenger seat. His keys were already in the ignition. I turned on the engine and turned the van around. Ben and Liam were still filling up the grave.

I drove back to the office. Isaac came to when we got there.

'We don't kill anyone. Criminals pay us to make bodies disappear. Good money.' He slurred.

I punched Isaac again and he slumped against the door. Out cold.

I parked the van behind the office, so that Ben and Liam couldn't see it from where they were working. Then I dragged an unconscious Isaac out of the passenger seat and locked him in the back of the van. I went into the office and called the police.

Through the window, I saw the light of the excavator swirling left to right. Moving earth. Taking the dead away from their families. Leaving them only with questions. I knew what that was meant to achieve. Painful lingering hope. The worst kind. I had sworn to myself that if I ever got the chance again, I wouldn't stand by while witnessing torture.

I sat down and waited till I could hear the sirens. At peace with my day's work.

BURY HIM BESIDE HIS BETTERS

Paul F. McNamara

Folk tremble when war comes calling but not me, not this blessed day, and mistake me not when I tell you how I was liberated by war. I was never a prisoner, not one of theirs anyway. Verily, I abhor kings and queens with their fêted dukes and knights and their flag-flying knavery. White rose. Red rose. English. French. Fie! I might yet be young but am in no doubt that people like me are mere blood and silver to them, placed upon this earth to fatten their coffers, fight their battles and fade meekly from existence. I may be condemned to service their wants from the cradle to the grave but today is my day and, I declare, those coddled overlings have repaid me full measure. Like a turd unto a cesspit, they have swallowed my foul deed in the enormity of their own, leaving no trace. I lie bruised and bloodied but I am alive and I am free.

My stepfather, Colwich, and the other shopkeepers despaired to see Warwick's army march into St Albans again. They recalled only too painfully the last time these scoundrels were here; how they'd rampaged through Market Place, blood-crazed with a morning's slaughter, stealing what they could carry, destroying what they could not. There was little reason to believe things would be different this time whichever hateful faction prevailed.

I hid in fear behind my mother that dread day as she clutched her kirtle about her distended belly, shrieking as Colwich was whipped for rendering his silver too slowly to the looters. I confess to taking some quiet pleasure in watching the old bully thrashed, but the disdain I held him in then was soon to be dwarfed by an all-consuming hatred that burgeoned in the years thereafter.

I know not whether it was the terrors witnessed that day or some monstrous seed Colwich planted in her, but neither mother nor babe survived the sweated agonies of childbirth in the days that followed. Colwich never recovered and, despite his seemingly unbounded love for my mother, he held not the slightest fleck of affection for me. I was the unwelcome dowry in his marriage to Widow Gammell and once she was gone, I became his burden.

Custom ensured he could not turn me out, but my very presence in his house gnawed at him. Worse still, since my countenance bears some semblance to my mother's, he was daily reminded that I was alive when his beloved was not. In time, he came to despise me, using me for only the meanest of tasks about the house. He delighted in chastising me. The slightest look askance or wayward word would drive him to fury until, one day, he grabbed me by the throat and hurled me down the stairs into his workshop leaving me forever with a twisted frame. 'Foolish Tom' became 'Crooked Tom' that day. And this was when he was undrunk! He was far more the beast after a night guzzling ale and playing dice. Rude and randy, he'd return from The Tabard or the Cornerhall, and drag me from my pallet to 'do my mother's duty!' Me, standing in the dark, tugging on his stinking pizzle with him barking instructions before slapping me away sorrowfully once spent. On such nights I was thrashed in lust if I resisted, in shame if I obliged.

Too numerous to recount, those everyday indignities clung to me like ticks to a dog's belly. They burrowed and burned and, today, they burst to release a vengeful fever. I had lain awake many a night fashioning a thousand revenges but, ere those fighting men returned last week, I had not the means to cloak my redress. Despite the constant misery suffered at Colwich's hands, I cradled life too dearly to risk hanging for his dispatch. Thus, where Warwick's men brought Colwich distress, they provided me hope.

So, consider my own despondency when those Cockney braggarts and that addle-brained king of theirs were wheeled through the town and set up for battle on Barnet Heath. God's nails! What use were they to me out there? If fighting was to be done, I needed it here, in town, not out on that god-forsaken scrag of moorland. I certainly couldn't see that raggy-arsed bunch of archers sheltering from the cold hereabouts serving my purpose at all but, as you shall hear, Crooked Tom isn't entirely without fortune.

No matter how long Colwich held his hand aloft, his slaps still smarted when they landed. So it was with the arrival of Queen Margaret's army. The presence of Warwick's troops and the increasingly lurid tales of pillage and rape from those fleeing south before the Queen's northern barbarians had driven the sober burghers of St Albans to frenzy awaiting the fight. But their panic remained undiminished when that picket scout appeared in Market Place at dawn, yelling about how, having marched overnight, the Queen's vanguard was already nearing Roomland with thousands more men crossing the Ver and marching up the Sallipath behind.

Well, that set Colwich squealing! Hearing his cries, I found him in his fusty bedchamber, hopping about like a palsied jangler, hauling up his threadbare hose and gabbling to no one in particular, 'The rumours were true! Those sneaky bastards were in Dunstable all along. Warwick's looking the wrong way!' I dared not open my mouth, of course, but comforted myself that, with Warwick freezing his cods off on Barnet Heath staring northwards for sight of her, the French queen had clearly come the *right* way....to further her and, I prayed, my own interests.

The two of us stood motionless, staring silently at one another as we listened to the growing hysteria in the Market Place below. As townsfolk raced home to board their windows and doors, we heard the archer's captain order his men to take up vantage points around the Vintry, the Waxhouse Gate and the clockhouse, instructing them to ready their bows and nock.

In the little time available to us before fighting began, Colwich ordered me downstairs to help drag his cutting bench behind the front door of the shop. Feeling I was somehow doubting the merit of doing so given what'd transpired last time, he delivered a hefty clout to my ear before demanding I go into the pantry and bring some dark bread and ale up to his chamber. When I got up there moments later, I found him crawling like a wary mutt towards the window where he eased back the shutter for a gawp at history.

An uneasy hush had fallen over Market Place by now and, wide-eyed with anticipation, we listened to the swelling rattle and clank of armoured men advancing towards the Market Place from the Abbey. As if it were some child's game, Colwich swivelled excitedly and whispered, 'They're here,' and, with a gulp, I prepared myself for the attack.

As the Queen's pikemen approached the Great Cross, we heard the archers' captain roar, 'Draw and loose!' to release four score arrows. Whistle and thump. Moments later came four score more and, to the swelling howl of men lying wounded on rain slicked cobbles, four score again. The noise of further volleys was then drowned out by the frantic clanging of the clockhouse bell alerting Warwick to the attack in town.

Carried away with the excitement of battle and plainly forgetting that Warwick's southern ruffians presented us with every bit the same personal menace as the Queen's northerners, Colwich stood to jeer as the attackers retreated. Almost upending his half-filled piss pot, he danced a clownish jig as he roared through the shutters, 'That's it, you whoresons! Get yourselves home to whichever shitholes you've slithered from!' But we both knew the soldiers would return again soon and, with inner satisfaction, I watched his smug grin fade as he regained his wits.

To the deafening clanking of the clockhouse bell, we bolted down our meagre breakfast and, between mouthfuls, Colwich expounded on what would happen next. All taproom bollocks, of course, as from the little we could discern, trapped as we were in the gloomy confines of his bedchamber, the Queen's men did not break through the houses onto Holywell Hill as he predicted. Arriving from exactly the opposite direction, they must've instead followed the Tonman Ditch around the west of town and broken in somewhere up by St Peter's.

The panic in the archers' voices was now clear as they shouted warnings to one another. With horsemen and foot soldiers approaching rapidly past the Moot Hall and the earlier attackers edging back up from the Abbey, the archers around the Market Place knew they were surrounded. Thankful that none had taken up positions with us, we heard their anguished cries as they were steadily flushed from their lairs. Some must have decided to make a run for it because, not long afterwards, there came the sounds of men fighting below our window. I watched Colwich turn and skulk back to his hidden lookout and decided that my time had finally arrived. It was now or never.

Believing him mesmerised by the carnage below, I tip-toed downstairs to his workbench and grabbed his prized head knife. Keen-edged with a broad half-moon blade, it would serve me well. My plan had been to fall upon Colwich immediately on return but, ever cursed by my twisted frame, I stumbled re-entering his bedchamber. Affrighted, he spun round to spy me standing over him, knife in hand. I froze. I had little chance of slaying him without the benefit of surprise but, with my second grant of good fortune that day, he misread my motives completely. Calling me a 'weak-kneed cretin,' he lambasted me for even thinking I could fight off any marauders breaking in and ordered me to put the knife away and forego any notion of resistance. But resistance was never my intent. I had no wish to waste my cherished hatred on any pox-ridden tyke or Scot. It was for him and him alone, and the instant he returned to his gawking I dropped on him, driving the knife down as hard as I could. Its fearsome blade tore a deep gouge into the side of Colwich's stubbled neck. As he bucked in shock to fend me off, he offered up his detestable fat wattles and I pounded the knife down into them, slashing hysterically, again and again. One. Two. Three. Four blows and more, forceful and deep, ripping criss-cross gashes into his throat.

To my amazement, he didn't call out when I stood away. Perhaps he couldn't. All he seemed capable of was rolling himself round into a splay-legged sitting position, chin on chest. Slumped there, he regarded me sombrely, a pathetic questioning in his eye, while pulsing gouts of blood embroidered his tunic with a spreading bib of red. Gasping for air, he gurgled over and over, 'You have wounded me.' Despite possessing one, I did not deign to reward him with any response.

Still clutching the bloodied knife, I retreated slowly to the opposite wall where, as the noise of battle outside died down, I leaned to watch him die. Panicked rasps of breath and a muttered entreaty for my eternal damnation heralded the end. Then, with a final shiver, the beast fell silent.

His curse on my eternal soul meant nothing to me. If hell truly existed, then it could hardly be worse than the one he'd made for me. No, my sole concern now was avoiding the gallows. I reasoned that any pillagers breaking in here after a day's fighting would be unlikely to pay more than scant attention to one more corpse, but I had no appetite for hazard in that regard. Thus, once I was sure Colwich was no more, I took hold of him beneath his oxters and, with all the strength my puny body could muster, I dragged him downstairs into the workshop and wrestled him into a prone position behind the front door.

Using my tunic and rags grabbed from the pantry, I dashed back upstairs to mop up the browning puddle of ooze where Colwich had sat to die, before descending to scatter the bloodied cloths around his injured head and neck.

Breathing hard now, I rinsed off my blood-spattered hands and face, donned a clean tunic and set about gathering together what silver groats and gold nobles I could find around Colwich's workshop and bedchamber. Once done, I placed half the sum into one earthenware pot and divided the remainder between two others before secreting all three around the house. My plan was to hand over as little coin as I could get away with. I would render the half pot first but the others only if compelled. This was a dangerous path. If I rushed too soon to hand over the half-pot, the looters might suspect they were being fobbed off, demur too long and I risked the kind of whipping I had watched Colwich endure years before.

Nearing exhaustion, I flopped down at a small table in Colwich's bedchamber to await the thieving rogues I knew would come. Remembering Warwick's men years earlier, I knew there'd be hungry days ahead. Lententide tomorrow or not, locusts like these would leave you precious little to eat at any time of year. What scran we had was better in my belly than theirs. So, cold though it was, I set about shovelling down as much of the previous night's potage as I could stomach, reminding myself that it was Shrove Tuesday after all.

Raucous halloos from outside made it clear that not all of the victors in town had decided to engage with Warwick on Barnet Heath. Inching my head out of the shutter, I surveyed the Market Place, its wet cobbles now bestrewn with stiffening corpses. Through February sleet, gangs of ruffians were moving from house to house, loading plunder onto waiting carts while others stalked, crow-like, from one recumbent figure to another, relieving them of their possessions and their last breath if foolish enough to stir.

Heart pounding, I noticed a sizeable group of looters working their way along Cordwainers Row towards me. Minutes later, I jumped to hear Hankin's widow screeching from next door and thought it a mercy that her recently married daughter was no longer at home for the pleasure of these miscreants.

A succession of low thuds at the shop door announced it was my turn. My jaw tightened to hear Colwich's workbench being steadily shoved back to permit entry. Moments later, seemingly oblivious to the cadaver they had to have stepped over, they were up the stairs and before me. Four screw-faced thugs, each sporting at least two pilfered jerkins, regarded me stonily. I noted immediately that the one thing these mobards lacked, on themselves or their weapons, was any sign of blood. These were brigands not warriors.

The gang leader suddenly sprang forward, grabbed me by the neck and, in a barely comprehensible garble, growled through broken teeth,

'Silver and gold! Bring me your silver and gold!'

Albeit terrified, I held to my plan. I pleaded for mercy, explaining that I'd been orphaned that very morning. But, as anticipated, such entreaties only provoked him and he crashed a mighty blow into the side of my face, pitching me sideways across the room.

'Don't waste my time, you little runt! Silver and gold coin. All of it. Now!'

With his comrades busying themselves cramming Colwich's brass plate, bed linen and other possessions into sacks, I stepped cautiously across the leader's icy glare to reach beneath Colwich's bed to retrieve the half pot of money. But these thieves had spent the last two months sacking towns from York to here, and it was immediately obvious that the gang leader knew that a shop like this, in a shrine like St Albans, should deliver more coin than he could see in that pot. Shaking his head almost ruefully, he tipped the contents of the pot into a bulging purse at his waist before unleashing a scything punch to my belly. As I lay in a heap at his feet, he bent down to bellow, almost rhythmically,

'Bring me all the coin, you little shit, or I will wring your scrawny neck, right here, right now!'

Eyes watering and perilously close to puking, I led him downstairs to the workshop where more of his henchmen were harvesting Colwich's stock of boots and shoes, along with his precious tools and lasts. As I stretched behind the kitchen hearth for one of the remaining quarter pots of coins, the gang leader nodded casually towards Colwich's bloodied corpse and, through a crooked smirk, quipped, 'I see father's not looking too healthy? What's happened there?'

'Sir, I begged the old dotard not to engage in the fighting but he had to play the hero. He came down here during the battle to stand in his doorway and defend his 'kingdom' but, as you can see, somebody's slotted him in the neck. I tried to stem the bleeding with those rags but...'

Displaying neither sympathy nor surprise, the gang leader just grunted. Wrenching the quarter pot from my hands, he quickly counted out its contents before calling out, 'Away now, lads. That'll do. Let's get next door before any other bastards show up.'

And, with that, they were gone.

Plenty of other desperate men followed once the fighting on the heath was done but, with the shop already in plundered disarray, none stayed long or harmed me further. The scarcer the scraps, the less time they could afford to linger. But I silently welcomed their visits because, after a dozen such gangs had passed through, I could tell any prying neighbours that Colwich had died a pointless death remonstrating with a bunch of northern cutthroats but I couldn't be sure which ones. They might express surprise at the old yelper's pluck given the beating he'd once taken from Warwick's men, but they'd have little reason to doubt me and precious little means to prove otherwise.

And, tomorrow, they will help 'poor orphaned Tom' carry his bloodied stepfather through the grieving streets of the town to St Peter's so some pasty-faced priest can bury him beside his betters. That undiscovered quarter pot of coin will help settle me in London where, Lazarus-like, I shall start my life anew. For I am alive, I am free, and Colwich, the beast, is no more.

***

Shrove Tuesday, 17th February 1461, remains the bloodiest day in St Albans' history. The main source for the story of the Second Battle of Saint Albans during the War of the Roses has been the excellent Burley P., Elliott M. and Watson H. (2007) The Battles of St Albans, Pen & Sword Books, Barnsley, South Yorkshire. The placenames used have been taken from their excellent text rather than modern day. Thus, the area we now know as Romeland was known as Roomland in the mid-15th century. Likewise, Fishpool Street was then known as the Sallipath, and Bernards Heath as Barnet Heath.

Albeit the geography of central St Albans has changed little since the 15th century, many of its medieval landmarks, like the Moot Hall, the Shambles and the Great Cross, have all disappeared, as have the names of many of the drinking houses. Those interested in examining a map of medieval St Albans should consult Chris Saunders' wonderful interactive map at http://www.salbani.co.uk/.

To inject a few words from the time into my tale, I've made use of the University of Michigan's Dictionary of Middle English:
https://quod.lib.umich.edu/m/middle-english-dictionary/dictionary

As will prove obvious to any expert, I am not an historian and any errors made in Tom's desperate tale remain entirely my own.

Finally, I would like to thank David Shiers, Janet Holdsworth, Martin Finnegan, Tanya O'Connor and Sarah Ward for commenting on an earlier draft.

#CRIMEORNOT

Sam Rostom

Dawn broke as Liberty crossed the street and headed down the narrow passage of Waxhouse Gate in silence. She could hear only her own breathing and the whirr of the great fans as they cooled the computer systems beneath her.

Is today the first day, or my last day?

Her black hair pinned back into a classic chignon, a nod to the old days, she thought, the good days, as she passed the Verdun tree opposite Vintry Gardens and around the crumbling walls into Sumpter Yard. The great cedar, standing stoic since 1803, had often comforted her, perhaps as a link to a simpler past—but not today, as she stepped into the first shadow of the Cathedral. It had itself stood the test of time for more than a thousand years, even as its purpose had changed; bending with the times like a willow in the wind, a post-religious monolith that had been reclaimed and repurposed. She looked up to it, as a child to a mother searching for an answer. What would this day bring? Humility? Vindication? Eradication? *They* now had the power, and she knew that no matter what the outcome, it was to be a day of reckoning.

Inside the building, the original flooring remained underfoot, producing an empty echo as Liberty crossed the flagstone, the stained windows bringing to life the past in vignettes—stories from a history that no longer existed. The space itself was vast, otherworldly even, and the ceilings tall with ornate carvings which had eroded, gently being erased by time itself. She passed the Abbot's door, marvelling at the detailed woodwork, and followed the sign '#CON' to cubicles that had taken over the area which had once been the Nave. Its gothic archways were almost hidden with cabling and speakers and dozens of numbered smaller box rooms running the length of the great hall.

This was now where justice lived.

She entered her assigned cubicle, AE78, and signed in with her iris and DNA print to await the judgement. It hadn't always been this way. Her grandmother had told her that years ago, laws governed what was right and what was wrong. Things were written down; a small group of people and a specially defined role called a 'Judge' then decided if you did something that was 'against' the written down rules. Things are different now; the world changed so quickly there was no sense in writing things down for posterity any more. It was 'People Power' that ruled now. If the People thought something was against the order of things—it was.

Everyone votes. Everyone.

It was dark in the cubicle. Every surface was a polished digital screen with black pixels a constant backdrop, as numerals counted down digit by digit whilst the final votes were entered and counted from across the country.

15

14

13...She knew it would be a close call; after all many people hated Professor Lucas for what he had made and what he had done—but was erasing him a stretch too far? Her stomach and its contents were in freefall, her anxiety doing a long-drop in her body, heart pounding in her chest as if it wanted to escape and spare her the agony of the wait, while the hair on her skin prickled intensely on high alert. The vote would be close, yes. Everyone had been commenting to say so in the chatroom and soon, Liberty would understand her fate.

12

11

10...

Oh god, how has it come to this? How did I not see what was going on? Just breathe Libby, not long now and it will all be over.

EV.E had been launched in 2054, only the year after Liberty had been born, so despite what her grandmother had told her, it was all she had ever known. 'Everyone Votes. Everyone', or EV.E, as it had since come to be known, was a platform that hosted a new judicial system, controlled by the People. It meant that the whole population became the jury in any case that people had an interest in, however big or small. All it took was an entry into the virtual ledger in EV.E and sufficient 'concur' swipes to agree that it was a matter of public concern. The accused then received a notification via the app to advise them that a #CrimeOrNot vote would be instigated against them.

...9

It was not lost on Liberty, the irony of her place of birth also being the birthplace of this new world order. Saint Albans City had for years been venerated as recording the first Christian martyr, Saint Alban, who had himself been judged by a Roman magistrate and sentenced to death for betraying the Empire. Liberty often wondered what his fate would have been if it had been up to EV.E. Now the city was known as the birthplace of arguably the most progressive form of a societal legal system ever developed. Many commentators had reported at the time that it had been the cumulative effect of a number of key moments in history, which had reached a tipping point into a different future. At school when she had been a child, Liberty remembered reading an old news article, which had put forward the set pieces that had created the conditions for evolution, and it seemed to her that perhaps there was some truth in that.

...8

What if I'm erased and all of this has been in vain?

The first of these events went as far back as the previous century, the 1980's or even earlier, when the 'network of networks' was first built, a clumsy system they called the 'internet'. It was crude and useless at first, filled with cat videos, viral memes and virtual reality videogames that eventually grew into the vast virtual communities that resembled the present. Over time, this online world had opened up a portal into modernity, a place where everyone had a voice and all voices were equal.

Virtual communities gained increasing power and influence, controlling society as culture gradually shifted into the binary space of zeros and ones.

The real world would still largely dominate public life until late 2053 when quite possibly the most significant event took place, opening the door to a parallel universe that humanity walked right through. In the spring of 2054, the Prime Minister of the United Kingdom was arrested and charged with causing death by dangerous driving. It was an especially tragic case; his Range Rover in convoy had hit a mother and her baby as they walked down a high street in London; the baby had died instantly and the mother a few days later as she lay in hospital. It was a public relations nightmare that caused substantial global interest, dominating the news headlines on both sides of the Atlantic. A further media frenzy ensued when someone close to the incident, possibly even a junior aide, leaked information to the press that a breathalyser test had revealed the PM to be twice over the legal limit and yet he had dismissed his aides and security detail and attempted to drive himself back home to Downing Street following a gala dinner. Serious concern was raised about the implications for both the PM and the Party as he was arrested and charged, all of which was live-streamed to millions. Weeks of speculation about the fate of the PM continued until the trial where a judge found him 'not guilty' on grounds of 'reasonableness' through virtue of his ministerial position. A tidal wave of anger followed, signalling an immense level of discontent in the judicial system at the time. A general election followed and the new party campaigned on being a party for the People, of the People. Their campaign slogan: Everyone Votes. Everyone.

...6

Did we build a machine that turned into a monster? Or did a monster build the machine?

When they got in with a landslide in the summer of 2054, it had already been decided that power would be distributed out from the centre; it was only a question of *how.* After all, why should only a few sit in judgement of the many?

Whilst all this was played out, Professor Lucas, who was an eminent academic teaching politics at the University of Hertfordshire, had been experimenting with new ways of empowering the population through collective decision-making and increasing civic participation. Disillusioned by the ever-decreasing levels of political engagement and diminishing voters over the years, he wanted to find ways of making politics more involved. He had also noticed that the basic principle of giving power to the people had already been tested in popular culture and it seemed to work. He teamed up with a tech giant, Facepage, and working together over the next 12 months developed a prototype that became the fastest growing start-up in history and would go on to become synonymous with law.

EV.E wasn't rocket science but perhaps that was the draw.

...5

A few years later, when Liberty left university after studying computer science, she had been so excited to work at such an important and prestigious company that had so much social value. By then it had branched out beyond politics; EV.E had its own cryptocurrency which supported a decentralised financial system, its own robotics institutes specialising in nanobots that focussed on improving the environment, and it had also purchased every human genome sequence ever mapped, with the goal of eradicating all human disease . EV.E was the Mother Teresa of industry and over time had built not only a cult-like following but also gained a level of trust from the population that was unwavering—and priceless. Liberty worked long days, weekends and even holidays alongside colleagues who became friends over the next few years. She lived for the company, gave her all to the company and truly believed in its mission, to give everyone a voice that could be heard.

However, there was a glitch. The problem was not the system; it was the human in the system. The ghost in the machine.

...4

Liberty had started to notice recurring #CON votes around particular themes and they always seemed to have the same benefactors. The EV.E ledger was often filled with duplicate requests for votes, 'concur' swipes registered to the same IP addresses became the norm and she and some of her colleagues began wondering what was going on. It appeared that although everyone voted, some votes now seemed to count for more.

When Liberty discovered that the ghost was Professor Lucas, she was heartbroken. She had started to delve into system archives for any signs of being tampered with so she could report it to the Professor and inadvertently stumbled on a memo in a folder on a hidden drive. It instructed him to plant a ledger and then use a piece of code that effectively copied selected votes and swipes, forcing #CONs to be set up on anything and influencing the out-comes, irrespective of what the voting population thought. Alongside it, an invoice for £32.4 billion. He was being paid off! How could he do this? How could he ruin such a beautiful system? Her heart-break turned to anger and anger turned to rage. He had to be exposed, ended, and EV.E with him.

...3

It was never meant to be a perfect crime; Liberty had known that. Even as she made her mind up to kill Professor Lucas, she knew that her virtual fin-gerprints would be traced back and she would be identified as the perpetrator. But that was the point. Like Saint Alban and all martyrs before and after him, she was prepared to accept any consequence for exposing the truth, even if it meant termination. For whilst all those around her saw the world for what it now was, she saw the world for what it had been and what it still could be. She and a groundswell of others in the company who had come to learn the truth believed they had to take things back in order to go forward. Professor Lucas and EV.E had to be destroyed.

She had arrived at work early the next day to her offices in the basement of the old museum on St Pe-ters Street. It was a prestigious place, the flagship building of this global empire that she alone would have to crush, exposing it to the population, and making old, this new world order. She had been up all night weighing up the alternatives but had come back around to the same conclusion. She knew that the corruption was so deeply embedded in the sys-tem from the top that that there was now no way back. Her mind made up, she wrote a passionate statement that she pre-programmed to launch across all platforms once she had completed her final task.

She ran her finger over the receptor in the entryway and the door slid open. Inside she sat at her computer, and instead of accessing her usual digital work areas she found the genome folder and searched for Professor Lucas' record. If she could corrupt just one letter of his DNA source code, he would cease to function in real time. She had seen it so many times before. After all, this is what happened to all those that were found guilty via a #CON vote. No need for guards, police, prison and no point in running, your DNA would be accessed via the central system and you would simply be wiped out, like you never existed. It was an open secret. An invisible stain on humanity, maintained through tacit silence, like so many human stains.

...2

Finding his file, she infiltrated it via an obscure source code she had taught herself whilst at university. It was all so easy. She hovered her cursor over the text. Delete. Delete. Delete.

...1

Is doing the right thing always the right thing to do?

Now here she was, in this dark cubicle awaiting the judgement of her people. The whole community was now aware of what Professor Lucas had been doing, what she had done because of what EV.E had become. All had logged in to vote on arguably the most important #CON in history.

...0

The result arrived.

She touched her face, her neck, her ribcage. She still existed, but something was different. A siren started to go off in the background; she knew this was only programmed to go off if there was ever a malfunction. The screen in the cubicle flashed the result, a result that had never before occurred. It said '50% / 50% - system failure'.

Now that quantum computing had been developed and scaled, there was a new kid on the block, Quantum Artificial Intelligence (QAI). QAI had been developed as a direct response to the failure of EV.E; the system relied on people and people were fallible. QAI was superior in every way. After all, why should a community decide on the fate of a person when a quantum supercomputer more intelligent than the greatest mind on earth could decide instantaneously and categorically? QAI would now determine right from wrong. Humanity was outsourced.

Welcome to the new dawn.

A new world order.

SOMETIMES QUIET. SOMETIMES LOUD.

Steven Mitchell

'Can you hear it?' I ask.

The noise fills the air—shrill, constant—passing through the streets and alleys as the sun rises over the distant clock tower. Its tiny sound waves ripple the surface of my morning coffee in the cupholder of my parked bus.

The passenger shakes her head, chestnut hair brushing her shoulders.

'I can't hear anything,' she says.

'Hold your breath,' I tell her. 'I'll hold mine. Try listening again.'

Shutting tight her hazel eyes, she smiles and inhales, happy to play the game. Her brow furrows in concentration.

She's a regular on this bus route, off to work today in a summer dress, yellow and floral. It'll be warm today, but the morning chill has raised goose bumps on her slim arms.

She lets out her breath.

'I'm sorry,' she says, laughing. 'I can't hear it.'

She pays her fare, dropping warm coins from her hand into my outstretched palm.

In my rear-view mirror, she walks to the back of the bus and takes a seat. She settles and studies her phone as the noise she can't hear burrows deep into my head. It'll be busier later, but this morning she's the only passenger on my route from St Albans to Hatfield.

The bus judders as the engine rumbles to life, and the noise is masked, a bit. But the doors close, squealing, adding to the clamour in my head, and I wince. As I release the brakes, I flinch at the sharp hiss. I grimace as the bus whines while pulling out from the bus stop onto the empty road. In my wing mirror, a man runs behind, hands waving, willing me to stop. I meet his eyes in the mirror. His mouth forms swear words as he shrinks into the distance. It's just me and her and the noise.

I turn a sharp left, heading down the hill of Victoria Street, the noise travelling with us. Opening my window, the rush of air softens the noise, but it's still there. Always there. But worse today. Today is a bad day.

A couple of cars pass but there are no people on the streets. The shops are shuttered. The takeaways, hairdressers and nail bars are yet to open for customers. It's a beautiful time of day.

A car pulls out in front, and I slam on the brakes. The brakes scream. A scream I know. The same as the noise in my head. Always the same scream. Sometimes quiet. Sometimes loud. The scream she'd made as the knife plunged into her chest, just above her necklace.

The bus jerks to a stop.

'Idiot,' I shout as the driver of the car avoids eye-contact.

I touch the gold cross beneath my uniform shirt. It calms me. But the scream remains, now ear-splitting. Painful. Stabbing. I rub my forehead. It's warm, sweating.

In the rear-view mirror, the woman in the back is looking at me.

'Some people just shouldn't drive,' I tell her.

She returns to staring at her phone as I start driving, glancing back at her. I hadn't noticed before, but she's the mirror image of someone I knew. The same hair. Same nose. Same figure. Wendy, the woman with the scream. The scream in my head. From whose neck I unfastened a bloodied gold cross necklace and used the folds of her skirt to wipe it clean.

Wendy had ridden the bus every morning. A different route to this one, a different town. We'd always laughed and joked, flirting. I loved to see her. I couldn't wait to see her. Then, one evening, I covered the evening shift, and there she was, on the night bus, drunk.

'Hello, you,' Wendy slurred, eyes lighting up when she recognised me.

I grinned.

'Have you had a good night?' I asked.

'Brilliant,' she said, giggling and toppling on her heels as she waved her return ticket at me. Gently, I took her swaying hand to still it. It was soft and warm. I stroked her thumb lightly with mine as I checked her ticket.

'Thank you,' I said, releasing her hand, closing the bus door, and preparing to depart.

She took the seat nearest to me and watched as I drove, a wide and beautiful smile on her flushed face. I grew embarrassed at the attention. And

Wendy's face changed when I turned off-route onto an unlit country lane.

Beeeeeeeeeeeeeeeeeeeeeeeeeeeeeeeeeeeeep!

A car coming in the opposite direction blasts its horn, and I jolt out of my Wendy daydream. I swerve back onto the correct side of the road just in time.

'Sorry,' I shout back to my alarmed passenger. She's clutching the top of the chair in front, eyebrows raised. Her eyebrows are just like Wendy's.

The noise is too much today. My head aches. My eyelids are heavy.

'I need to stop for a minute,' I say, turning off Hatfield Road on to a lane. 'There's something wrong with the bus,' I lie. I can barely hear my own voice through the noise.

She looks at her watch and tuts.

We pass a field of ripening wheat and pull up off the lane beside a gated woodland.

I release myself from my driving compartment and lumber up the bus aisle towards my passenger, head and shoulders heavy with the noise.

She glances up before looking back at her phone.

The noise is intense. Penetrating deep into my skull.

'Are you sure you can't hear that sound?' I ask.

'No,' she says, annoyed, before she sees the knife raised in my hand.

I grab her hair and pull her, yelling, from her seat and down the aisle. She flails, trying to release herself, but the pain of pulled hair is too much. Opening the doors, I drag her down onto the bare ground outside. Birdsong, like alarms and sirens, adds to the cacophony in my head. The gate to the wood is ajar and I pull her deep into the trees before releasing her hair and throwing her to the ground.

'What are you do—?'

My arm swings and she screams. A beautiful scream. A painkiller to my aching head.

The knife slices through the skin of her raised forearm. She screams again. It is bliss. I stab and stab in ecstasy, her chest, her stomach, her thighs, the pitch of the screams lowering, until the screams stop.

I feel incredible. Tingling, almost rippling with pleasure.

From around her neck, I break a simple diamond pendant. It'll sit well upon my chest with Wendy's gold cross, another passenger's silver locket, and the schoolgirl's St Christopher charm.

The scream in my head can't be silenced. But I can drown it out with the screams of others.

ABOUT THE CONTRIBUTORS

BEN BERGONZI

A regular writer and reviewer, Ben has a strong interest in history, having previously worked as a museum curator and a digitization consultant. He now works at a university and also as a Reviews Editor for Historical Novels Review. He can be found on Linkedin and on Twitter @bergonziben.

RACHAEL BLOK

Rachael Blok grew up in Durham and studied Literature at Warwick University. She taught English at a London comprehensive and is now a full-time writer, living in Hertfordshire with her husband and children. She writes a psychological
crime series set in St Albans.
https://www.rachaelblok.com/

GERWIN DE BOER

Gerwin tells tales about crime and pushing back hard, sometimes with a hint of the fantastic. Criminals, spies, intelligence officers, and folk with unique perspectives on the world are the focus of his stories. Gerwin was born in the Netherlands and now lives and writes in St Albans.
www.gerwindeboer.com

JOAN CROOKS

Joan has worked as a psychotherapist. She was always interested in writing stories and has found being a member of Verulam Writers very supportive. She lives in Boxmoor, Hemel Hempstead and enjoys walking and dancing.

CANDY DENMAN

Candy spent most of her life as an NHS nurse but now concentrates on writing full time. She has written extensively for television programmes such as The Bill, Doctors and Heartbeat and has published a medical mystery series, featuring Dr Callie Hughes as a police doctor investigating murders in Hastings.
www.candydenman.co.uk
www.facebook.com/CrimeCandy/
www.twitter.com/CrimeCandy

SAM ELLIS

Sam has been a member of Verulam Writers since 2009 where he is currently editor of the newsletter Veracity. He studied Literature at Essex and Exeter universities, works in the media industry and is often found in the garden with his dog Maggie and husband Aaron, to whom his story is dedicated.

JUDITH FOSTER

For all of Judith's life, she has been a linguist and reader of classic literature of all periods; in retirement a painter; now, in second retirement, a writer. When she writes poems, she likes them heroic. When she writes a story, she likes to make the reader do half the work.

CÉCILE KEEN

Cécile started writing short stories in November 2021 and joined Verulam Writers in January 2022. Encouraged by her husband and two teenage sons, she entered two VW competitions for which she won First and Third prizes, to her great surprise. It gave her the confidence to carry on writing with no other ambition than just enjoying it.

CLARE LEHOVSKY

Clare read Classics at BA and MA level and is currently doing an MA in Museum Studies. She writes mainly historical fiction, sometimes fantasy and occasionally poetry.
Email: clehovsky@btopenworld.com

HOWARD LINSKEY

Howard is a best-selling author published in eight countries. Howard writes crime fiction novels set in the north-east of England for Penguin Random House. He also writes historical fiction and non-fiction. Originally from the north-east, Howard lives in Hertfordshire with his wife Alison and daughter Erin.

YVONNE MOXLEY

Yvonne enjoys writing non-fiction and has had a book published on the town of Aylesbury, its people, places and history; and two books on Windsor and Eton. She is currently researching and writing about Rochester and then Dorchester as well as desperately trying to finish a historical novel.

KEN OSBORNE

Ken took up fiction writing as a challenge following a career in civil engineering in The UK and overseas where communication had to be concise and factual. The colourful characters encountered and the humour of the construction site have become a rich source of material.

PAUL F. MCNAMARA

Paul is originally from Middlesbrough. He moved to St. Albans in 1987. Following a long career in academia and finance, he attended the creative writing course at Oaklands College and began writing fiction in 2018. Paul is a songwriter and one half of successful folk duo, Na-Mara.

JL MERROW

JL Merrow is that rare beast, an English person who refuses to drink tea. She writes award-winning contemporary gay romance and mysteries and is frequently accused of humour. Her Plumber's Mate Mystery series has been translated into French and is set in and around St Albans. https://jlmerrow.com/

STEVEN MITCHELL

Steven is a writer from St Albans via Peterborough and has been the chairperson of Verulam Writers since 2020. His real name is Phil Mitchell but he often uses a pseudonym to avoid confusion with his popular EastEnders namesake. His debut novel, Under The Moss, was published in 2022, closely followed by his debut short story collection, Little Islands. www.stevenmitchellwriter.com

JANE PALMER

From very young, Jane swam like a fish and watched seabirds along Bushman's River. She biked in the Rhodesian bush and surfed at Beira. Study of Art, English and French literature led her to London publishing. Nurturing her children, she ran Live Lines, promoting innovative products, and charity work took her around the UK and to West Africa.

ROBERT PATERSON

Robert has been a member of VW for 11 years. He has twice been the overall winner in their writing competitions and sits on the committee as vice chairman. He has been a library assistant for 13 years, a St Albans resident for 35 years and a writer for even longer. Outside writing, his chief joys are books, animals, culture, music and travel. Examples of his writing can be found on his blog on Wordpress: rpatersonwriting.

KATHARINE RIORDAN

After studying for an MBA and a global career in sales & marketing for 5-star and boutique hotels, Katharine became a full-time mum and homemaker to 3 small people. She is currently writing historical fiction and a self-help guide for parents of children with special educational needs.

SAM ROSTOM

Sam Rostom was born in north London and now resides in St Albans with her family. She writes a range of fiction as well as poetry and whilst forging a writing career, works for the NHS. Sam also has a first-class degree and an MA. You can follow Sam at @starterforpen

STEVE SEATON

Steve has lived and worked mainly in St Albans for over 50 years. Originally an English teacher, he later re-trained as a psychotherapist, and has loved both careers. He has hence enjoyed a long professional life in which stories, both those of literary fiction and people's own personal life narratives, have played a rich part.

TINA SHAW

Tina was born in St Albans during the war, returning to London as a toddler. When she married in 1967 St Albans was slightly cheaper than Enfield, and she's lived here, moving twice, ever since. Tina is a retired Social Worker who enjoys writing for pleasure.

JOHN SPENCER

John is a published author of over 30 non-fiction books on the Paranormal and Business topics. He is currently President of Verulam Writers. He joined Verulam Writers to develop skills in writing fiction and now has four books completed which are seeking publishers/ agents. He can be contacted at john@connorspencer.com

WENDY TURNER

Wendy enjoys picking non-fiction bones apart and writing up articles for People's Friend, This England, Evergreen and The Countryman magazines. You can find her A-Z of St Albans in the Cathedral, Museum and St Albans bookshops. Wendy is sure to welcome you at Verulam Writers with a cup of tea and biscuit for which she bears sole responsibility.

DAVE WEAVER

Dave has had five novels released by the Dartford-based speculative fiction publishers Elsewhen Press. He's also been featured in various anthologies and self-published three short story collections in ebook, available at online retailers, plus his latest novel, *The Transference.*

ABOUT VERULAM WRITERS

St Albans has always been stuffed with literary talent. So, almost seven decades ago, the local writing community formed Verulam Writers.

Taking the name from the name of the Roman town where St Albans is now located, Verulam Writers meets in-person every two weeks and online in the alternate weeks. Evenings include manuscript critique sessions, competitions, workshops, social events, and guest speakers.

All writers are welcome. Members write fiction, non-fiction, poetry, and screenplays. In fiction, members write in genres including crime, fantasy, sci-fi, historical, romance, literary fiction and everything in-between. Some members are at the start of their writing journey, and some are prolific and professional novelists. It's a mix which makes for a friendly and broad critique of manuscripts and lively workshops.

The in-house magazine, Veracity, available for free to non-members, is packed with articles on the craft of writing and showcases our members' work.

New members are always welcome. So, to find out more about the group and read Veracity Magazine visit:

www.verulamwriters.org

ALSO BY VERULAM WRITERS

COVIDITY edited by JL Merrow, Phil Mitchell and Wendy Turner

THE ARCHANGEL AND THE WHITE HART edited by Jonathan Pinnock

Printed in Great Britain
by Amazon

21744175R00162